Also by Jenna Hartley

<u>Love in LA Series</u>
Inevitable
Unexpected
Irresistible
Undeniable
Unpredictable
Irreplaceable

<u>Alondra Valley Series</u>
Feels Like Love
Love Like No Other
A Love Like That

<u>Tempt Series</u>
Temptation
Reputation

For the most current list of Jenna's titles, please visit her website www.authorjennahartley.com.

Or scan the QR code on the following page to be taken to her author page on Amazon.com

SCAN ME

Unexpected

jenna hartley

ISBN: 9798386498726

Editing: Lisa A. Hollett
Cover Artwork © 2022 Indie Sage Designs

For Charlie Puth.

No, really. Thank you for writing (with Jacob Kasher) and singing the song, Boy, which inspired this novel.

You don't know who I am and will probably never read this, but my daughter is your biggest fan. She's two.

Content Warnings

This story contains explicit sexual content, profanity, and topics that may be sensitive to some readers.

For more detailed information, visit the QR code below.

PLAYLIST

"Boy" by Charlie Puth
"Light" by Sleeping At Last
"Delicate" by Taylor Swift
"Like I Did" by JC Stewart
"Someone To Stay" by Vancouver Sleep Clinic
"Don't Give Up On Me" by Andy Grammer
"Hold On" by Chord Overstreet
"Sex on Fire" by Kings of Leon
"Someone You Loved" by Lewis Capaldi
"Falling Like The Stars" by James Arthur
"Where's My Love" by SYML
"Hands To Myself" by Selena Gomez
"You & Me" by James TW
"Someone To You" by BANNERS
"I Like Me Better" by Lauv
"Wherever You Are" by Kodaline
"Say You Won't Let Go" by James Arthur
"Chasing Cars" by Snow Patrol
"Ruin My Life" by Zara Larsson
"Arcade" by Duncan Laurence

"Tired" by Gavin James
"Beautiful People" (featuring Khalid) by Ed Sheeran
"Dusk Till Dawn" (Radio Edit) by ZAYN, Sia
"Brother" by Kodaline
"Fix You" by Coldplay
"Silhouette" by Aquilo
"Stand By You" by Rachel Platten
"Can I Be Him" by James Arthur
"Safe in My Hands" by Eli Lieb
"Back To You" by Selena Gomez
"Underdog" by The Script
"Someone" by Michael Schulte
"Still Falling For You" (From Bridget Jones's Baby) by Ellie Goulding

You can find this playlist and more at
https://www.authorjennahartley.com/playlists

CHAPTER ONE

Alexis

"You look like you could use a drink."

I glanced up to see Christine leaning against the door of my office and grimaced. "I could use a hell of a lot more than a drink."

"Rough day?" she asked, pushing off the doorframe.

I laughed, but it was without humor. "Rough week."

And I didn't see it getting easier anytime soon. "Wolfe keeps changing his mind on what he wants. I've shown him no fewer than twenty properties. Shelly is still out on maternity leave, and the city is fighting me on the plans for the new property on Sycamore."

I leaned my head back against the chair, sick of all the drama, the bullshit. I loved my job, had worked my ass off to get to this point in my career, but it never seemed like enough. There was always another challenge to conquer—a newer, bigger client to court, more money to be made.

I used to think that if I had five hundred dollars in the bank, I'd be set. Now, I had five hundred so many times over, I'd lost count. Despite the number of zeros in my account, it was never enough. *I* was never enough.

I was always running from one thing to the next. Hair appointments to cover the premature gray. Spa appointments to keep my skin firm and glowing and my bikini line clean. The gym to stay in shape. Client meetings. School conferences. Plays. The list went on and on.

"Wolfe will be happy in the end," Christine said, breaking me out of my thoughts. "You'll find the perfect property. You always do."

Deep down, I knew she was right. But sometimes it felt like I had to sell my soul to get there. Like I wasn't just selling the client a property with every deal, but a little piece of myself.

"Thanks," I said, and I meant it.

Christine was my employee, and she was a good sounding board. She was a hard worker, good at her job. She reminded me a lot of myself at her age.

"I'm sure you'll find your footing with the developmental side," she said. "You just need to make the right contacts."

I nodded. I'd been wanting to branch out to developing properties for years. I'd waited until Sophia was in school full time. And with her visiting her dad for the summer, I'd finally felt confident enough to take on the extra work it would entail. It was a big gamble, but I was hoping it would pay off.

My phone rang, and I glanced down at the screen to see my ex-husband's name. "I have to take this," I said to Christine before connecting the call. "Cal."

"Alexis, hey." I knew that tone—he needed a favor.

"What do you need?"

"This huge opportunity came up, once in a lifetime, really." I could hear people talking and laughing in the background. Loud music. He was probably in a bar.

I pinched the bridge of my nose. I knew what was coming

next. And I was tempted to hang up the phone just so I wouldn't have to hear it.

"I got a music gig I can't pass up."

I blew out a breath. I wanted to be happy for him, honestly. His passion for music was one of the things that had initially drawn me to him. But over time, I'd realized he would always put it above everything—and everyone—else.

And I'd had enough of playing second fiddle. I'd had enough of feeling like a single parent, working to support our family while he was off galivanting. Off chasing his dream. Divorcing him had helped—our relationship was better now than when we were married. But he would always be an artsy free spirit, and I would always be the worker bee; the bad cop to his good.

"Cal," I chided. "Sophia's all packed, and she's so excited to spend time with you."

"Maybe I could—" He was quiet, but the background noise was overpowering. "Maybe she could come with me for part of it, since I'll be touring for the next eight weeks."

My eyes went wide. "Eight weeks? That's the whole summer."

In my business, summer was selling season. I often moved more properties during the months of May to July than the other three quarters combined. With the school year over, families were looking to move. And properties showed well during the summer, when most buyers were generally more relaxed. Plus, I'd been counting on having this time to iron out some of the issues on my Sycamore property.

"I know, babe. I'm sorry. But I could still take her for part of it."

"Absolutely not," I ground out, standing so I could close the door to my office. "Our six-year-old daughter is not going to be a groupie."

"Yeah. You're probably right. The tour bus is going to be crowded as it is."

Was he… Did he seriously think that taking a six-year-old on a cross-country music tour was a good idea? It was times like this I wondered what I'd ever seen in him. Opposites might attract, but what happened after the initial appeal wore off?

"What am I supposed to tell her?" I asked, knowing just how upset she'd be. I could already picture her tear-stained face.

"Tell her…I'll catch her next time. Tell her I'll make it up to her. I promise."

I rolled my eyes. How many times had he said that before?

"Cal, you can't do this. She's counting on you, and so am I. I'm working on closing a huge deal, and I gave Gabriela the summer off because you were supposed to be spending time with our daughter."

Gabriela was our live-in nanny, and Sophia adored her. I adored her. She treated me like a daughter, and I'd be lost without her. I might attend parent-teacher conferences and school plays, but she knew all the ins and outs of Sophia's routine. She knew where Sophia's favorite outfit was and what her favorite food was.

Sometimes I felt like a bad mom for not being as involved, but then I reminded myself I was affording her a life I could never have dreamed of. I was ensuring she'd never have to work as hard as I did. I loved her, and I showed that love by providing for our family financially.

"Summer camp!" he said, as if it were that simple.

"Camp?" I shook my head. "It's too late to register, and most of the good ones had waitlists months ago."

I heard him talking to someone else in the background, and I knew I'd already lost him. It didn't matter what I said or how much I begged, Cal was going to do what he wanted. The problem was, I was going to pay the price. *Again.*

Yet again, he was having all the fun, and I was doing all the work. Yet again, he was bailing on our daughter, and I was having to scramble to pick up the slack. Yet again—

"Hey, Lex. You still there?"

I clenched my fist, staring out at the skyline beyond my window. "I'm still here. *I'm* always here."

"Can't you offer to pay Gabriela more or something? I bet she'd be happy to watch Sophia."

"No, Cal. I can't. She's already halfway to Colombia by now," I spat back, getting madder and madder the longer this conversation dragged on. It didn't matter that our nanny had gone home to visit her family in Colombia; it was the principle of it.

"All right. All right." His tone told me he thought I was being irrational, which only incensed me further. "Calm down, babe."

"Don't call me babe. Don't call me Lex either. I'm not your wife. I'm not your groupie." My voice rose with every word, my anger becoming something tangible. Something living and breathing. "I'm just the mother of your child, and I'll figure it out without you. I always do."

"Look," he sighed. "I'm really sorry, but I have to go. I'll FaceTime with Sophia when I can."

"Cal… Cal!" I shouted into the phone when he didn't answer, only then realizing he'd already hung up.

Shit. I continued to stare at the phone as if he'd call back and tell me it was all a big joke.

I laid my head on the desk and took a few deep breaths, trying to center myself. It wasn't just the change in plans or the lack of notice, I thought. Though those definitely pissed me off. It was the impact on Sophia. I knew how devastated she'd be. And how guilty I felt even though none of it was my fault.

I should've known better than to trust him.

My phone chimed, and I lifted my head to see a calendar entry for "Drinks with the girls." For a moment, I considered bailing. But then I remembered Sophia was sleeping over at a friend's house, and I could really use a drink.

When I arrived at the bar, Lauren was already waiting, drink in hand. She waved me over, and my red-soled shoes clacked against the floor, drawing attention. I straightened, tossing my caramel waves over my shoulder as I strode toward her. I felt powerful, confident, sexy. Even when my life was spinning out of control, I could at least look like I had it together.

"Alexis!" Lauren's bronzed skin glowed beneath the lights, her brown eyes sparkling. "Honey, you look good." She spun her finger in a circle, indicating I should do the same. "Mm. Mm." She shimmied her shoulders as if enjoying a decadent dessert.

It made me laugh as I slid into the high chair across from her, knowing I'd made the right decision in coming. Lauren and I had been friends since what we lovingly referred to as "the college internship from hell." We'd bonded while working for a property developer. And we'd stayed friends since, even as we formed our own businesses. I often referred my clients to her for interior design, though her real talent was staging. Which was why, as much as I'd wanted to go home tonight and crawl into bed, I knew I needed to come out.

"Hot date?" she asked.

"Annoying client," I said, knowing her question was in reference to my fitted sheath dress and sky-high heels.

She flashed me a wicked grin. "Even better."

I rolled my eyes. "I'm not sleeping with him, if that's what you're implying."

"Maybe you should," she said. "If you dress like that for meetings, I'm positive he'd be interested."

"Oh," I said, waving the bartender over to order a drink. "He's interested. I'm just more interested in business."

She smirked. "Maybe you could mix a little business with pleasure. It might close the deal faster."

I knew she was only kidding—at least, I hoped so. But I wasn't interested in sleeping with my clients. It would only end in disaster.

"You know I never mix business with pleasure."

"That's not true." She gestured between us.

"That's different," I huffed, thanking the bartender when he returned with my drink. She and I had been colleagues first, then friends.

"Well, you look hot, girl," she said, raising her glass to toast.

"So do you." I grinned, following suit. I took a sip of my drink, relishing the burst of flavors on my tongue. The salty olive, the gin. It was divine. "I love that color on you."

"I do look pretty fabulous, don't I?" She laughed, and we both knew she was only half kidding. That was one of the things I loved about Lauren—her confidence.

"Where are the others?" I asked, glancing around for Juliana and Harper.

"Juliana had a work emergency. And Harper—"

I cut in, already knowing the answer. "Don't tell me... Brett called at the last minute. And yet again, she dropped everything for him."

She took a sip of her drink and nodded. "For a hot second, I thought you were going to stand me up too. Not that I'd mind. There's a delicious piece of man candy at the bar I'd love to sample."

I rolled my eyes and laughed. "Yeah, sorry. Long day, then Cal called."

"Ugh. What's he bailing on now?"

"The summer. Sophia." My shoulders slumped, and I fiddled with the stem of my cocktail glass. "How am I going to tell her? She's going to be crushed."

Her jaw fell open. "He bailed for the entire summer?"

I nodded, still wondering what I was going to do. Gabriela wasn't an option. Summer camp was out. And I sure as hell couldn't take time off to watch Sophia twenty-four seven, even if I'd wanted to.

"You're not looking to hire a six-year-old summer intern, are you?" I teased.

She threw her head back and laughed, the rich, lusty sound drawing the attention of several nearby men. "Um. No. How about a nanny service?"

"I don't know," I hedged. Sophia had only ever known Gabriela. And the idea of finding someone else—trusting someone else—seemed daunting.

"They run background checks and have a crazy vetting process," she said, surprising me with her knowledge. "And you don't even communicate directly with the nanny. The agency handles everything, like a vacation rental."

I wanted to point out that my daughter wasn't a vacation rental, but I needed details. "How do you know all this?" I asked. Lauren didn't have kids, and I wasn't sure she ever planned to.

"One of my clients—the house I did recently over on Hummingbird? She owns one. Hartly... Harlot... Hartwell Agency," she finally settled on. "Rumor has it her clients include several major celebrities." She dug in her purse, grabbing her phone and tapping on the screen. "I'm sending you her info now."

"Thanks," I said, not sure I'd ever use it. But at least it was something. I mean, if it was good enough for the celebrities of the world…

I opened my mouth to say something else, but Lauren held up a finger. "Hold that thought. There's a hottie two tables over, and he is checking you out."

I turned my head, curious to see what he looked like.

"No!" Lauren reached out, grabbing my chin and forcing my attention back to her. "Don't look. Then he'll know we were talking about him."

"And now he's going to think I'm a lesbian." I made a goofy face, letting her know I was joking. She could be so dramatic.

"You want to kiss?" she teased. "Give him a little show? Some guys are really into that."

I backed away. "Yeah. That's not the type of guy I'm trying to attract." I took a sip of my drink. "Actually, what am I saying? I'm not trying to attract men. I'm trying to repel them." I pressed against an imaginary force field. "Stay away, men of the earth."

Lauren grabbed my arms and pulled them down. "That's crazy talk. You've been divorced for a year, and your relationship with Cal was over long before then. It's time."

I glared at her. "My life is good. Full. I don't need a man."

"I didn't say you needed a man. You need sex."

I scoffed. "I don't have time for that."

"Honey," she said, holding up a finger. "Everyone has time for sex. And you, my dear, desperately need to get laid."

Did I miss the companionship? Yes. But I barely had time to sleep. I was running a highly successful brokerage firm, as well as taking on a new property development. Between that and Sophia, I had enough on my plate without adding a man.

Besides, being a mom added a whole other set of challenges to dating. Men my age were either in a relationship or looking for someone younger. Someone without children.

And the idea of introducing Sophia to a man I was seeing… the idea of that was enough to have me downing the rest of my drink and asking for another.

Lauren's expression softened, and she leaned forward. "Is this about Cal? Are you still hung up on him?"

"What?" I jerked my head back. "No. Absolutely not. I mean, the sex was good, but… I don't…" I closed my eyes briefly before reopening them. "No." This had nothing to do with my ex.

"Then, what?" she asked. "Because you certainly don't lack for interested partners. Nearly every man—and even a few women—stopped to watch you when you walked in."

I blew out a harsh breath. "I'm just…overloaded. Exhausted. I have my job and Sophia."

"You know what's great for helping people relax?" She grinned, but I rolled my eyes, already anticipating her answer. "Sex."

"Keep your voice down," I hissed, feeling the stares of nearby patrons.

"Sex. Sex. Sex," she chanted, mocking me.

"All right," I said, moving her drink away. "You're cut off."

"And you, my friend—" she pointed her finger at me "—are no fun."

"Hey." I pouted. "We're having fun now, aren't we?"

"We are. And you know I love you, but you need to relax. You need to let loose every now and then."

Easy for her to say. She didn't have a mortgage, private school tuition, college to plan for. And she didn't have a daughter to consider. I didn't have the luxury of dating, and I wasn't interested in casual sex.

"*No.* I need to stay focused."

"I admire your drive, Alexis. I do. But sometimes you have to slow down and appreciate the scenery." She waggled her eyebrows.

I laughed. "Oh my god, that was so cheesy."

She smirked, throwing back the rest of her drink. "Cheesy or not, it made you smile. Now—let's go shake our booties. I see a hot man I'm ready to grind up on."

I let her pull me out onto the dance floor. "We're getting too old for this," I said over the music.

"You're never too old to have fun!" She shouted over the thump of the bass.

She was right, but sometimes I felt older than my thirty-five years. I had the weight of the world on my shoulders, and as much as I wanted to let go sometimes—I couldn't.

CHAPTER TWO

Preston

"Come on," Hunter said. "You're not really going to pass up a week of endless pussy, are you?"

I rolled my eyes. "How many times do I have to tell you, dickweed? I'm not going."

Hunter was spending the summer in New York, opening a new location for a business he'd started with a couple friends from business school. The four of them worked hard, but they liked to play hard too. And I knew Hunter would be living the life out there this summer.

He backed away from me, holding his arms out wide as he neared the entrance to the kitchen. "Fine." He smirked. "More for me."

I shook my head, marveling at how different the two of us were. We'd been best friends since fifth grade. Hunter had been with me through everything. Had stood by my side when everyone else left—just him and my parents. Well, and Sam. But I hadn't met him until later, until after the shit hit the fan.

"I don't need to go to New York to get laid," I said,

dodging a flip-flop he'd tossed in my direction. "There are plenty of girls on campus to choose from."

"Yet, you never bring any home."

I lifted a shoulder. What could I say? "They all seem so young."

Hunter scoffed. "Dude. You're twenty-six. Which means they're like…what? Five, maybe six years younger? Younger —and hot. What more could you want?"

"I'm not interested."

"Well, what kind of woman are you interested in?" I thought he was genuinely curious until he said, "I mean, if you're into dudes, that's cool too. I'm not, but hey—more power to you."

I rolled my eyes, turning my attention back to the sandwich I was making. "I want a woman who's confident, smart, sexy."

"Mm-hmm." He'd crossed his arms over his chest.

"A woman who knows what she wants and isn't afraid to ask for it. And those," I said, giving him a pointed look, "aren't the types of girls I've met on campus."

I had an image of the woman I wanted, though I didn't know her name. Didn't know anything about her other than the fact that she had a daughter who attended the same school as Theo. She was sophisticated, self-assured, and sexy as hell. I'd only seen her a few times—at school plays and such, but the image of her stuck in my mind.

Hunter waved his hand in front of my face. "Earth to Preston."

"What?"

"Wait…do you want an older woman? Is this because you want to be a kept man?" he asked, amusement coloring his tone.

"No. Money has nothing to do with it. I'd happily support my wife."

Not that I really had much to support a hypothetical spouse with. Not yet, anyway. Between tuition and rent, I was lucky to be staying afloat. I had a scholarship, but it wasn't enough to cover everything. And I refused to ask my parents for money—not after all they'd shelled out for me already. As it was, they'd be working for the rest of their lives. Something I hoped to change.

"Whoa. Whoa." His eyes went wide. "Back up. Marriage?"

"Yeah. One day." Hopefully sooner rather than later. "I want to get married, have kids. Don't you?"

His eyes went wide. "No way. No fucking way."

"Well, I do. I know how short life can be. I don't want to waste it chasing meaningless relationships. I want more."

His expression softened. "I know. I just think that—" He blew out a puff of air. "That you were forced to grow up so fast, you kind of skipped straight to adulthood."

I nodded, knowing he had a good point. I *did* grow up fast. That's what cancer did to you.

"I don't want you to miss out on anything life has to offer," he added. "Besides, I could use a wingman I can trust."

I smirked. "Nice try, but it's not happening. Theo's family offered me extra hours this summer, and I need them. Besides, I can't bail on him."

He rolled his eyes. "I still can't believe my best friend's a manny."

"I'm not a 'manny.' I'm an in-home childcare provider," I said.

"Call it what you want," he said. "You're a manny."

It worked well with my schedule, and the money was good. More than good. The only opportunities I'd found that paid more involved stripping—no thanks. And bartending, which didn't appeal to me either. Being a nanny was satisfying, fulfilling.

"It pays well. And after the kids go to bed, I have time to study."

"It gives you time to learn to crochet too," he teased.

He had no idea the time and energy it took to care for a child day in and day out. A child who wasn't your own, yet you felt attached to. When I'd started the job, it was because I thought it would be easy. I liked kids. I enjoyed spending time with them.

Now, I appreciated just how difficult the job was. But how rewarding it could be too. And, like I'd told him, it paid well.

"Do you know how many single moms there are? *Hot* single moms?" I flashed him a wicked grin, enjoying his stupefied expression.

His jaw dropped. "Dude," he said, drawing out the word. "No fucking way. You're banging the moms?"

I lifted a shoulder, leading him to infer what he wanted. I wasn't *banging* anyone, but this would get him off my back. It might not be for the right reasons, but I was tired of having to defend my job. Maybe after this, he'd finally stop giving me shit about being a manny.

Damn it. In-home childcare provider.

"Is that why you change diapers? So you can fuck mommy after the kids go to bed?"

I cringed at his crude language. Sure, some of the moms were attractive, but I was their employee. And besides, I mostly worked for Theo's family, and his parents were married, happily so. They seemed to have it all—dog, big house, nice cars. Even a boat.

"You're such a pig."

He burst out laughing. "I fucking knew you were lying. You should see your face."

I shoved his shoulder as I moved past him for my bedroom. "Fuck off."

"Hey," he said, snagging a piece of apple from my plate before halting with it in midair. "Maybe you should consider it."

I furrowed my brows. "Consider what?"

"Fucking the moms. With your body, I bet you could make good money. It could be a nice little side business." He bit into the apple slice, chewing obnoxiously.

"Okay. I'm done," I said, going into my room and shutting the door behind me. "More than done," I muttered to myself.

"Oh, come on. Preston," he said from the other side of my door. "Don't sulk."

"Enjoy your summer. I hope you fall in love," I called, taking a seat on the bed and switching on the TV.

"Take that back!" His tone was insistent as he banged on my door. "Take it back, fuckface."

I smirked to myself, setting my feet on the bed. "Nope. See you in a few weeks."

"See ya," he called. "And don't forget to call me if you bag a cougar."

Not a chance in hell, I thought.

LATER THAT AFTERNOON, I HEADED OVER TO THEO'S HOUSE. I'd been taking care of him for the past year, and I knew how excited he was that school was almost over. We'd been talking about our plans for the summer—the camps he was going to attend, the movies he wanted to see. He was only six, but he wasn't short of ideas or enthusiasm.

I let myself in the side door, using the key his parents had given me. The house was oddly quiet; even their dog hadn't come to greet me. *Huh.*

"Hello?" I called, wondering if I'd missed a message through the agency portal.

I found Theo in his room. When he spotted me in the doorway, he rushed over to me for a hug and burst into tears.

"Hey, bud. What's wrong?" I asked.

He was crying so hard, I could barely make out the words he said. Though, I heard "moving" and "not see you… anymore." I rubbed his back and held him close, a deep worry sinking into my gut.

"Preston, hey," Amanda said, coming into the room.

She had dark circles under her eyes and wore her hair in a ponytail. She never wore her hair in a ponytail, unless she was working out. Even then, it was always perfectly styled. But she wasn't wearing her latest pair of Lululemon leggings. Nor did she look like she'd even showered, for that matter.

"The agency didn't call you?" She unscrewed the lid from a bottle of prescription pills and popped one in her mouth, chugging some water to swallow it.

I frowned. "What's going on?"

I kept my arm around Theo, wanting to console him. Was it odd that he sought me out for reassurance instead of his mom? I didn't know; I was just glad he felt safe with me.

"My husband lost his job. And…" She sucked in a harsh breath. "Our assets are being seized."

I couldn't help it; my eyes went wide. "What happened?"

"I'm sure you'll see it on the news in the coming days," she said, wiping away a few tears. "But he's been charged with tax evasion."

"Steve?" I asked, still trying to wrap my head around it.

She nodded, waving a hand through the air. "I'm sure it's all just a little misunderstanding. But until we get it sorted out, we won't be needing your services anymore."

Right. Of course. All I could do was nod.

"We so appreciate everything you've done for us. And

Theo, clearly, adores you," she said. "I just wish we—" She hiccupped a sob. "Well, we're going to move in with my parents for the time being."

"I'm sorry you're going through a difficult time. It's been a pleasure working for your family."

She nodded, though she seemed a bit dazed. A bit off, somehow. I wondered what kind of pills she'd popped earlier.

"I hope you'll find another placement soon."

Me too, I thought.

Until then, I wasn't sure what I was going to do. Though last-minute placements could—and did—happen, it was rare. Plus, being a male in this profession made it even more difficult to place me. Most families requested a female; they weren't accustomed to the idea that a guy could be a caregiver. It had taken months to be placed at all.

But it was better than the alternative—not using an agency. I shuddered at the memory of my experience before signing up with Hartwell. The parents were so disconnected from their kids, it was heartbreaking. They were disconnected from each other. The mom flirted with me constantly and then threatened to fire me if I didn't sleep with her. I didn't, but the entire experience had been eye-opening.

Something like that would never happen with the Hartwell Agency. Placements might take more time, but they paid more, and they were a much better environment to work in. Hartwell vetted both potential nannies and families, and there were safeguards in place, expectations.

Theo sniffled, and I tried to focus on him instead of my fears about my own future. I hadn't come this far to give up now. I would find a way to pay my tuition.

Theo, on the other hand, was going to lose his home, possibly his dad. And this scandal would follow them for the rest of their lives. So, I set aside my fears, my worries, and tried to do my best to reassure him.

"Hey, buddy." I turned to look him in the eye. "It sounds like you're going to have some new adventures. And you're going to get to spend more time with your mommy and your grandparents. That will be nice," I said, knowing how much he adored his grandparents.

"Will you come visit me at my new house?" he asked.

Once a placement ended, any contact had to go through the agency. Still, I needed to find a way to soften the blow. "I'm not sure I'll be able to. But you know what?" I asked. "I will think about you every time I drive by the yellow park." It had been one of his favorite places to go.

"The yellow park." He nodded. "Our place."

"That's right." I held out my fist. "It will always be our place."

Instead of a fist bump, he wrapped his little arms around me, squeezing me tight. "I love you, Preston."

A little piece of my heart shattered, and I knew I wouldn't get it back. "Love you too, bud." I squeezed him tight, hoping he wouldn't forget me.

"Thank you, Preston," Amanda said as she escorted me to the door. "Theo's really going to miss you. We all will."

I nodded. "He's a good kid. I'm really going to miss him too."

I shuffled out to my car, feeling deflated. I hadn't just lost my job; I'd lost a friend. And it was yet another setback on the path to getting my degree.

CHAPTER THREE

Alexis

My alarm blared from my nightstand, and I reached over to shut it off. I glanced at the clock on my phone: five thirty. Despite the fact that it was my day off, it certainly wasn't the weekend for me. So, I dragged my ass out of bed.

Workout clothes on, I hopped on my exercise bike in my home gym, going through the prompts. As I pushed myself harder and harder, I focused on the music. On the screen in front of me. It was my escape—my outlet. One of the few things I did for me.

An hour later, after I'd stretched, I showered and checked my emails. Nothing new from my nightmare client, which was a miracle in and of itself. But I knew it was only a matter of time. There was no way he'd let the day pass without finding some new way to torture me. In fact, I was beginning to suspect he enjoyed it.

I made a protein shake and carried it and my tablet over to one of the lounge chairs surrounding the pool. Sophia would be home from her sleepover in a few hours, and then I would have to figure out how to break the news about her dad. In the meantime, I was going to figure out a solution for the summer. I wanted to have a plan in place by the time she arrived home, impossible as it seemed.

I'd been right about overnight summer camps—all booked. Au pairs were out of the question. I should've requested one months ago. At least I'd put in a call to the Hartwell Agency. It really was my last hope.

Still, I remained hesitant. Sophia was used to Gabriela. I was used to Gabriela. She'd been taking care of Sophia since she was six months old, and she adored my daughter. She provided continuity; she lived with us, knew our routines. She was available any time, day or night, and I couldn't imagine so easily handing that trust over to someone else.

I leaned my head back against the chair, soaking in the California sun. My backyard was beautiful—clean and classic, with a large pool that shone a pale blue. It was my favorite thing about the house, and I loved relaxing on the chair with the palm trees swaying in the breeze and the waterfall cascading in the background. It was so peaceful. So tranquil.

My cell phone rang, shattering the calm. It never stopped. It was barely eight o'clock in the morning, and It. Never. Stopped. With a deep sigh, I connected the call.

"Alexis Black."

"Alexis, hi," a woman replied. "This is Renata from the Hartwell Agency."

"Yes." I sighed with relief. "Thank god. I mean, thank you for calling me back. Please tell me you have someone."

"Unfortunately, most of our caregivers have already been placed for the summer, but there is someone." I sensed hesitation on her part, and I wondered why.

"Someone…yes?" I was practically hanging on her every word.

"Yes, well, it's a bit of an unusual situation," she hedged.

Spit it out, woman.

"His name is Preston. He's been with the same family for the past year, but they—" She cleared her throat. "They, um, are moving. He's a bit older than most of our nannies, but he has a great track record. Every family he's worked for has given glowing recommendations, always citing him as reliable, responsible, and caring. Would you like me to send you his file?"

I was still trying to get past my surprise that it was a guy. "Um…sure. That will be fine."

"Great. Please call with any questions, or let me know if you'd like to schedule an interview."

"Okay. Thank you so much," I said, trying not to feel discouraged.

A guy? How would Sophia feel about having a guy as a live-in nanny? How would Cal feel?

You know what? Fuck Cal. He was the one who'd put me in this position in the first place. He'd lost the right to have a say in the matter the moment he ditched his daughter.

By the time I navigated to my inbox, Renata's email was waiting. Preston's background check was spotless, not that I'd expect anything less from the Hartwell Agency. In addition to Lauren's recommendation, I'd done some research of my own. A few of the other parents at Sophia's school had nothing but good things to say about their experience.

Preston's file was even more encouraging. He was an honors student studying for his bachelor's degree in social work and spoke Spanish fluently. When Renata said he was a bit older than most of their nannies, I'd expected a senior citizen, not a senior in college. And the more I read, the more intrigued I was. The more hopeful, too.

I opened one of the attachments—a personal letter. He wrote with passion and enthusiasm, and he seemed genuine. I'd already wanted to interview him, but this sealed the deal. Assuming he and Sophia clicked, I was ready to hire him.

My mind was whirring with possibilities. I wasn't sure I'd be comfortable with him staying in the house, but... I glanced toward the pool house, which had a fully furnished apartment. The previous owners had used it as a mother-in-law suite, but I'd never needed it for that purpose. And while I'd considered renting it out over the years, I never had. Now, I was glad it had remained vacant.

I emailed Renata, and we scheduled an informal interview with Preston for this afternoon. By the time the doorbell rang, announcing Sophia was back from her friend's house, I wasn't dreading it as much as I'd feared.

I opened the door and pulled Sophia in for a hug as I waved at her friend's dad, Nate. Why couldn't Cal be more like him? Dependable, loving—present.

"Hey, baby," I said, helping her carry her stuff to the laundry room. "Did you have fun at Brooklyn's?"

She nodded. "Tons. When's Dad coming?" She skipped through the house, her presence like a ray of sunshine. I didn't say anything, wishing this brief moment of bliss could've lasted longer.

"About that..." I finally said, knowing it was inevitable.

She stopped skipping, and her face fell. "He's not coming?"

I shook my head slowly, crouching down to her level so I could peer into her beautiful blue eyes. They were so like her father's. "Daddy loves you very much. And he wishes he could be with you more than anything, but he had to work."

It wasn't an outright lie, but it wasn't the entire truth either. Still, I wanted Sophia to feel loved. I wanted her to know that her parents were there for her, supported her. It was one of the reasons I'd stayed with Cal long after I should've ended it.

A few tears slid down her cheeks, and I swiped them away with my thumbs. "Don't cry, Soph. You're going to have lots of fun this summer."

"With Gabby?" she asked hopefully.

I gripped her shoulders, rubbing my thumbs back and forth. "No. Remember, she went home to visit her family. But you know what, I have someone new for you to play with."

"You do?" Her eyes were wide, and I sensed her curiosity. "Who?"

"Well, his name is Preston, and he's coming over this afternoon."

"Does he go to my school too?" she asked, and I realized then that she thought he was her age.

"No." I laughed. "But he's friends with one of the boys at your school. And if you have fun with Preston, we'll ask him to hang out for the summer. Okay?"

She nodded, but I sensed she was still upset about her dad. Understandably so.

"Besides," I said, scrambling for something that would make up for it. Or at least give her something positive to focus on. "This gives us more time to plan your birthday party." I ruffled her hair.

"Yay! Yay!" she shouted as she jumped around. "I want to do a pool party. With mermaids. And shells. And—"

I laughed. "Okay. We can do whatever you want."

"Can we have Juliana help?" she asked, referring to my friend, a party planner to the stars and occasional wedding planner.

"Sure," I said, relieved she was more focused on her birthday than Cal bailing. "But first, let's go pick out an outfit for this meet-cute."

She sped toward the stairs but then paused. "Mommy, what's a meet-cute?"

I laughed, more at myself than anything else. "It's when

two people… You know what, never mind. Let's just go pick out a cute outfit. 'Kay?"

"Okay!" she squealed and bounded up the stairs to her room.

The rest of the afternoon, Sophia played dress-up, while I worked on my laptop. "Mommy, Mommy," she said.

I was so close to finishing this email, but she kept interrupting me. If this thing with Preston didn't work out, I didn't know what I was going to do all summer. As much as I loved Sophia, I didn't have the time or luxury to dedicate my full attention to her right now. Work was just too busy.

"Yes?" I ground out, forcing a smile. It had only been a few hours, and already my patience was waning.

"Watch this!"

She did a cartwheel in her dress, then took a bow while I clapped. "Very nice. Look, Soph, Preston will be here soon. I need to finish up a few emails first. If you let me get some work done now, we can have fun later. Deal?"

"What kind of fun?"

I smirked. My daughter—the great negotiator. I couldn't wait to see what she'd do with her life. She was full of potential. And I was working my ass off to provide her with the opportunities I'd never had. Opportunities I never could have dreamed of.

"Well," I said. "We could go out to eat at Zaza's."

She frowned, and I was surprised. She usually loved getting dressed up and going to Zaza's. It was a special treat, something we did just the two of us.

"Would you rather do something else?" I asked.

"Could we…could we build a fort and watch a movie?" She was practically bouncing on her toes.

"That sounds great."

"And…and no phones allowed." She raised a hand triumphantly into the air.

Talk about mom guilt.

I hated to let her down, but I needed my phone. I had clients relying on me, employees relying on me. I'd built my business from the ground up, and the pace was relentless. I was lucky to be able to agree to watching movies. Even so, it meant I'd be staying up late into the night answering emails. Still, it was a sacrifice I'd gladly make to spend time with Soph, especially after Cal bailed on her.

"Sweetie, I'd be happy to build a fort and watch movies. But I have to keep my phone on me. You know that."

She huffed, crossing her arms over her chest. "Cece's mom doesn't have her phone on all the time."

I wanted to retort that Cece's mom was married to a well-known movie producer who would prefer she be nothing more than a trophy wife. But I bit my tongue.

"Well, it's part of my job." I wouldn't apologize for it. I just had to hope that, one day, she'd understand.

"Sometimes I hate your job," she huffed and stomped off down the hall just as the doorbell rang.

Great. I sighed, pinching the bridge of my nose. This summer was already off to a great start. And it would be just my luck that she'd hate Preston too. Unfortunately, we didn't have many options.

Okay, no options. He was our only option. I had to make this work.

I spied a man's silhouette through the frosted glass of my front door as I approached. Tall. Muscular. Surely this wasn't the new nanny.

I opened the door, expecting a college kid, but he was all man. And I couldn't stop my eyes from roaming his features. Dark chestnut hair that was longer on the top than the sides. Skin with a golden hue. He was dressed professionally— wearing a pair of fitted chinos and a button-down shirt with the sleeves rolled up to his elbows. But it did nothing to hide the magnificent body beneath the clothes. He looked like someone who belonged on a Hollywood set, not…I swallowed…a nanny. Still, he could just be my new neighbor. My new, incredibly hot neighbor.

"Hi," he said, and my knees nearly buckled at the richness of his baritone voice. At his dazzlingly white smile. "I'm Preston Hawthorne. From the Hartwell Agency."

My mouth went dry, but I forced myself to speak. "Yes." I smiled. "I'm Alexis Black. Please," I said, opening the door wide. "Come in."

I could feel his eyes on me as I led him through the house. "Soph," I called. "There's someone here I want you to meet. Sophia?" I called out again when she didn't answer.

I turned to Preston. "She's probably in her room."

He smiled, and I couldn't tear my eyes away from him. Seriously, the man was hot. Like, fry-my-brain hot. And I realized he was staring at me expectantly, as if he'd asked me a question and was waiting for an answer.

"I'm sorry. What?"

More like, what the hell was wrong with me? We lived in LA—Hollywood. I interacted with beautiful people all the time, especially in my line of work. Beautiful, wealthy, successful people. And I never felt intimidated. Never got tongue-tied. But Preston seemed to have a strange effect on me, and I wasn't entirely sure what to make of it.

He chuckled, the rich sound sending vibrations through me that resonated deep in my core. "I asked if we should go find her. The first time I meet a kid, I like to do it on their turf—where they play."

I smiled brightly, wondering how much of a disaster Sophia's room was. Usually, she and Gabby would play and then pick up. But I'd just been thankful she'd entertained herself while I worked. I hadn't cared about the cleanup. *Until now.*

I resisted the urge to rush up the stairs ahead of Preston to check. It was tempting, but…if he was going to spend the summer with us, he deserved to know what he was getting himself into. Especially if he was going to be sleeping here.

Not here, I reminded myself. In the pool house. With at least two locked doors between us.

"Have you nannied for many girls, or has it mostly been boys?" I asked when we reached the upstairs landing.

I could hear Sophia talking to her toys in her room, and I leaned against the banister, interested to know more about Preston.

"I spent the last year with a little boy Sophia's age. But it was part time. I watched him after school and during breaks, as well as the occasional evening."

"So, it wasn't a live-in situation."

"No," he hedged. "But I did travel with his family to the Bahamas over spring break. And, yes, I've nannied for girls. It's just that my longest, most recent, placement was for a boy. He goes to the same school as Sophia. Well, at least, he did."

I nodded. "And they're moving, right?"

"Yes."

His blue eyes were so expressive, framed with dark lashes and dark brows. I was tempted to stare into them all day.

"Well," I said, pushing off the banister. "I hope you're comfortable with dressing in drag," I teased. "Because Sophia loves all things pink, glitter, and dress-up."

He coughed a few times. "I'm game for anything." He leaned in, brushing against me as he passed.

My heart was racing, and I stood there a moment, staring after him. Had I imagined the seductive lilt to his tone?

I closed my eyes and took a few calming breaths. *Get it together, Alexis.*

When I entered Sophia's room, she was in her closet.

Dresses and accessories were flying through the open doorway. I watched Preston's expression for annoyance or surprise, but he merely seemed amused.

"Princess Sophia," he said, projecting his voice.

All movement stopped. There were no more flying shoes. No boas or tiaras being tossed from the closet. She peeked her head around the doorway, tentatively glancing between Preston and me. I gave her a reassuring smile.

"Princess Sophia," he said again, addressing her as though she truly were royalty. She perked up, straightening. "My name is Sir Preston, and I've been sent to your kingdom on a noble quest."

Her eyes went wide, and I knew she was eating this up. "You have?"

He nodded, and I watched their interaction with rapt interest. Sophia was outgoing by nature, but it often took her a while to warm up to new people. With Preston, she seemed as captivated by him as I was.

I couldn't help but stare. The sight of this tall, muscular man sitting on the floor and playing with my daughter while wearing a crown was almost more than I could handle. He smiled at her the entire time, spoke with an impressive British accent, and made her laugh. I didn't know if Sophia liked Preston as much as I did, but I was already under his spell.

Was he attractive? Yes. But I didn't think it would be an issue. As Lauren would say, "I can appreciate the candy without sampling it." I needed help, and Preston was willing to step in. He was here to do a job, nothing else.

CHAPTER FOUR

Preston

"Sir Preston," Sophia said in a very serious tone. "I have another quest for you."

"Does it involve raiding the pantry again?" I teased.

She giggled. "Maybe."

She was entirely too precocious for her own good, or maybe just for my own good. I hadn't been offered the placement yet, but I had a good feeling. Sophia and I had clicked, and I found myself feeling hopeful for the first time in days.

This girl was too adorable. And her mom… I shook my head, stealing a glance at Alexis. What were the chances I'd be placed with *her*? The mystery woman who regularly inhabited my fantasies.

I couldn't believe it when she'd opened the door. I couldn't believe the same woman who was seeking a new nanny was the same woman I'd often seen at Theo's school. The same woman I often found my mind drifting to.

And now, I not only knew her name and address, but I was in her home. Talking to her, getting to know her. And the reality was even better than my fantasies. Well, except for the fact that in my fantasies, I wasn't her nanny. And she was usually wearing a hell of a lot less.

She stood against the doorframe, scrolling through her phone. She was deep in concentration, her brow pulled together. I used the opportunity to watch her, admiring the loose waves in her hair, the bow of her lips, the swell of her breasts. She was wearing some kind of short-shirt combo that revealed a large expanse of bare skin on her back. And that wasn't even the best part. The best part was her toned, tanned legs, which were begging to be touched.

Her phone rang, snapping my attention away from her and back to her daughter. The one I was supposed to be keeping my eyes on.

"I have to take this," Alexis said before excusing herself to the hall.

I wasn't trying to eavesdrop, but I could hear snippets of the conversation. She sounded confident, in her element, and she seemed to be negotiating something—a property deal. It only made me more curious about her, and I was already extremely curious as it was.

I wanted to know everything about her. More than anything, though, I wanted to know if she was single. Her ring finger was bare, and I hadn't once heard her refer to a husband. One hadn't been mentioned in the file either. Not that I'd spent a ton of time reading it, but I certainly would now.

"Does your mom spend a lot of time on her phone?" I asked.

I'd worked for a number of affluent families, and I'd seen the crazy hours the parents sometimes pulled. Working evenings and weekends was often the norm. And Alexis had a nice home, more than nice. It was a stunning two-story with pale wood floors, lots of natural light, and a huge pool. Considering the location and the size, I knew it wasn't cheap.

Sophia nodded. "Like you wouldn't believe. I asked for a phone for my birthday, but she says I'm too young."

I nodded, though I was surprised by her answer. A number of the kids I'd nannied for had their own phones, even one as young as four. "That's a bummer. Do many of your friends have phones?"

"Tons of them," she said. "I'm the only one without a phone."

I tried to school my features into a neutral expression. I couldn't understand why anyone under the age of maybe twelve needed a phone. What they needed was less screen time and more human interaction. But, hey, I wasn't a parent. At least Alexis seemed to have a sensible approach.

"Who would you talk to if you had a phone?" I leaned in, whispering conspiratorially. "Do you have a boyfriend?"

"What?" She jerked her head back, scrunching up her nose. "Eww. Gross."

I laughed, gratified by her response. But then her expression turned more serious, and I wondered what she was thinking.

I nudged her shoulder with mine, surprised by how quickly we'd developed such a good rapport. How could we not? She was a cute kid with good manners. And I was happy to do anything and everything she wanted. Only an hour into the placement—correction, interview—and I was already wrapped around her little finger. If it were up to Sophia, I was pretty sure I'd already have the job.

"I wish I had a phone so I could FaceTime with my dad."

"You don't get to see him much?"

My heart was beating rapidly, but I was pretty sure Sophia didn't notice. She was too absorbed in her own thoughts.

She stared at the floor, her lips pulled into a frown. "He travels a lot for work."

"I'm sure you and your mom both miss him very much," I said.

"My parents are divorced." Her voice was completely devoid of emotion, and I realized this likely wasn't a recent thing. "My dad is a musician."

"Whoa," I said, latching on to how proud she was of that fact. "That's cool."

"Yeah. He's pretty amazing. What do your parents do?" she asked, as if we were friends, as if she were an adult and we were having a conversation.

She seemed so mature for her age. Whip-smart and funny. She was a firecracker for sure.

I chuckled to myself. "Nothing quite so glamorous," I said, relaxing. "My dad is a construction manager, and my mom is a teacher."

Sophia adopted a serious demeanor. "Teachers are very important."

I smiled. "Yes, they are."

"Are you having fun?" Alexis asked, returning to the room.

"Oh yes, Mommy." Sophia hopped up and skipped over to Alexis, grabbing her hand. "Preston is the best!" She frowned. "I mean, Sir Preston."

Alexis tried to hide her smile, her eyes meeting mine over the top of Sophia's head. "I'm glad to hear that."

So was I.

We played for a while longer, and then Alexis said, "Hey, Soph, let's go get some snacks. You can play a game on the tablet while I talk to Preston."

"Mom," Sophia whispered. "It's Sir Preston."

"Right." Alexis grinned at me. "Excuse me, *Sir*."

My dick twitched with excitement at the husky sound of her voice. *Fuck. Down, boy.*

I followed them downstairs, greedily drinking in the

sight of Alexis's bare shoulders, the curve of her ass. My attraction to this woman was off the charts. But I couldn't be lusting after her, not if I wanted this job. And I *wanted* this job. I needed the money to cover my tuition and rent.

And while I got the feeling she was attracted to me—at least if her "sir" comment was any indication—I doubted she'd act on it. She might not be married, but that didn't mean she didn't have a man in her life. She was too beautiful, too alluring, not to.

"Would you like a drink?" she asked.

"Water would be great." *A cold shower would be even better.*

She bustled around the kitchen, filling a glass for me before getting Sophia set up on her tablet. Alexis was full of energy, but her movements were gentle, nurturing. Even from my brief interaction, Alexis's love for her daughter was apparent.

"Why don't we take a seat outside," she said. Sophia was already immersed in her tablet, and I followed Alexis to the pool area. She left the glass doors open, allowing a nice breeze to flow into the house.

"This is gorgeous," I said, admiring the space. It was an outdoor oasis, with sparkling blue water, swaying palm trees, and a waterfall. I could definitely see myself spending lots of time out here.

"Thank you." She smiled as she took a seat on a lounge chair, folding one of her legs beneath her.

I knew I should stop staring, stop coveting something I'd never have, but I couldn't seem to help myself.

"The whole house is," I said as I joined her. "Love these dark window sashes and the light wood floors with the cream walls. It's very…relaxing," I said, finally settling on the word.

She tilted her head to the side, appraising me with a

curious gaze. "You speak the lingo like a pro." She tapped a finger to her lips. "Let me guess—HGTV fan?"

I chuckled, leaning back to rest my arm across the back of the chair. "My dad's a general contractor for a custom builder back home."

"Ahh." She angled her head back to display the long column of her neck. "That explains it."

"Though I do enjoy watching HGTV from time to time," I said.

"Favorite show?" she asked, and I felt like I was being quizzed.

For a moment, I considered lying. "*Christina on the Coast.*" I cringed, bracing for her reaction.

She appraised me a moment, as if to see if I was joking. "Really?"

"Yeah. I just think Art is so sweet to Christina, and I love seeing their blended family. I think it's brave that she gave love a second chance."

Her eyes sparkled, and I could tell I'd said the right thing. I thought she was going to say something more about it, so I was surprised when she shifted gears to business. "Thank you for coming over today."

My heart plummeted to my stomach. Was she going to tell me she wasn't interested? The Hartwell Agency was like a matchmaker. Sometimes they set up playdate interviews which led to a placement, sometimes not. Though I'd thought I'd hit it off with Sophia—Alexis too.

"Renata told me you're available for the entire summer," she said, though she didn't sound excited. "After meeting Sophia, are you still interested in the placement?"

It took everything in me not to jump out of my seat and tell her yes. But I forced myself to remain still and answer calmly. "Yes." I leaned forward, noticing the way her eyes darkened at my proximity. "I'm very interested."

She sucked in a jagged breath, and I leaned back, gratified I wasn't the only one affected. Still, she was now going to be my boss, which meant she was officially off-limits. At least, until the end of summer when the placement ended.

Not that it mattered anyway. Alexis was so out of my league, it wasn't even funny. She was smart, successful, sexy. God, was she sexy, especially when she laughed.

I took a sip of water in a futile attempt to cool myself down. Something about this woman got me all hot and bothered like no one else had. *If Hunter could see me now,* I thought.

"Excellent." She smiled. "When can you move in?"

I choked on my water, coughing a few times before catching my breath. "Move in?" My chest was tight. "Here?" I glanced back at the house. "With you?"

Her brows pulled together. "Yeah—in the pool house. Didn't Renata tell you? This is a live-in position. I have crazy hours and work weekends, so I need someone available twenty-four seven."

Oh, I can be available twenty-four seven, I thought. I felt light-headed at the onslaught of images that idea sparked in my mind. Alexis in a black lace bra and matching underwear. Her caramel waves sprawled out across a white pillow. My hands on her hips. My lips tracing a trail down her—

"Preston." She placed a hand on my thigh.

I glanced down at the connection, loving the way her long, delicate fingers were splayed over my muscles. I swallowed. Hard. If my thoughts had been hot, my skin singed from that simple touch.

Off-limits. Off-limits. Off-limits, I chanted in my head like a mantra.

Focus on the job. The money. Focus on your goals and your future.

She retracted her hand, brows furrowed. "I'm sorry. I, um…are you okay?"

I met her eyes, the sun making them seem more golden than brown. "Yes. I'm fine." I smiled. "And yes, that will be fine."

"Great. I can't tell you how much I appreciate this." She seemed so relieved, it made me even more glad I'd agreed. Though I couldn't deny, part of me was disappointed. I'd secured the placement, but that meant she was now my boss.

Fuck.

She glanced to the open doors where she could see Sophia playing in the living room, then lowered her voice. "Sophia's father bailed on her for the summer, and she was devastated."

I nodded. "She said he travels a lot for work."

She smiled, but I could tell it was forced. I hadn't been around Alexis that long, and already I could read her. "He does, but—" She closed her eyes briefly before reopening them. "He knew how important this was to Sophia. I should've known better than to believe he'd actually follow through."

"Hey," I said, resisting the urge to touch her. "Don't beat yourself up. It says a lot about you that you were willing to give him the benefit of the doubt."

She puffed out a breath, ruffling some of her hair. "Yeah. It tells me I should've had a backup plan."

"Well…" I smiled. "I'm here now, and I'm happy to help in any way I can."

Her shoulders relaxed, a genuine smile playing at her lips. "Thank you. Seriously, Preston," she said, placing her hand on my shoulder. "You're a life-saver."

We stared at each other, and I could feel the connection between us as if it were a tangible thing. It was more than the weight of her hand on my shoulder; it was a pull—deep and unexplored. My body thrummed with excitement, and I sensed Alexis felt it too.

Sophia ran outside, ending the moment all too soon. She chattered on, all excited about her latest creation. Alexis smiled at her and stood, and I followed suit.

"I'll have Renata send over the contract. Once it's signed, you can move in."

"Great."

I watched Alexis a moment longer, captivated by the way her honey-colored strands blew about her face. I'd just agreed to spend the summer with the woman of my dreams —as her daughter's nanny. But, like she said, she worked a lot. I'd been hired to do a job, and I consoled myself with the thought that, in all likelihood, I'd barely even see Alexis.

CHAPTER FIVE

Alexis

I cupped my coffee mug in my hands, warmth spreading through me. I stared at the designs without truly seeing them.

"Well," Lauren said. "What do you think?"

"Hmm?"

"The drawings?" she asked, tapping her finger on the design plans scattered across the surface of the table. "Girl, you sure are distracted today."

"Sorry," I said, taking a sip of my coffee. "I stayed up too late answering emails because I'd promised Soph we'd watch movies together." Which was partially true.

"You're such a good mom," she said, and I knew she meant it.

"Hah." I barked out a laugh. Somehow, no matter how much I did, it never felt like enough. "Thanks."

"So, did my girl at the Hartwell Agency hook you up?"

I coughed a little, thinking of the word hookup and Preston in the same sentence. "Yes. Thank you again for recommending them. Sophia's new nanny will be moving in today." I glanced at the clock on my phone. "Soon, actually."

As if on cue, the doorbell rang, and Sophia bounded down the stairs. "I'll get it!"

I shook my head and laughed. At least I knew she was excited about seeing Preston again. And she wasn't the only one. I'd spent way too much time reliving moments from yesterday. He hadn't been at all what I'd expected—in a good way. In the best way.

Sophia skipped into the kitchen a moment later with Preston in tow. He was dressed more casually than yesterday, but he still looked nice. His shorts were fitted, but not so tight that it looked like he'd raided the women's department. And his T-shirt stretched over the muscles of his chest, highlighting his golden skin.

"Hey." I smiled, feeling like the atmosphere of the room had changed just by virtue of his presence.

"Hey," he said. And we stood there for a beat, just smiling at each other until Sophia tugged on his hand.

Then Lauren cleared her throat, and I remembered she was standing there. Watching us. I started bracing myself for her comments.

"Preston, this is my associate and good friend, Lauren. Lauren, this is Preston." I hesitated a moment, debating whether to call him the nanny. *Manny?* Instead, I decided to avoid the topic altogether. "He'll be looking after Sophia for the summer."

"Friend?" She turned to stare at me, her expression indignant. "Friend?" Her voice rose. "Girl, I'm not just *a* friend. I'm your best friend."

I laughed, throwing my arm around her shoulder. "Yeah. I know."

She turned her attention back to Preston with an appreciative glance. "Nice to meet you." She held out her hand to shake.

"Take good care of our girl," she said, tightening her grip

on his hand. And for a minute, I felt like she was referring to me, not Sophia.

"Of course." His voice radiated sincerity.

I saw a gleam in Lauren's eye that I knew meant trouble. I needed to get him out of here before Lauren ran her mouth.

"Oh," I said to Preston, rounding the island and grabbing the spare key from the drawer. "This is for you."

I handed it to him, and our fingers brushed in the process. That simple touch had lightning racing up my arm, across my skin. And when I glanced up at him, his eyes seemed to flicker with the same surprise I felt.

"Thanks." He added it to his key ring, and I admired the dexterity of his long fingers. "I'll go through the gate."

"Can I help?" Sophia asked, practically jumping up and down.

"Soph, I'm not sure that's a good idea," I said at the same time Preston said, "Of course."

He chuckled, placing a hand on her shoulder. "It's fine, really. I didn't bring much, and this will allow you to get back to your meeting."

"Are you sure?" I asked.

I hadn't expected him to start working until tomorrow morning. And while I didn't want him to feel like I was taking advantage, I appreciated the offer.

"Absolutely." He turned to Sophia. "Come on, princess. You can help me organize my clothes."

"Really?" she practically shrieked, and I watched them disappear toward the front door.

"Mm. Mm. Mm," Lauren said after they'd gone. "Girl, he is foine."

I laughed nervously, feeling my cheeks heat. Was my attraction completely obvious?

"It's okay," she said. "I'm not going to judge. You can

admit it—you were totally checking him out. He has a good ass. And face. And, well, pretty much everything."

I laughed, this time a more genuine one. "He's the nanny. Manny?" I shrugged. "I don't know what to call him."

"I think he'd let you call him whatever you want." She arched an eyebrow. "Because boy, is he into you."

"He is not," I responded quickly, too quickly, and my cheeks flushed with heat. Though, really, I wanted to know. Was he? "And besides, he's just a boy."

"Handsome, hardworking, and he calls your daughter princess." She held her hand to her heart and pretended to swoon.

"Okay," I said, grabbing her bicep and picking her up off the floor. "I think we're done here."

"No way." She wagged her finger at me. "Nuh-uh. You're not kicking me out now. Not when the show's about to start."

"What show?"

"He's going to be *moving* in to your pool house." She said each word slowly, enunciating as if I couldn't understand her.

"And…?"

"And so, he's going to be lifting and bending and being all sexy and sweaty. And you, my dear," she said, spinning me toward the large sliding glass doors that faced the pool, "have a front row seat. *I'm* not going anywhere."

I rolled my eyes and took a seat on the barstool, returning my attention to the real reason we were here—work. It was Wednesday morning—my Sunday—and I wanted to get the designs finalized before my week officially started. "Where are we on these?"

"You tell me." She assessed me over the rim of her coffee mug.

I glanced through the materials and sketches. "I love what

you did with the kitchen—definitely want to keep that California-chic vibe. But I'm not sure about the bedrooms."

"Okay. What are you thinking? What do you want to change about them?"

"Considering the neighborhood and price point, I think we should target couples who want to entertain, not families."

"So, nix the kids' rooms." She made some notes on her tablet. "Done. Maybe make one a study?"

I nodded, and movement out of the corner of my eye drew my attention. I turned to watch as Preston carried Sophia in a firefighters's carry, his other arm wrapped around a box of books. He was laughing, and it looked effortless.

"Damn…" Lauren said the word long and low.

I nodded my agreement before shaking my head and turning my attention back to the designs.

"I think I need to hire myself a nanny," she joked. "Though, knowing my luck, I'd probably get a grumpy old woman."

I laughed and went back to the designs for the next house. It was a huge, modern home in the Hills.

"So, what are you going to do about it?" Lauren asked.

"About what?" I kept my eyes focused on the designs, feigning ignorance though I knew what she was referring to. Or rather whom—Preston.

"The attraction between you two." She fanned herself. "Whew. I'm getting hot just thinking about it."

At least I wasn't imagining the chemistry, I thought.

Was I attracted to him? Absolutely.

She leaned over, butting my shoulder with hers. "So…?"

"So, nothing," I said. "I'm not going to do a damn thing. He's Sophia's nanny and a college student."

"He looks nothing like the boys I went to school with." Her eyes were focused on the backyard. She had no shame.

I couldn't resist looking, and I immediately wished I hadn't. Because I knew the image of him chasing Sophia across the yard, both of them laughing, would be etched in my brain from here forward. Preston had known her less than twenty-four hours, and already he had a better relationship with her than her own father. Not that it took much effort.

Cal loved Sophia, but he was off living his life, doing his thing. He called when he could. He showed up when it was convenient. He knew how to have fun; he didn't know how to parent. He couldn't handle the hard stuff.

"How old is he anyway?" Lauren asked.

"He's too young for me, that's for sure."

He was twenty-six. Twenty. Six. The number had been seared in my brain as a reminder that he was nearly a decade younger than me.

"Is he a grad student?"

I shook my head. "Studying for his bachelor's."

"Hmm." She crossed her arms over her chest. "That seems a bit odd. Want me to have my PI friend look into him?"

"Lauren, the Hartwell Agency already ran a comprehensive background check. Who cares that he's a little older than your average college student?"

Okay, not just a little. A lot. Most students graduated by the age of twenty-two, twenty-three, max. But he was twenty-six. I knew there had to be a story there, but I also realized the less I knew about his personal life, the better.

She pursed her lips. "Still...why would a guy like him, a guy who could be a freaking model, want to be a nanny?"

I lifted a shoulder. "It wasn't in the file. And maybe he is a model, but he needs to pay the bills between gigs."

"As a nanny?" She gave me an incredulous look.

"He had glowing recommendations from every family he's worked with. And clearly," I said, gesturing toward the backyard where he and Sophia were talking as they rolled a suitcase across the yard, "he loves children."

"When he called Sophia 'princess'…" She placed a hand to her chest and sighed. "So sweet."

"I know," I said. "He's so, so good with her. Which is why this relationship can never be anything but professional."

"I know. I know." She held up her hands. "You don't mix business with pleasure."

"That's right." I stood and rinsed my mug in the sink, hopefully putting an end to the discussion. Even if I'd wanted to pursue something with Preston, I couldn't. I needed his help.

Lauren started packing up her stuff. "Thanks for the coffee. And the eye candy."

"Any time," I said, walking her to the door.

"Really?" She perked up. "I'm going to take you up on that."

I laughed, knowing she wasn't serious. *Right?*

She slid into the driver's seat of her white Mercedes coupe and rolled down the window. "Good luck with the new manny." She winked.

I rolled my eyes, and I couldn't help but smile. "Thanks."

"Hey, I'm just excited to see you finally interested in a guy. I was beginning to think you were secretly in love with me," she teased.

"Oh, Lauren." I leaned into her window and puckered my lips as I squeezed her cheeks. "You know I love you, pookie."

She laughed, pulling away from my touch. "Don't mess up my makeup," she said in a threatening tone.

"What makeup? Your skin is naturally flawless."

"Damn right. Thank you, girlfriend. If we're both still single when we turn forty, we're getting married."

I laughed. "Fine. But I hope it doesn't come to that."

"Oh, I'm fairly certain it won't," she said with a knowing glance toward the backyard.

"Go on." I backed away as she pressed the *Start* button, firing up the ignition. "Get out of here."

I returned to the kitchen feeling restless before deciding I should check on Preston and Sophia. I could hear them talking from the open door of the pool house, and I couldn't resist listening to their conversation.

"These books are heavy," Sophia panted, and I could picture her trying to lug around some of the textbooks I'd seen Preston carrying across the yard earlier.

"Yeah, well. As you get older, the books you read will get bigger too."

"Yeah, but mine won't. Weigh," she grunted. "A ton."

He chuckled. "Here let me help you with that."

"Haven't you ever heard of something called an e-reader?" My Sophia, always full of sass.

"I have," Preston said matter-of-factly. "But you know what? I actually prefer a paperback."

"You're weird," she said, and I covered my mouth to stifle a laugh.

"Knock. Knock," I called, rapping my knuckles on the doorframe.

"Hey." Preston glanced up at me and smiled. "Come in."

"Yeah, Mommy." Sophia grabbed my hand. "Come in."

She led me on a tour of the place as if I'd never been there. It didn't take long. There was a bedroom with a bathroom attached. And a small kitchen and sitting area that doubled as the dining room. It was simply furnished, but at least it was nice, clean.

"Are you settling in okay?" I asked Preston once we'd returned to the living room. Sophia had resumed organizing his books, placing them in alphabetical order on a shelf below the TV.

"I wasn't sure what to expect, but this is very nice. Much nicer than my apartment, so thank you." He smiled, rubbing the back of his neck.

"Wait. Apartment?"

"Yeah. I have a place near campus. Eventually, I'd love to have a house, but, yeah, real estate in LA is insane. Didn't really think about that when choosing a college."

I laughed. "Yeah. LA is certainly an expensive market. Good for people like me—agents and brokers. Not so much for struggling models...or, um, students," I added, feeling like my cheeks were on fire.

He gave me a bemused smile. "Maybe if I weren't on an eight-year degree program, it wouldn't be so bad."

I wanted to ask more, but I kept my mouth shut. Business —this was nothing but business. But surely, I should have a good relationship with my employees? I was certainly close to Gabriela. She was like family.

"I'm just thankful to be getting my degree," he said, and I sensed there was more he wasn't telling me.

"Mommy," Sophia called. "I'm starving."

"You're starving?" I asked, mimicking her tone and inflection. It was easy to tease, but she had no idea what it meant to be truly starving. Something I swore to myself she'd never know.

"Can we order from Celebration?" She wrapped her arm around my waist, blinking up at me with her gorgeous baby blues. "Please?"

"Why not?" I turned to Preston. "Would you like to join us?"

"I wouldn't want to intrude," he said. "Besides, I should probably unpack."

"Of course." I tried not to let my disappointment show.

"Come on, Soph." I pulled her into my side. "Let's go get ourselves some dinner."

"Yay!" She jumped around. "Night, Preston. See you tomorrow."

"Night, princess." He waved. "Sweet dreams."

"Goodnight, Preston," I said. "Thank you again. And please, don't hesitate to knock if you need anything."

Why was my voice so husky? And had I really said that?

He arched a brow, a subtle tilt to his lips. "Anything?"

I wondered if I was reading more into his tone than was actually there, but I didn't think so. I'd been around the block before, and I knew when a man was interested in me. And Preston was clearly interested. The idea that someone so much younger than me—and so hot—was attracted to me made me giddy, made me feel younger than my age.

"Mom," Sophia called, dragging out the vowel. It was like being doused with a bucket of ice water.

It didn't matter how hot Preston was, or how much I liked him, he was here for Sophia—not me. His attention, flattering as it was, could never amount to more. This was business. And as I'd told Lauren time and again, I absolutely did not mix business with pleasure.

CHAPTER SIX

Preston

"Hey, man. What's up?" I held the phone to my ear with one hand, while making the bed with the other. "How's New York?"

"Awesome," Hunter said. "Hotter than I expected, but man…this place is crawling with models."

I laughed. "And LA isn't?"

"True. But I've already slept with half of them." He wasn't kidding.

"So, what's up?"

"Some fucker at my sister's apartment building decided to light some candles and forgot to blow them out."

"Is she okay?"

"Yeah, and so is most of her stuff. But they decided it was a good time to renovate. And now everyone has to relocate. Would you be okay sharing the apartment with her this summer?"

"Yeah. The hot one, right?" I teased, knowing it would get a rise out of him. I assumed he was referring to Kate, since his older sister was married. Not that it mattered—they were both like sisters to me.

He growled. "She's too young for you."

She was twenty.

"I might be willing to make an exception. You know, since she's your sister and all." I smirked, picking up a few items as I walked toward the front room.

"Not funny, man. I'm seriously rethinking this."

"Nah," I said, figuring I'd tortured him long enough. "I'm not even going to be there this summer."

He lowered his voice, and I could imagine him walking down a hall to find some privacy. "Is everything okay? Are you okay?"

"Yeah, I'm fine." I rushed to reassure him. "I got a new placement, and it's a live-in position."

"Really? What happened with Theo?"

"Aww." I paced by the windows. "You do listen."

I didn't hear anything he said after that because Alexis was standing on the lawn in leggings and a sports bra. Her bare feet were nestled in the grass like her instructor's. As if that weren't torture enough, Alexis bent over to unroll her yoga mat, putting her perfect ass on display.

"Fuck," I said, dragging out the word.

"What?" Hunter asked.

I knew I should look away, but I couldn't. Especially not after she started going through a series of poses. I didn't know much about yoga, but it was clear that Alexis was incredibly flexible.

"My, um, new neighbor is doing yoga on the lawn," I said, settling on a version of the truth.

That got his attention. "Is she hot?"

"Mm-hmm." My dick strained against my zipper as she leaned forward, giving me a straight shot into her sports bra. Was she trying to torture me?

"What's she wearing?" Hunter's husky voice snapped me out of the trance.

"We're not having this conversation," I said, cringing that it had even gotten as far as it had.

"Why not?" I could imagine his expression—genuinely perplexed. "You know what—you're right. I have a better idea. Send me a picture."

My vision clouded, and I clenched my phone in my hand. "I'm not sending you a picture of Alexis."

"Alexis, huh? You sure are getting friendly with your new neighbor. Unless…" He was quiet for a moment, and I knew the wheels were turning. "Wait, is Alexis your boss?"

"What?" I scoffed. "No."

"Ha! She is." I could imagine his shit-eating grin. "Trying to bag a cougar after all?"

"Don't call her that," I hissed.

"Tell me one thing…" I could imagine him leaning back in a chair, his feet propped up on a desk, wearing a smug grin. "How old is she?"

I spotted Sophia, hopping across the grass. She bypassed Alexis and her yoga instructor and headed straight for my door. Guess this was just a regular day in her world. Mine too, now.

"She's… I'm not doing this with you." I spun away from the windows, suddenly feeling like a pervert for watching.

Could I really do this? Could I spend the next two months living in her pool house and not act on my desire for her?

I didn't have a choice. If I wanted to finish my degree, if I didn't want to completely fuck myself over financially, I needed to focus on the job, on Sophia. Sophia—not Alexis.

"Preston," Sophia called, knocking on the door. "Preston," she said in a singsong voice.

Since it was summer, Sophia could sleep in. Since she was supposed to be spending the summer with her dad, she had nowhere she needed to be, no schedule she needed to follow.

I wondered what her summers were typically like. I wondered if she was the type of kid to get bored easily or if she was good at independent play. I wondered if this summer —living and working so closely with Alexis—was going to be pure torture.

"I have to go," I said to Hunter.

"Have fun with your MILF."

I covered the mouthpiece with my hand, careful not to cuss in front of Sophia, even if there was a door separating us. "Shut the fuck up," I whispered just before I opened the door with a big smile. "Hey, princess."

"Oh man. You are so screwed." He chuckled.

"Catch you later." I disconnected the call, but not before I heard his laughter reverberating through the phone.

Sophia cocked her head to the side. "Who were you talking to?"

"My friend Hunter." I closed the door behind me.

Don't look up. Don't look up. Don't look—shit.

Alexis had her hips pressed to the ground, her chest lifted. And she was looking right at me. For a brief moment, it was as if a thread stretched between us. I was tethered to her, pulled in her direction.

And then Sophia's voice severed the connection.

I glanced away, returning my attention to Sophia. "Did you already eat breakfast?"

"Nope."

I steered her toward the house, doing my best to ignore Alexis. A nearly impossible task when her lips parted slightly on an exhale, her head lifted toward the sky.

She was stunning. Her body, sculpted and lean. And so incredibly flexible. Watching her move through the yoga poses had my imagination working in overdrive. And her apparel wasn't helping matters. Leggings that clung to her every curve, much like I wanted to. A sports bra that hugged her breasts, pushing them up so her cleavage nearly spilled over.

"Preston," Sophia said.

I cleared my throat and turned my attention back to her. "Um, yeah?"

"What do you want to eat for breakfast?" she asked.

Your mom.

So bad. So, so inappropriate. But seriously...those leggings were going to be the death of me.

"Um, I typically have eggs or oatmeal, like this morning. What do you like?" I followed her into the kitchen, which was immaculate.

"Gabby usually makes me an omelet," she said it with little to no enthusiasm.

"Do you want an omelet?"

She bit her lip, and in that moment, she looked so like Alexis.

"Well, then, what would you like? I am at your service, princess." I bowed low, and she giggled.

She glanced toward the backyard where Alexis was still showing off just how pliable her body was before turning back to me. "Could we..." She hesitated, and when she spoke again, it was with more confidence. "I'd really love some pancakes. Please," she added.

"Then pancakes you shall have." I glanced around the kitchen for supplies, relieved she hadn't requested an ice cream sundae or something I knew would absolutely not fly.

"Really?" she squealed.

Her reaction only confirmed my theory that pancakes weren't something she was typically permitted. I wondered if it was because of her food allergies—gluten, wheat, and oats. Or if it was something else, perhaps a ban on carbs? In California, you never knew what crazy diet people would come up with next.

"You want to help?" I asked.

She lit up. "Really?"

"Yeah." I nodded. "Of course. Everything tastes better when you make it yourself." I pulled the eggs from the fridge. "Can you grab us two bananas?"

"Bananas." She ran over to the counter and grabbed two. "Check."

"Great. We'll also need some cinnamon, salt, and olive oil."

She directed me to the pantry, which was both well stocked and incredibly well organized. Like the rest of the house, it looked like something straight out of a magazine. I grabbed the remaining ingredients, including the rice flour.

"Okay," I said, placing everything on the counter. "Two bowls. Two forks."

She grabbed them, and then, standing side by side at the counter, I showed her how to make pancakes. The last one was coming off the pan when Alexis strode through the door. Her cheeks were flushed, and her skin glistened. Her hair was in a high ponytail that bared her shoulders to me. And she looked good—good enough to eat.

"Mommy, Mommy," Sophia said. "Look! We made pancakes!"

I smiled, happy to see her pride and excitement over making breakfast. I turned off the gas range and added the last one to the stack.

"You did?" Alexis asked, and I could tell from her tone she wasn't entirely thrilled by the idea.

Meanwhile, she was pulling the most random stuff out of the fridge—spinach, grapes, some juice. It looked healthy, but also, disgusting.

"And they don't have wheat, gluten, or oats?" Alexis glanced to me for confirmation.

"Nope." I grinned. "None of the above."

"We made some for you too." Sophia slid a plate across the counter.

Alexis looked down at the stack of pancakes, eyeing them hungrily. "Thank you, baby. But you know I have a protein shake for breakfast."

She pushed the plate away, and I watched as Sophia disappeared into herself. Her shoulders slumped, her head down.

"These are actually very healthy pancakes," I said. "They have just a few ingredients: banana, egg, rice flour, and some seasonings."

"That's it?" Alexis's expression showed surprise.

I understood. When I'd first seen the recipe, I'd been skeptical too. A pancake with no butter or milk? And you could use alternative flours, but you didn't even have to add those.

"Sophia did such an amazing job making them." I gave Alexis an encouraging smile and inclined my head toward the pancakes. "Maybe you could just try a bite."

"I suppose one bite wouldn't be the end of the world." She grinned and picked up a fork.

Sophia and I watched as Alexis wrapped her lips around the fork. Sophia was waiting for the approval she so desperately sought. And I...I was just plain desperate.

She chewed then swallowed and finally smiled. "These are amazing. Seriously. Good job, Soph."

Alexis took another bite, and Sophia glanced up at me and grinned. It was like a sucker punch to the chest.

"These are so good," Alexis moaned, taking a seat on the barstool next to Sophia and pulling the plate closer to her. "So, so good."

I grinned to myself, giving them a moment to enjoy their breakfast while I wiped down the counter. They talked and ate their pancakes, and I was thrilled that the summer was already off to such a great start.

"Any questions about today?" Alexis asked.

"Nope. I think we're good. And if we can't figure something out, we'll call." Not that I intended to call unless it was an emergency.

"Actually—" She paused to swallow the bite she'd been chewing. "I'll be working from home this morning, and then I have a few showings this afternoon. So, I'll be around most of the day if you need anything."

I gripped the sponge. "Great."

"Also, I meant to tell you… You're welcome to use the pool or the home gym anytime. I know you weren't expecting a live-in placement, and I want to make this transition easy for you."

"Thank you," I said. "I appreciate it. And I'll definitely be taking you up on that offer."

She slid off the barstool and ruffled Sophia's hair. "Thanks, Soph."

I grabbed her empty plate and turned to stack it in the dishwasher. When I spun around, I bumped into Alexis. She wobbled on her feet, and I reached out to steady her.

She sucked in a quick breath when my hands gripped her hips, peering up at me with surprise. This close, I could see that her eyes were a deep brown at the center and fanned out with golden rays toward the edge. They were striking.

"Preston," she rasped, and the sound of her voice went straight to my dick. She cleared her throat. "Thank you."

I nodded, and with great reluctance, I removed my hands from her hips. I spun, putting my back to her and Sophia so I could adjust myself discreetly. "You're welcome."

I would never admit it to him, but Hunter was right. I was so screwed.

CHAPTER SEVEN

Alexis

"This is really good, Mommy," Sophia said. "You should try it."

"Try what?" I asked, pouring a glass of wine for myself. I took a sip and rounded the counter, taking a seat on the barstool next to her.

It was Tuesday, which meant Preston had the night off. His car wasn't in the driveway, and I wondered what he was doing. Who he was with. He hadn't mentioned a girlfriend, but that didn't mean he was single.

"This pizza Preston made. It's *delicious*." She took a huge bite.

I sipped my wine. "Pizza, huh? What's in it this time?" I asked, knowing Preston's "pancakes" and "cookies" were often much healthier than their name implied.

He'd been watching Sophia for several weeks now, and the pull between us hadn't lessened. If anything, it was stronger. I often escaped to the office to work just so I could avoid him—avoid this insane attraction to him. He was so sweet with my daughter, and Sophia adored him.

But it was more than that. He was smart and handsome,

caring and patient. And he made me laugh. He made me feel like I could be myself around him.

"Take a bite. See if you can guess." She sat up straighter, wiggling a little in her chair.

I cut my eyes at her as I lifted a piece to my mouth. "Somehow, I think this is a trick."

She giggled a little, and I took a bite. The flavors exploded on my tongue—tomato, oregano, onions, and mushrooms. Salty Parmesan. It was delicious.

"It's made with garbanzo bean flour?" It seemed like a reasonable guess. I knew it was an ingredient Gabby often used when making things for Sophia.

She shook her head, covering her mouth with her hands as she giggled. "It's a sweet potato crust."

I glanced down at the pizza, which looked rather ordinary. "Really? Sweet potato?"

She nodded. I took another bite just as my phone rang. Sophia groaned as I walked over to pick it up, expecting that it was another work call. I had a house closing soon, and there were a lot of balls in the air with the lenders, the client, and a few remaining issues that had come back on the inspection.

"It's your dad," I said, holding up the phone so she could see his name. I connected the call and set the phone in front of her.

"Daddy!"

"Hey, sweetheart." Cal's voice rumbled through the phone.

"Can you FaceTime?"

"Um, sure. Give me just a second." A moment later, Cal's raven hair and blue eyes filled the screen. "Hey." He smiled. "What are you up to?"

"Eating dinner with Mom." She turned the screen so the camera was focused on me, and I gave a little wave.

"Hey, Cal."

"Hey, Lex," he said, but he didn't see my eye roll because Sophia had already turned the camera back on her. He knew I didn't like it when he called me Lex.

"I don't have long to talk, but I wanted to call and say hi. I miss my girls."

I ground my teeth. I was poised with a retort, but this was Sophia's time with her dad. I knew how precious it was to her, and I didn't know when he'd call again. It had been over a week since the last time he'd checked in.

"Where are you, Daddy?" Sophia asked, squinting at the screen.

"Dallas, Texas," he said. "It's hot here."

"It's been nice here. The pool is perfect. Will you come for my birthday party?" she asked.

Sophia had thrown herself into planning it, and Juliana had readily agreed to help. I had a feeling the mermaid-themed pool party was going to be completely over the top. But it was what was expected, and it had given Sophia something to look forward to after Cal had bailed for the summer.

"Of course I will."

Her whole face lit up.

"Can I talk to your dad for a minute?" I held my hand out for the phone.

"Here's Mom," she said. "Bye, Daddy. I love you."

"Love you too."

I turned my back to Sophia and walked down the hall. "Take me off FaceTime please." I lowered my voice, holding the phone to my ear. "Why did you tell her you'd be at her birthday party?"

I could already see it all play out, probably because this was his pattern. This was what he did. He'd promise to come. She'd get her hopes up. And then, like always, something would come up at the last minute, and he wouldn't be able to make it.

"Because I will. Lex—Alexis," he huffed. "I'll be there. Promise."

I clenched my jaw. "Don't make promises you can't keep."

"Mom!" Sophia called, darting past me for the front door. "I heard a car. Maybe it's Preston."

"Preston?" Cal asked. "Who's Preston?"

It was on the tip of my tongue to tell him that Preston was Sophia's nanny. But "our new neighbor" came out of my mouth instead.

"Oh. That's nice," Cal said, not questioning it further. "I'm so glad Sophia has someone else to play with this summer."

I squeezed my eyes shut, grateful we were no longer on FaceTime. I could've used the opportunity to correct him, but I didn't want to get into a fight. Not when I'd come to rely on Preston. Not when I'd come to look forward to seeing him every day.

"Yes. Yes, it is." I craned my neck toward the front door, hoping maybe Sophia was right and Preston was home. "Look, I have to go."

"Yeah. Me too." He sounded tired. "See you in August."

I didn't respond because what was there to say? I'd believe it when I saw it.

Sophia returned to the kitchen with her shoulders slumped. "Not Preston."

I let her watch TV for a while before going through her bedtime routine. When she climbed into bed, I tucked the covers around her and leaned down to place a kiss on her forehead.

"I miss Preston," she said as I leaned back, sitting on the edge of her bed.

I would've been concerned by how attached she was to him, did I not feel it too. He'd become a fixture in our home, taking care of Sophia. But also, taking care of me. I'd lost count of the number of meals he'd prepared, the chores he'd done to make my life easier. He was incredibly nurturing and considerate, and any doubts I'd had about a male nanny had quickly vanished.

"You'll get to spend all day with him tomorrow." That made her smile.

"He tells the best stories," she said around a yawn.

"Better than Gabby?" I asked.

She nodded, her eyes already closed. "Gabby just reads straight from the book, but Preston makes them up."

"Wow," I said. "Sounds pretty awesome."

"Mm-hmm," she hummed, but she was already half asleep.

I sat there a minute, just watching her as she drifted off to sleep. My beautiful baby. My Sophia.

I couldn't believe how quickly she was growing up. Sometimes it felt like I was missing out. Like I was so busy trying to give her the life she deserved that I sacrificed spending time with her. It was something I grappled with a lot, but more so this summer.

Maybe it was because she was home instead of with Cal. Maybe it was because Preston was watching her instead of Gabby. Whatever it was, I'd noticed a shift in my priorities. And I found myself trying to carve out more opportunities to spend time with my daughter. To show her just how much she mattered to me.

Finally, when her breathing evened out, I switched off the lamp and crept out of her room. I grabbed my glass of wine as I passed through the kitchen, heading toward the pool with my laptop. The lights in the pool house were off, and I hadn't thought to check if Preston's car was in the driveway. I reminded myself it didn't matter; I shouldn't care. He was my employee, and his personal life was just that.

The moon cast shadows on the lawn through the palm trees, reflecting on the surface of the pool. I took a seat in one of the chairs and opened my laptop, only to shut it again. I had a million things to do, but with a warm breeze in the air and the water cascading gently into the pool, I didn't want to do anything. And as I looked out over my beautiful backyard with the perfect grass and the perfect pool, I felt a deep sense of loneliness.

With a heavy sigh, I downed the rest of my wine and stood from the chair. Sophia was tucked safely in her bed, and most of the things on my to-do list could wait. And the rest—I could handle first thing in the morning. Right now, there was a hammock calling my name. It was a fabric one that was incredibly comfortable, yet I rarely used it. Rarely made the time.

I padded across the grass, enjoying the sensation of the smooth blades flicking across the bare skin of my feet. An airplane hummed overhead, but it seemed distant. As if part of a different world.

I angled my head toward the sky, watching the plane as I leaned back to sit in the hammock. I realized a moment too late that it was already occupied. It swung wildly, and we were a tangle of arms and legs, the scent of cedar filling my nose. I knew it was Preston, knew it was his strong arms that caged me in, holding me close. Knew he was the one keeping me from falling.

The hammock finally stilled, but my heart didn't. No, my heart clamored against my ribs as Preston continued to hold me long after the threat of toppling had passed. He didn't move and neither did I.

I blinked up at him. "I didn't realize you were out here."

He stared at me, and even in the dim light, I felt the intensity of his gaze. "I must have fallen asleep."

"I gave you one hell of a wake-up call." I shot him a sheepish grin. "I'm so sorry."

"I'm not," he rasped, lifting his hand to tuck a strand of hair behind my ear.

"You're not?" I felt a little silly for repeating him, but it was as if all rational thought had fled my brain the moment I'd found myself tangled up in the hammock with him.

His blue eyes locked on mine. "No."

One hand was tucked beneath his cheek, but he used the other to caress my face. He traced my jaw with his thumb before brushing it over my lips. I felt like I was locked in a dream, an alternate reality. And I wanted so badly to embrace it, to embrace him. I wanted to believe it was real.

"Kiss me," I blurted.

His eyes darkened, and he leaned forward, his breath feathering over my skin. He bypassed my lips, opting to place delicate kisses along the corners of my eyes, over my nose, on my cheeks. His touch was so light, so reverential. And I felt it all the way to the depth of my very being. I'd never felt more connected to someone.

I relaxed into his arms, reveling in the moment. It felt so decadent—to lie in a man's arms without a care in the world. To be kissed and worshiped as if it were his sole purpose in life to cherish me.

Unlike any of the other men I'd been with, there was no rush. If anything, Preston seemed intent to slow down and savor the moment. And I found myself noticing more—the feel of his scruff against my skin. The way my nerve endings tingled, reaching out for him.

I was on the verge of begging him to kiss me when he finally slanted his lips over mine. My body hummed with excitement, but he continued to keep his movements slow. We sampled each other, our bodies forced together by the fabric of the hammock, making it feel like we were in a cocoon. Even when he teased the seam of my lips with his tongue, it was a languid movement. It felt like we had all the time in the world, and he wanted to spend it with me.

He didn't push for more, and neither did I. Instead, we explored each other, our legs and tongues tangled together.

I could've stayed there all night. But then, I heard Sophia calling for me, and I bolted upright.

"Mommy?" Her voice was more insistent, and she sounded upset.

I rushed to find my footing, one of my feet getting stuck in the hammock. "I'm coming!"

Preston helped free me, only for me to fall flat on my face. I scrambled to my feet and rushed over to where Sophia was standing by the back door.

My heart was racing as I wrapped my arm around her. "I'm here, baby. What's wrong?"

She sniffled. "I had a nightmare."

Talk about a nightmare. I'd just experienced the most amazing kiss of my life—with my daughter's nanny. My employee. A man who was nine years younger than me.

But overriding all of it was guilt. I hadn't been there for my daughter when she needed me. When I should've been comforting her, I was making out with her nanny.

"It's okay." I held her close to me. "You're okay. Why don't we go inside and cuddle for a little bit?"

She nodded, allowing me to lead her toward the doors. "Mommy." She sniffled. "Why is there grass on your shirt?"

I glanced down, brushing it off quickly. "I, um, was doing some yoga before bed."

I could hear Preston's quiet chuckle in the dark, could feel him watching me as I shut the glass door behind me. I shook my head, more at myself than him. This couldn't happen again. But the way his low laughter threaded through my belly told me that would be easier said than done.

CHAPTER EIGHT

Preston

The click-clack of Alexis's heels against the tile floor was the only warning I had. I glanced up, expecting her to look amazing as usual. But I wasn't prepared for the way her black sheath hugged her curves and her leopard-print heels emphasized her spectacular legs.

Fuck me.

"Hey, Soph." Alexis dropped a kiss on her daughter's head before going over to the fridge. My eyes tracked her every move, lingering on her every detail.

"Good morning, Preston." She gave me a smile, but it was forced.

Just like every interaction we'd had since the night of our kiss. It had been three days of stilted conversations, averted gazes, rushed goodbyes. She was never rude; she was always on the go, always busy. And if I weren't mistaken, avoiding me.

"Good morning," I said, handing her a mug of coffee. I'd prepared it just the way she liked—a splash of almond milk and no sugar.

"Thank you, but I already had some," she said, green smoothie in hand.

She smiled, but it didn't quite reach her eyes. I knew she was embarrassed about the kiss—maybe she even regretted asking me to kiss her. But if she'd just talk to me, maybe we could do it again. Or at least, maybe things wouldn't be so awkward between us.

She returned her attention to Sophia. "What are you up to today?"

Sophia wiggled in her chair. "We're going to see the new exhibit at the Natural History Museum. Right, Preston?"

"Right." I nodded.

"Great," Alexis said. "I won't be home until late. I have that closing today, and then I'm sure the client will want to go out for drinks."

"Do you have to?" Sophia asked.

Alexis's expression faltered before she quickly masked it with a smile. "Yes, baby. Somebody has to pay for the big mermaid extravaganza."

Sophia was excited now, her earlier disappointment easily forgotten. "Can I wear a mermaid tail?"

"You can wear whatever you want. We can go shopping next Tuesday, when I'm off."

"Yes! Yes! Yes!" Sophia chanted. She wrapped her arms around Alexis's waist and squeezed. "Thank you, Mommy. I love you."

"I love you too." Alexis closed her eyes, breathing her daughter in. "So, so much," she whispered. I considered looking away, feeling like I was watching an intimate moment between the two of them.

"All right—" Alexis straightened, and I already sensed a shift. "I've got to get to work. Call me if you need anything." Where was the warmth from a few days ago? The lingering glances?

"Will do, boss."

She flinched as if she'd been slapped and quickly grabbed her things before bolting for the door. I stood there feeling like a jackass, until I noticed she'd left her smoothie on the counter. I grabbed it and rushed after her.

"Alexis," I called, but that only seemed to spur her to move faster. How she could walk so quickly in those damn heels was a mystery. "Alexis. Wait."

She paused at the front door with her back still to me. Her shoulders were hunched, and I hated that I'd been the one to cause her pain. That was the last thing I wanted.

She spun around, her expression fierce. She was intimidating, and I could see how she was so successful. "What?" she snapped.

"I… You forgot your smoothie," I said.

"Oh." Her expression fell, and I watched as she deflated. "Thank you."

She went to grab the smoothie, but I held it just out of reach. It had the effect of bringing her closer to me. I stared down at her, thinking that if I moved just a little closer, we could be kissing.

"And I'm sorry." My voice was gravelly when I spoke. "My comment was uncalled for."

Her eyes were fixed on the floor, and what I wouldn't give for her to look at me. She hadn't looked at me in days, not since we'd kissed under the stars. It was slowly killing me. That and her yoga sessions on the lawn, and the way she dressed for work, and…

Okay, everything about this woman was killing me. Especially the fact that we'd shared such an incredible moment, and she preferred to act like it had never happened.

She lifted a shoulder. "It wasn't untrue."

"Yeah, but…still," I huffed. "I shouldn't have called you 'boss' in that tone. I certainly don't think of you as my boss."

She straightened, and I could see her armor sliding back into place. "And maybe that's the problem. Look," she sighed. "I'm sorry if I gave you the wrong impression, but I had a little too much to drink, and—can't we just forget about it?"

I wanted to call bullshit, but instead, I said, "I don't think I can."

And judging from the conflicted look in her eyes, she couldn't either. Even if she wasn't ready to admit it.

Her phone chimed, saving her from a response. She snagged the cup from me. "Thanks. I have to go."

She left me standing there, staring after her, until Sophia called my name. I huffed and returned to the kitchen, wondering where we went from here.

A few days later and I was no closer to figuring out the answer. Alexis was still as busy as ever, though she did seem more relaxed since the closing. Sophia was happy, but I could tell she missed her mom. And it made me feel guilty—like my role in the kiss had not only pushed Alexis away from me, but Sophia too.

To compensate, I did my best to keep her busy. We'd spent the day at the children's museum, and the way her shoulders drooped told me she was getting tired.

"You ready, princess?"

Sophia nodded, taking a long drink from the water bottle I'd handed her. She'd been running around, exploring, and playing with other kids all day. She'd had a blast, and it made me realize how much she needed time with kids her own age. Something I intended to work on.

"Can you keep a secret?" she asked on the way home from dinner.

I glanced at her in the rearview mirror. "Can I keep a secret?" I scoffed. "It's part of the sacred oath of nannies. Anything you tell me gets locked in the vault."

She was quiet a moment, considering it. "So, you won't tell, right?"

"No, princess." I smiled. "I won't tell. What is it?"

"Do you think my mom's happy?" Her question surprised me. It was easy to forget how insightful children could be.

I frowned. "Why do you ask?"

"She just always seems... I don't know," she huffed. "Maybe lonely."

I'd noticed it too, but I didn't want Sophia to worry. So, I turned the question back around on her. "Do you think she's lonely? She has you. She has friends like Lauren, right?"

"Yeah, but...I think she needs a boyfriend. Ben's mom got a boyfriend, and she's so much happier now."

I chuckled. "If only it were that simple."

"Why not?" she asked. "Couldn't you be her boyfriend?"

"Sophia," I said, trying not to let any emotion show. "Do you know what a boyfriend is?"

"Yes." Even without looking back at her, I knew she was rolling her eyes. "It's when a guy is really nice to a girl. And he takes her on dates. And, and he does nice things for her—like buy her flowers or call her on the phone."

I nodded. "That's actually not a bad description."

She preened. "See. And you already do nice things for my mom."

"I do?"

"Yeah. You make her coffee every morning—just the way she likes. You cook her breakfast and sometimes dinner. You hang out with me. And you make her smile more than she has in a long time."

I grinned, but then my face fell. Maybe Alexis had been happier lately, but then I'd ruined it with the kiss. As much as the kiss meant to me, I'd take it all back if it meant we could go back to the way things were again.

"Anyway…" She yawned. "Just think about it. 'Kay?"

I didn't know what to say, so I kept my attention focused on the road.

Not long after, her eyes drifted shut, and she was deep asleep by the time we returned home. I pulled into the driveway and unbuckled Sophia before carefully picking her up. She mumbled something in her sleep, but otherwise, she was out.

I carried her up the stairs and set her on her bed. After removing her shoes and tucking her in, I switched off the light and crept out of the room.

I sank onto the couch, flipping through the channels until I found HGTV. It was an episode of *Fixer Upper* I'd already seen but didn't mind watching again. I wondered when Alexis would be home, wondered if I should try to talk to her and clear the air.

As I was debating all that, my phone rang. My mom's picture lit up the screen. I was tempted to let it go to voice mail, but I hadn't talked to her in a few days. And I knew if I didn't answer, she'd worry.

"Hey, Mom," I said, lowering the volume on the TV.

"Hey, sweetie. How are you?"

"I'm good. Tired." I yawned, rubbing a hand over my face.

Being a live-in nanny was so much more demanding than the part-time placements I'd had in the past. Entertaining an energetic six-year-old all day, instead of after school or for a few hours, was no small feat. But really, it was emotional exhaustion. I was exhausted from the tension that seemed to stretch endlessly between Alexis and me.

"Are you eating okay? Sleeping okay? Any pain?" Her

questions came rapid-fire, and I should've known better than to say I was tired.

"Mom." I interrupted her mid-question. I understood why she was freaking out, and I felt bad for alarming her.

"I'm just…tired. Chasing after a rambunctious six-year-old is hard work," I said, hoping my answer would reassure her.

"You're sure? Do you think we need to set up an appointment with Dr. Patel?" I heard her voice wobble, even as she tried to cover it.

"I'm fine, really."

"Okay, but—"

"I know. And I'll schedule an appointment if I need to," I said.

"Thank you," she sighed, and I could sense her relief through the phone. "Don't wait for your six-month scan. If you think you need to be seen sooner, go sooner."

I understood her concern, but still… "Okay, Mom."

"Any updates on Sam?" she asked, knowing he'd started another round of treatment.

I shook my head before remembering she couldn't see me. "He's struggling. Indy says he's losing a lot of weight."

"Hmm," she said, and we both knew that wasn't good. "Let me know if I can do anything."

"I will." I appreciated the offer, even if I wasn't sure there was much that could be done. It was heartbreaking to watch a friend struggle, to know their pain, their fear. "So, what's up with you? How's Dad?" I lay down on the couch, tucking an arm beneath my head.

"Good. Good," she said, sounding lighter. "I want to hear more about your adventures with Sophia."

I laughed. "Today we went to the children's museum. She loved it. She's so inquisitive and clever. And man is she funny."

Mom laughed, and I felt myself relax. "You were just like that at her age."

"Yeah?"

"And you were always so sweet to the other kids, especially the littler ones. Which is why it doesn't surprise me at all that you're a nanny." I felt my chest warm from her comment.

"It doesn't embarrass you that your twenty-six-year-old son is a nanny?" I asked.

"No," she said immediately. "It's a noble job. What you do is hard work. To love a child, to care for them as if they were your own, but ultimately to know you'll say goodbye—that's not an easy thing to do."

I nodded, knowing how much I'd miss Sophia when the summer was over. Gabby would come back from Colombia, and I would return to classes full time. And Alexis… I sighed.

"What's wrong?"

It wasn't something I wanted to discuss, especially not with my mom. "Nothing. I should probably get going."

"Wait," she said. "A letter arrived for you from the university. I didn't open it, but it looks important. Do you want me to forward it to you?"

"Can you just tell me what it says?"

"Of course."

I could hear the sound of paper tearing and then a pause. She sucked in a shaky breath, and my anxiety grew with every moment that passed.

"What is it?" My heart pounded, and I bolted upright. "What's wrong?"

"Oh, honey." I knew from the tone of her voice that I wasn't going to like what she'd say next. But I was completely unprepared for the words that came out of her mouth. "Your scholarship. It's gone," she whispered.

My eyes went wide, and I leaped up from the couch. "What do you mean…gone?"

I was trying not to panic as I paced the floor. Surely there must be some mistake. I needed those funds. I was counting on them to finish my final year of school.

"Dear Mr. Hawthorne," she read. "We regret to inform you that your scholarship will no longer be available. The money was invested with a brokerage firm that mismanaged the funds and has now gone defunct. We are working with law enforcement to try to recover the funds, but it may take some time."

This was a joke, right? I was waiting for someone to pop out and yell "Gotcha!" Yet, no one did.

"The FBI has informed us it may take years to recover, but even that is unlikely. We apologize for any inconvenience, and we hope this will not prevent you from continuing your education."

She finished reading, and we were both quiet after that.

Shit.

"What are you going to do?" she finally asked.

"My placement with Sophia pays well. I'll just have to try to get placed quickly when this one ends."

"Your dad and I—"

"No, Mom," I interrupted. "I'm not taking any more money from you and Dad."

She sighed. "Okay. Well, I guess the important thing is keeping your placement with Sophia. That will help, and hopefully her mom will give you a great recommendation."

Not at this rate, I thought. At this rate, I was going to be lucky if I kept my job. Which meant that I needed to back off with Alexis. I needed to go back to being professional. I needed to start thinking more about my future and less about screwing my boss.

CHAPTER NINE

Alexis

Lauren raised her glass for a toast. "To new developments." She grinned. "Your new property—gorgeous, by the way. And congrats on closing that big deal. Ten mil—that is sick."

I laughed, clinking my glass against hers. "Thanks."

It was sick. It was the most expensive home I'd listed to date, with a commission to match. And since I owned the real estate brokerage, I wouldn't have to share my earnings with anyone. It was also a ton of pressure.

"This is huge for you, for your office," she said.

I nodded, sipping my cocktail. It was. It was the type of opportunity I'd been working for. It was the type of opportunity most would kill for. Now I just had to find a buyer.

She frowned. "Why aren't you more excited?"

"I am. I'm just…" I sighed.

"Just…?" She pushed her head forward, moving it from side to side.

I couldn't keep it in any longer. And I knew Lauren would never judge me, even if I was totally judging myself for what I'd done.

"Something happened with Preston the other night." I kept my attention focused on the wineglass as I toyed with the stem.

"With you and Preston?" she asked.

I nodded, unwilling to meet her gaze. "He sort of, um, kissed me."

"Sort of?" she asked. "How does someone 'sort of' kiss you?"

"Okay," I huffed. "He kissed me."

"Did you kiss him back? How was it?"

I met her eyes, knowing there was no turning back now. "Yes. And it was amazing."

"Oh, girl." She grabbed my hands, nearly bouncing in her seat. "Give me all the juicy details."

I told her a condensed version of what had happened. At first, I felt lighter for sharing my burden. But by the time I finished, I didn't know what to think.

"Damn. That sounds hot. Most guys are so wham, bam, thank you, ma'am. It's like, um, hello. I have needs too." She pointed a perfectly manicured nail at herself, and I laughed.

"Seriously." Her expression was contemplative. "Who knew the younger manny would take things slow?"

Oh god. I'd kissed the manny.

I groaned, sliding my hands forward so my head was resting on the table. "What is wrong with me?"

"Girl, there is nothing wrong with you. It's biology. Your body is wired to seek out a potential mate. And Preston is hot, young, and great with your kid. Of course, you're going to be attracted to him," she said, as if it were really that simple.

I hadn't ever really considered having more children. Not that that's what this was about, but now that Lauren had mentioned it, my mind automatically went there. And

Preston—I had a feeling he'd want kids, or at least want the chance to decide.

I pushed myself up, meeting her eyes, which were kind, understanding. "But I don't even want to have more kids. I love Soph, but I'm getting too old to have more babies."

"Too old," she scoffed. "Says who?"

I groaned. "Everyone."

She crossed her arms over her chest. "Bullshit."

"Okay, well, even if you want to ignore prevailing medical research regarding the risks, I'm still too old for him."

"And again, I say, bullshit." She stared at me, hard.

She could be unrelenting. It was something I valued about her in business, but as a friend…

"He's what—six years younger than you?" she asked.

"Nine. *Nine*," I said again, sobered by the fact. "When he was born, I was about to start middle school. When he was being potty trained, I was going through puberty." My chest tightened. "When he turned twenty-one and could legally drink, I was…" I couldn't breathe. "Thirty."

"Sweetie." Lauren placed her hand over mine. "Alexis," she said in a calm but firm tone. "Take a deep breath. A few deep breaths."

"Oh my god. What am I doing?"

"Right now, you're freaking out," she teased, but I didn't laugh.

What the hell was I thinking? Was this some sort premature midlife crisis? What was next—a sports car and a boob job? My life was spinning out of control.

"Alexis," Lauren said in a stern tone. I snapped my eyes to hers. "It's going to be okay. It was just a kiss."

Just a kiss? Ha! It was so much more than just a kiss. It was *the* kiss. The best kiss of my life. With a man nine years younger than me. With my daughter's nanny. I was turning into a perverse sort of cliché.

"Okay? No, this is not going to be 'okay,'" I said, using air quotes. "Things have been so awkward since."

And I hated it. I hated that I missed his smile. I hated that I missed his flirting. I hated myself for wanting to kiss him again.

"So, talk to him," she said.

"And then what? He could quit, and then I'd be really fucked." My eyes went wide as another thought occurred to me. "Oh my god. What if he tries to sue me for sexual harassment?"

Lauren rolled her eyes. "He's not going to try to sue you. He likes you. And besides, you said he initiated it."

Yes, I thought, remembering back to that night. *But only after I'd asked him to kiss me.*

"This is such a mess." I buried my face in my hands and shook my head. "And this is exactly why I don't mix business and pleasure. Sophia adores him, and I need his help."

She was quiet for a moment, sipping her drink as she nodded thoughtfully. But then she got a gleam in her eye, and I knew I wasn't going to like whatever she was about to suggest.

"So, treat it like a business proposition."

My brows pulled together. "Um…what?"

"Yeah," she said, growing more animated. "Treat it like a business proposal."

I waited for her to elaborate, but when she didn't, I asked, "Treat what like a business proposal?"

"Sex," she said, and I swallowed hard. "With Preston." She flashed me a wicked grin. "All you have to do is set up guidelines, conditions."

I stared at her a minute, waiting for her to tell me she was joking. When she didn't, I finally said, "You're serious."

She nodded. "Dead serious."

"I can't do that."

"Well, what are the alternatives? Act as if nothing happened? Continue to be tortured for the rest of the summer? Fire him?"

"No," I rushed to say.

She smirked, like she'd expected me to say that. "Just think about it or, actually, don't. For once in your life, let go. Have a summer fling. Come fall, Gabby will be back, and Preston will have moved on."

A knot formed in the pit of my stomach. *Moved on?* I didn't like the thought of that—not one bit.

"There is another option," she said. "But I don't think you're going to like it."

"What is it?" I was desperate. Desperate for a way to fix this situation. My head might be clear on the fact that Preston was off-limits, but I wasn't sure my heart was on the same page.

"Go on a date with Mateo."

She'd been trying to set us up for months, and I'd always said no. Not that he wasn't handsome or successful. I'd just never been interested. I was content with my life—it worked for me. And between work and Sophia, I didn't have the time or desire for a relationship.

"He's a nice guy. Hot as fuck and…older."

Not hotter than Preston, I thought before chiding myself.

"How old?"

"Forty-two." She took a sip of her drink. "It's just one date. Go out, eat, see if any sparks fly. If they do—great. You can move on from your crush.

"If not, at least you tried. And you'll have shown Preston you're unavailable."

I knew she was right—I had to do something. But was this really the answer? A little voice in the back of my head said that screwing the nanny wasn't the right answer either.

"Fine," I sighed. "Set it up."

"Eek!" She clapped her hands together. "You won't regret this. You'll see."

Somehow, I doubted that.

A FEW NIGHTS LATER, SOPHIA CAME INTO MY ROOM AS I WAS getting dressed. She flopped down on the bed, propping her chin up with her fists. "Where are you going, Mommy?"

"Out with a friend," I said.

I hadn't dated much since the divorce. The few times I had, I always said I was going out with a friend. I'd never introduced a man to Sophia as my boyfriend or even someone I was dating. And I didn't intend to, unless it was serious.

"With Lauren?" She watched me as I flicked through my clothes, debating my options.

"No, but he's friends with Lauren."

I considered wearing a floral-patterned dress but realized it was too daytime for a romantic date. Too…tame.

This wasn't what I'd wear if I were going on a first date with Preston, so why would I wear it with Mateo? I pushed that thought—and the floral dress—aside and grabbed a red dress with a plunging neckline. If I was going to give this a real shot, I needed to pull out all the stops. I needed to treat it like a real date, even if my heart wasn't in it.

I zipped up the dress, then selected a gold necklace that drew the eye down to my cleavage. Finally, a pair of five-inch nude heels completed the look.

Sophia's eyes were wide as I crossed the room to my dresser. "Wow. You look…fancy."

I laughed and sprayed on some of my favorite Jo Malone

perfume. She hopped off the bed, holding out her wrist as she came over to me.

"Can I have some?"

"Sure." I smiled and gave her a small spritz. "Come on." I grabbed my purse off the bed. "Let's go talk to Preston."

When we reached the bottom of the stairs, he was already waiting. He stared up at me with a need so powerful, I felt it all the way to my core. I'd never had a man look at me with such longing, and it was a heady feeling.

"Wow." He swallowed hard, and I was thankful Sophia had already skipped off to the living room. "You look—" His eyes darted from my lips to my breasts to my hips and my heels. But then he seemed to recover himself, straightening as if remembering our roles. "Nice."

Nice? That's all?

I'd spent two hours getting ready, and the best he could do was "nice"? Then again, why did I care? He wasn't the man I was trying to impress. Right?

"Thanks. And thanks again for agreeing to watch Sophia so I could go out tonight."

"No problem. I'm always happy to hang with my favorite girl, and I know you sometimes have work functions in the evening."

"Actually..." I brushed my hair away from my face, debating whether to tell him the truth. But then I remembered Lauren's advice. "It's not a work dinner. It's a date."

A look of pain flashed in his eyes, then it was gone. It happened so fast, I almost believed I'd imagined it. Almost like I'd begun to believe I'd imagined the kiss.

I'd noticed a shift the past few days. Preston seemed more professional than ever lately, and it honestly kind of pissed me off. Yes, I'd pushed him away, but was he really going to give up that easily?

I'd always believed that if you wanted something—truly

wanted it—you had to be willing to work for it. Whether it was a sale or a relationship, you had to show up and prove how much you cared. And if you didn't…well, that was a huge reason Cal and I hadn't worked out.

"Bye, Soph." I waved to her from the hallway.

"Bye, Mommy," she called, but her attention was focused on the TV.

"Have a nice evening," Preston said as he closed the door behind me.

I stood on the front porch for a few moments, feeling torn. My best friend had set me up on a date with a successful, handsome, and—more importantly—older man. At least on paper, Mateo was perfect for me. Yet…I couldn't help but feel that if Preston were maybe ten years older and not Sophia's nanny, I would be going to dinner with him instead.

I took a deep breath. I might be attracted to Preston, but attraction wasn't the foundation for a lasting relationship. I'd fallen into that trap once before, and I wouldn't do so again. I didn't have that luxury now that I was a mom.

No. Mateo was the smart choice. The safe choice.

I might take risks in my professional life, but in my personal life—I preferred to play it safe. So even though my heart told me to cancel the date, to stay home with Preston and Sophia, I knew I couldn't.

I took a few steps toward the car, telling myself it was the right thing to do.

CHAPTER TEN

Preston

I glanced at the clock again. Only five minutes had passed since I'd last checked the time. Sophia had been a good distraction, at least until she went to bed. Then, I'd spent the last hour and a half alternating between staring at the clock and watching the door like Alexis would walk through it any moment.

It was after eleven, and she still wasn't back from her date.

Date.

When she'd told me her plans earlier, it felt like a punch to the gut. Even though I knew it was for the best, the thought of her on a date with someone else nearly killed me. I didn't want her to go out with another man, especially not looking the way she had.

That red dress and those red lips…drove me wild. I could just imagine the dress on the floor, her lips wrapped around my cock.

I'd even briefly considered asking her not to go. But then I remembered—I was just the nanny. And she…she was so out of my league, it wasn't even funny. Still, it hadn't stopped me from wanting her. From imagining a future with her.

I heard a noise, and my eyes darted to the front door for the millionth time. A moment later—quiet. I raked my fingers through my hair. This was maddening.

For all I knew, she might stay out all night. I doubted it, but that didn't mean they wouldn't kiss. Touch. Have sex. The thought had crossed my mind—numerous times.

I'd even been tempted to call her with a fabricated emergency, so she'd have to come home. But I wouldn't do that. Not only would it tank my chances of keeping this job for the rest of the summer, but it would cause more stress for her. And that was the last thing I wanted to do. Her life was stressful enough as it was, between running a successful brokerage firm and being a single mom.

I rested my elbows on my knees, cradling my head in my hands. This was pathetic. I was fucking pathetic. She didn't want me; at least, she said she didn't. And I certainly shouldn't want her.

Yet, I did.

Despite the fact that she was on a date with another man. Despite the fact that she ran hot then cold. Despite the fact that she was my boss and this was a terrible idea, I wanted her, and I knew I'd regret it if I let her go so easily. Life was precious. *Time* was precious. Sam's recent bout of treatment was proof enough of that. I didn't want to always wonder "What if?"

Besides, there had to be a reason why our paths had crossed. And not just because she'd needed a nanny. I wouldn't waste my time with someone who wasn't interested. But I had to know—*was* Alexis interested?

The sound of the key turning in the lock echoed in the hall. Followed by the chime of the alarm system. It felt like hours until she walked into the kitchen, but it was probably no more than a few minutes.

"Hey." She set her keys on the counter.

My heart was racing, but I tried to appear outwardly calm. This was the first time we'd been alone together in days. The first time we'd been alone together since the kiss.

"Hey." I glanced back over the couch to look at her. Even in the dim light, she looked immaculate as ever, not a hair out of place. No smudged lipstick. No smile either.

She grabbed a bottle of wine and two glasses from the kitchen and carried them over to the coffee table. She kicked off her shoes and folded her leg beneath her when she sat on the couch. The material of her dress rose higher up her thigh, revealing more of her sun-kissed skin. I wanted to track the material's path with my fingers, taste her skin with my tongue.

"Can we talk?" she asked.

My eyes darted from her face to the wine, trying to decide what was going on. If she was going to fire me, I didn't think she'd offer me alcohol first. "Sure."

She poured us each a glass. There was no toast. There was no hint as to her thoughts. I took a large gulp.

"This," she said, gesturing between us, "isn't working for me."

Shit. She was firing me.

It was on the tip of my tongue to apologize, to beg for my job, when she asked, "Why did you kiss me?" She sounded angry, but her expression betrayed nothing.

Was she serious? When she continued to stare at me expectantly, I told her the truth. "Because I've been imagining what it would be like for almost a year."

She jerked her head back. "What?"

I nodded. "As you know, I used to nanny for a boy who

went to the same school as Sophia. So, I saw you a few times at school plays, when he invited me.

"I know it was completely unprofessional, and I'm sorry if I made you uncomfortable. But I had to know if it was as incredible as I'd imagined."

I held my breath, awaiting her response.

She leaned forward. "Was it?"

I shook my head. "It was better. Beyond anything I'd ever dreamed."

She groaned, dragging a hand through her long waves. "You can't say things like that."

"Why? Because I'm your daughter's nanny?"

"That's certainly a big part of it." She took a large gulp of wine.

"I won't always be her nanny." We both knew my placement would only last until the end of the summer.

"True, but..." She seemed hesitant to tell me. She closed her eyes and drew in a deep breath.

I wasn't sure I wanted to know, but I had to ask. If there was any way to overcome her objections, I wanted to at least try.

"But what?"

She opened her eyes again, and I knew she was stalling. "You're so...young."

I set my glass on the table and leaned forward, looking her straight in the eye. "I'm old enough to know what I want. And I want you.

"Tell me you don't feel this." I scooted closer to her, gesturing between us. "Tell me you don't want me too," I rumbled, challenging her to deny it.

We stared at each other for a moment. Then we seemed to move at the same time, gravitating toward each other as if our collision were inevitable. Inescapable.

Unlike our first kiss, there was nothing restrained about

it. We were all hands and teeth and tongues. It was like a seal had been broken and the dam came crashing down.

I pulled her onto my lap, needing to be closer. She tugged at my shirt, and I reached behind my neck to yank it off. Her fingers scorched my skin, a fire blazing in the wake of her touch.

"This," she said, breaking the kiss. "Is such." Another kiss. "A bad idea."

"Do you want to stop?" I asked, needing to know.

I couldn't stop kissing her. Didn't want to contemplate the loss of her touch. But I needed to know that she wanted this just as badly as I did. I needed to know that she wanted me.

She stared at me a moment, my hands resting on her hips, her arms wrapped around my neck. Her lips were swollen from my kisses, her hair deliciously mussed from my fingers. I liked seeing my imprint on her, liked knowing I'd affected her.

She pulled me closer, rubbing her nose against mine. "I don't think I could stop even if I tried."

"Thank fuck," I muttered, returning my attention to her neck, kissing my way down to her breasts.

She arched her back, and I loved how responsive she was. I'd barely gotten started, yet her body seemed to come alive beneath my touch.

"You're not going to ghost me after tonight, are you?" I teased, trailing my fingers along the tops of her breasts, her collarbone.

"I can't exactly ghost you when you live in my pool house." She laughed.

She slid her hand up my neck and into my hair, pulling me closer. I shivered at her touch, at the molten look in her eyes. God, she was sexy.

"So, no. I'm not going to ghost you. But we should lay down a few ground rules if we're going to do this."

I smoothed her hair away from her face. I didn't want her to overthink this. I wanted to keep her in the moment—with me. Still, I knew Alexis well enough to know she was the type of person who wouldn't relax without some sort of plan. And I wanted her to relax.

"Such as?" I pulled down the straps of her dress, revealing creamy skin encased in a thin layer of lace.

I placed the lightest of kisses along the swell of her breasts, and I could tell from the way her breathing picked up that I was driving her mad.

"Gorgeous." I met her gaze. "You are gorgeous. And *that's* what I should've told you when I met you at the bottom of the stairs."

"If you're trying to distract me," she said in a serious tone, though she was smiling. "It's not going to work."

I grinned, taking it as a challenge. "I guess I'll just have to try harder, then."

I picked her up and spun her before gently setting her on the couch. Her golden-brown hair fanned across the cushions, her brown eyes blinking up at me. I smirked, knowing I had her right where I wanted her.

I sucked on her nipples through the lace, gratified by the way she tugged on my hair. I was eager for more, eager to feel her wrapped around me. But I was also patient. I wanted to enjoy this moment. I wanted to make our first time together special.

"Preston." It came out as half sigh, half plea. "Preston." This time, her tone was more insistent, and she yanked on my hair, forcing me to look at her. "I'm serious."

"So am I." I moved my attention to her legs. I started massaging her feet, slowly working my way up her calves to her thighs.

By this point, she'd stopped talking. I glanced up her body and smiled when I saw her lips were parted. I loved pampering her, finally being able to touch her the way I'd dreamed of. Because I had a feeling despite all the expensive spa treatments, Alexis rarely allowed anyone to take care of her like this.

"Would you still like to discuss conditions?" I mocked.

"Yes," she said on a moan.

I withdrew my hands.

She opened her eyes slowly and pouted. "Hey. Why'd you stop?" She grabbed my hands, moving them to where she wanted me to touch her.

"Nope." I crossed my arms over my chest to prevent myself from giving in. "You have conditions. Go."

She propped herself up on her elbows. "*If* we're going to do this—"

"We're doing this," I said, pressing my lips to hers.

I'd meant for it to be a quick peck, but it turned heated. My hands were in her hair, hers on my chest.

"Okay," she panted when she gently pushed me away. "But no one can know, especially not Sophia."

I wasn't thrilled about the idea of keeping our relationship a secret, but I understood. Especially since I didn't think the Hartwell Agency would be supportive of the fact that I was screwing my boss. It wasn't specifically outlined in my employment contract, but that didn't mean I wouldn't be fired if it came out. And I couldn't afford to get fired. I needed the money to finish my degree, especially now that my scholarship funding was gone.

"Fine. But no more dates. And you definitely can't sleep with anyone else."

"Same goes for you," she said, dragging a finger down my chest.

"Of course."

The idea of me wanting to sleep with anyone else was laughable. Why would I want anyone else when I had this woman? She was everything. Brilliant, savvy, sexy. But she was also caring, hardworking, and so much more.

I teased her breasts, moving her bra aside to circle her nipples. I was growing tired of this conversation. "Anything else?"

"I'm on the pill and I'm clean." Was she… I swallowed, searching her eyes. Was she really suggesting I could have sex with her bareback? *Holy shit.*

"But this is just sex," she added.

"I'm clean too," I said, not wanting to acknowledge her last statement. I'd take her any way I could get her. Even if that meant agreeing to the fact that this was a fling, when I wanted more.

"Good." She grinned.

"Good."

We stared at each other, wearing matching dopey smiles. I leaned forward, our chests brushing as I kissed her. After that, we didn't talk; we communicated with our bodies.

She slid her hand down my chest, cupping me over my shorts. My dick hardened even more, if that was possible, begging to be released. But I wanted this to be about her. I wanted to make her feel incredible.

When she started to unbutton my pants, I shook my head and moved out of her reach. Sweat prickled along my forehead, but I wanted this so badly. I wanted her so badly. But I also didn't want to ruin it with the conversation that would inevitably follow when she realized I only had one ball.

"Tonight is about you."

She gripped the edge of the couch, and I sensed her desperation as she ground out, "You're torturing me."

I pushed her dress up over her hips, biting the inside of my cheek when I saw the red lace of her panties. I kissed the inside of each thigh before nipping at them gently. As I worked my way higher, I could smell her arousal, and it made my chest puff with pride—knowing I'd done that to her. And when I finally moved her panties to the side so I could taste her, I growled.

"So fucking wet."

"Mm. Someone has a dirty mouth," she teased, but I could tell she liked it. It was clear from her short pants and the way her back arched as I lapped at her clit, feasting on her.

I inserted one finger, then another, curling to hit that magic spot. She writhed on the couch, and it didn't take long for her to fall apart, clenching around my finger as she quietly chanted my name.

Her head fell back on the cushions, one arm flopped over her forehead. "That was…oh my god, that felt amazing."

"Good." I grinned, unzipping my shorts but not removing them. "Because we're only just getting started."

CHAPTER ELEVEN

Alexis

"Holy shit," I panted, falling back on the rug. Preston lay down beside me, cradling me in his arms. I marveled at the contrast between his strong exterior and the tender lover he'd been. That was the best sex I'd ever had. Hands down.

I didn't know if it was his endurance, the stamina that came with being a younger man, or just him. But I'd never felt so sated. That didn't mean I didn't want more. I wanted much, much more. I told myself it was just because it had been a while since I'd slept with someone.

"Where'd you go?" he asked, tracing the line of my jaw.

I smiled, loving his ability to ground me in the present. "I'm here."

I glanced at the time on the microwave, groaning when I saw how late it was. "I should get to bed. I have to be up in four and a half hours to work out." I shifted, glancing around for my underwear.

"Can't you skip?" he asked.

"Unlike some people," I teased, trailing my finger over his

muscular shoulders and down to his six-pack abs. "I don't have the luxury of skipping."

"Hey." He frowned. "I work hard for this body."

"I know you do." I'd seen him in the home gym several times a week, usually chatting with Sophia. And I saw how healthily he ate—mostly home-cooked meals, lots of protein and produce, no carbs, and minimal dairy.

"Maybe I could join you?" he offered as he zipped up my dress.

I considered it a moment, wondering if that would be unprofessional. *Unprofessional?* I nearly laughed aloud. I'd just had sex with my nanny on my living room floor. Working out together seemed tame in comparison.

"I'll be down at five thirty," I said, closing my eyes as he kissed the skin behind my ear. "If you're willing to get up that early, be my guest."

He turned me so I was facing him, pulling me into him. Nestled in his arms, I felt safe, a sense of security I hadn't had in a long time, maybe even forever. I breathed in his scent, enjoying the warmth of his skin beneath my cheek, the sound of his heart thumping in his chest.

"Come on." He released me, only to link our hands as he tossed his shirt over his shoulder.

Preston seemed intent to touch me, even in small ways, and I secretly delighted in it. But when he headed toward the stairs, I froze. I thought I'd made it clear that this had to be a secret. That Sophia absolutely could not find out.

He glanced back at me, and I shook my head. "We can't."

He pressed his lips to mine, tangling his fingers in my hair. Despite the fact that we'd spent hours kissing, I was still desperate for more.

"If you're trying to change my mind…" I whispered. "It's not going to happen."

He leaned his forehead against mine. "Tempted as I am to

try to persuade you, I wanted to walk you to the stairs and wish you goodnight."

I bit back a smile. "Oh."

He backed away, a roguish smile on his handsome face. His chest was bare, his shorts hanging low on his waist. He was stunning.

"Goodnight, beautiful."

I blinked up at him. "Goodnight."

Preston headed for the pool house, while I floated up the stairs to my room. I still thought this was a terrible idea, but after multiple orgasms, I couldn't muster the energy to care. It might be wrong, but it felt oh so good.

The next thing I knew, my alarm was chiming, alerting me that it was time to wake up. I groaned, feeling like I'd barely gotten any sleep. I stretched, my body telling me just how sore it was as memories of the night before with Preston flashed through my mind.

His hands caressing my skin, worshiping me. His large frame hovering over me. I'd never felt more cherished.

I remembered his mention of working out with me, and that got me out of bed. I selected my favorite leggings with mesh cutouts. On top, I wore a sports bra that really lifted my breasts. Then I put my hair in a ponytail and swiped on a fresh coat of lip gloss.

I bounded down the stairs, and into the...dark, empty home gym.

I switched on the lights and blew a raspberry, surprised I was so disappointed. Regardless of whether Preston came, I had a workout to do. Maybe he'd still show up.

I went through a short stretching routine, stalling as I kept checking the time. The room was a nice size, though not as cavernous as some of the ones in the homes I sold. But the wall of mirrors certainly made it seem larger than it was.

After a few minutes had passed, I hopped on my bike,

getting into the program. My back was to the door, so when Preston's deep voice rumbled, "Good morning," I nearly jumped out of my seat.

"Good morning." I smiled as he leaned in for a kiss. His hair was mussed, his smile sleepy.

He went over to the rack of weights and removed his shirt before picking up two large dumbbells. I watched in the mirrored wall as his muscles flexed, mesmerized by the way they moved beneath the skin. I didn't realize I'd slowed down, until the trainer on my bike computer yelled at me to pick up the pace.

"You seem…distracted," Preston said over the whir of the bike.

"And you seem intent on distracting me."

"Who, me? I'm just working out." He did another rep and then another. Then, he dropped to the floor and started doing push-ups.

I held back a groan. He was trying to torture me. But two could play at this game. With my warm-up out of the way, I went over to the weights.

"You know…" He jumped to his feet and came to stand behind me so I could see our reflection in the mirror. "I can think of a way to burn calories that's much more enjoyable."

"Is that so?"

He leaned in, brushing my ear with his lips. "You interested?"

"I might be. I do enjoy trying new things."

He licked the shell of my ear, grazing it with his teeth and setting off a chain reaction in my body. I'd never considered the ear a sensual part of the body, but I was beginning to think otherwise as he continued to send goose bumps racing along my skin.

He smoothed his hands over my breasts, my hips, my stomach, and back up again. My nipples hardened beneath the thin material, and I was positive he could feel them every time he brushed past.

"I want you," he rasped. "I want you so fucking bad."

"Then take me," I said, meeting his eyes in the mirror—dark, piercing, filled with desire. "I'm yours."

Preston held me in place with his stare and his touch. He dipped a hand beneath the waistband of my leggings, and I watched as he continued to touch me, tease me.

"Leg up," he commanded.

I complied, placing my foot on the bench, spreading myself wide for him. He slid a finger inside me, pumping in and out as I continued to watch our reflection. And as I stared at us in the mirror, I wasn't thinking about the fact that he was younger than me, or my daughter's nanny. All I could see was how hot we looked together. How attractive he made me feel—wild and carefree.

"Fuck, you're sexy," he grunted, his hard-on digging into my back.

And the idea that Preston—someone so insanely hot, so much younger than me—found me desirable pushed me over the cliff.

My muscles clenched around him, and I bit my lip to keep from screaming. When my knees sagged, Preston held me. He was there to catch me when I came down from one of the most intense orgasms I'd ever experienced.

I spun to face him, smoothing my hands over his chest. He smiled down at me, tempting me to kiss him. Instead, I pressed him down onto the bench, wanting to make him feel as incredible as he made me feel. As I massaged his shoulders and arms, his head lolled to the side. I marveled at the feel of his smooth, tanned skin beneath my hands. And when I dug my fingers into his hair, he moaned in appreciation.

"That feels—" he swallowed "—so good."

"Good. It's about to feel even better." I sank to my knees before him. "Now, strip."

His eyes popped open, his entire body stiffening when he realized what I was offering. "You don't have to reciprocate."

"I know I don't have to. I want to."

He didn't move. "No, really. It's okay."

I frowned at him, trying to understand. What guy in the history of—well, ever—turned down a blow job?

"Did I do something wrong?" I sat back on my heels, struggling to make sense of it all.

He reached out, grabbing my hands to stop me. "No. Not at all." He cupped one of my cheeks, and I leaned into his touch. "I was just trying to be careful. I should probably get back to the pool house before Sophia wakes up."

I glanced at the clock on the wall. It wasn't even six-thirty. We both knew she wouldn't be up before eight.

"She likely won't be up for another hour—at least. So why don't you tell me what's really going on?" I asked. "I mean, it's not like I haven't seen your dick before."

"Yeah, but…you were distracted. It was dark."

Okay. So, he felt more comfortable having sex with the lights off. *Interesting*. But also, completely fine. It wasn't the worst quirk to have.

I went over and switched off the lights, so that only the natural light from the sunrise came in through the window. I resumed my position in front of him and tugged playfully at his waistband. "Now then. Where were we?"

Instead of removing his shorts as I'd expected, he turned and walked away. He rested his forehead against the opposite wall, banging it gently with his fist.

"Preston?" I went over to him, placing my hand on his back. "What's wrong?"

"I-I," he stuttered. "This is harder than I thought it would be."

I rubbed circles on his back, trying to give him some space while also showing my support. "It's okay. We don't have to do anything you don't want to. I'm sorry if I pushed."

"You didn't do anything wrong," he sighed, his voice full of sincerity.

"Will you talk to me? Help me understand?" Because the scenarios racing through my mind were absolutely terrifying.

He drew in a deep breath, and I tried to prepare myself for whatever he was about to tell me. "I only have one testicle."

"The last girl you dated must have been a real ballbuster," I teased, assuming this was some kind of joke.

I mean, how could I not have noticed something like that? The lights had been dimmed, sure. And he'd never taken his clothes completely off. I hadn't thought much of it at the time—I was kind of distracted. But now I wondered if it had been intentional.

He turned to face me and barked out a laugh. "You know, I don't think I've heard that one before." He wagged his finger at me. "I wish I were kidding. But I'm not."

He lowered the front of his waistband, giving me a full view of his semi-hard dick. I was momentarily distracted by the sight of it—long, heavy, and really just perfect. And, yep —there it was—only one testicle.

"Oh my god," I breathed. "Preston, I'm so sorry. I swear I thought you were joking. I had no idea."

He huffed. "Well, I guess I did a better job of hiding it than I thought. I, um, well, you're the first woman I've slept with since…"

I watched him struggle with his emotions, desperate to comfort him. The man who always made my daughter smile, made her laugh and have fun, was baring himself to me. And here I'd turned his struggle, his pain, into some kind of joke.

"Since I went into remission," he said.

I held my hands to my lips, tears pricking my eyes as I swallowed back emotion. *Cancer?* He was so young. *Too* young to have gone through something like that.

And I'd made fun of him—a man who'd survived testicular cancer. I'd never felt like more of an ass.

"Though your joke was pretty clever." He glanced up at me from beneath his long, dark lashes.

"I'll have to work on my comedic timing." I tried to keep it light, sensing this was difficult for him. I placed my hand on his forearm, needing to touch him. "But seriously, I'm sorry."

"It's okay. Really. Trust me, I've cracked many jokes about it over the years. Sometimes you have to—it's the only way to cope with something so terrible."

"Do you want to talk about it?" I asked.

He shrugged. "Maybe another time. I didn't mean to start your day on such a heavy note. And I'm sure you need to get going soon."

"Thank you for trusting me with this," I said. "I can't imagine how hard it was for you, but I'm here if you want to talk. Or not talk." I waggled my eyebrows.

He laughed, and I felt my heart lighten. "You're just trying to get in my pants."

"You know it." I winked. "But seriously, I think you're so incredibly brave and..." I wasn't sure I was ready to admit this to him, but he'd opened up to me. "I'm pretty sure last night was the best sex I've ever had."

He closed the distance between us, placing his hands on my hips. "Only pretty sure?"

"Well..." I wrapped my arms around his neck. "You know, it could've been a fluke."

He captured my lips in a kiss that was both sweet and sensual. It was a reminder of the passion from the night before and a promise of more to come. It was addictive, and I wanted more, craved it as I played with the hair at the back of his neck.

I broke the kiss, only to press my lips to his cheek, his chin, his neck. I kissed my way down his chest, admiring every ridge and divot. When I reached the waistband of his shorts, I glanced up at him, silently asking for permission.

I didn't want to make him uncomfortable. I wanted to show him the same pleasure, the same reverence he'd shown me. I wanted him to know that he could trust me. That I would respect his scars, like he'd respected mine.

He didn't fight me when I pushed down his shorts and boxers. He didn't protest when I stroked his dick, licked all the way up from the root to the tip. And when I took him into my mouth, while gently massaging his ball with my hand, he moaned.

"Fuck."

I could taste him, salty and yet somehow sweet. And I licked and sucked, drawing him as far into my mouth as I could handle. His grunts and the way he gripped my head, thrusting into my mouth at the same time, spurred me on. I was hungry for him, but more than that, I wanted him to feel as confident and sexy as he'd made me feel.

He tugged my ponytail gently. "I'm coming. Oh god, I'm—"

I swallowed it all down, licking every inch of him clean. He stared down at me, dazed.

"Um, wow. Okay," he panted. "That was… Blew my mind."

I laughed, standing up to pat him on the cheek. "So glad I could return the favor."

My phone chimed with an incoming message, and I groaned. I wanted to ignore it, but I knew I couldn't. Not when I had another closing coming up.

"It's okay. Go," he said, but not without tugging me back

to him first. "Have dinner with me tonight—after Sophia's gone to bed."

I nodded, falling into his denim-blue eyes. "I'd like that very much."

He slanted his mouth over mine, and as much as I wanted to stay, to fall into this incredible kiss with this amazing man, I couldn't. I pulled away, knowing I'd get to see him again later.

"Later." I smirked.

"Later." His eyes were hooded, and I knew there would be a lot more on the menu than just dinner.

And I couldn't wait to dig in.

CHAPTER TWELVE

Preston

"Ooh. What do you think of these?" Sophia held up a hot-pink candle coated in glitter.

"Um—" My phone rang, and I pulled it out of my pocket to see the Hartwell Agency flashing across the screen. "Hold that thought."

I connected the call, holding the phone to my ear. "This is Preston."

"Hi, Preston. This is Renata with the Hartwell Agency."

"Yes. Hi, Renata. How are you?" I asked, following Sophia around the store as she picked up nearly every pink candle and added it to the basket.

Who knew there were so many shades of pink? But hey, I guess if there were fifty shades of gray, why wouldn't there be an equivalent for pink?

"Good. I wanted to check in and see how your place-ment's going."

"It's great. Sophia and I are having a lot of fun together."

"Excellent. Well, I just wanted to let you know that we're still searching for a fall placement for you."

"No prospects yet? No one I can interview with, even?" I

asked, desperate for anything. The university had emailed earlier in the week to remind me that tuition was due soon, scholarship debacle or not.

"I'm sorry, but no."

I could read between the lines to know that most parents preferred a female caregiver. There might be placements available, but parents weren't interested in a twenty-six-year-old man. I respected it; I just didn't like it.

I sighed. "I understand. I just really need to find a placement before this one ends."

"I know. And we're doing everything we can to make that happen. In the meantime, focus on your current position and getting a good review."

I nodded, hating that I felt so powerless. Hating that I was often overlooked just because I was a guy. I knew the Hartwell Agency did everything they could to promote me as a candidate, but it was certainly an unusual situation.

"A positive review carries a lot of weight with families. For you—being a little different from our typical nanny—it's even more important."

"I understand." I grabbed a candle from Sophia and placed it back on the shelf.

She stuck her tongue out at me, and I smirked.

"Please feel free to call with any questions," Renata said. "Have a good night, Preston."

"Thanks. You too." I disconnected the call.

"Was that your friend Hunter?" Sophia asked.

"No. And we're not getting pink candles," I said when she tried to add yet another one to the basket.

"Why not? You said you wanted to impress this girl. Girls love pink. Trust me, I'm an expert." She said it all with such an air of authority, it took everything in me not to laugh. Still, I had to admire her confidence.

"Yes, but not this girl." I placed a few more candles back

on the shelf. "I mean, your mom's favorite color isn't pink, right?"

She scrunched up her nose, considering it for a moment. "No. Her favorite color is black."

"It is not." I poked her in the side, which made her giggle.

"Okay, you're right, but she does wear a lot of black." She tapped a finger to her lips. "You know, actually, I think her favorite color is blue."

Good. This was good.

"What's her favorite dessert?"

"Dessert?" Sophia laughed. "Mommy doesn't eat dessert."

My jaw dropped. "Ever?"

"Nope. I mean, I couldn't live without cupcakes and chocolate. But she's like…allergic to sugar or something."

"Hmm. We'll see about that," I muttered.

"Did you say something?"

I pushed the cart farther down the aisle, grinning to myself. "Nope."

When we got home, I fixed dinner, and we played some games before she went to bed. All evening, I'd been watching the clock, waiting until the moment Alexis would come home. She didn't return until a little after nine.

"Hey." She dropped her keys on the counter, setting her purse next to them.

"Hey." I grabbed her hand. "Come with me."

She kicked off her shoes and gave me a smile, but I could see she was tired.

"How was work?" I led her toward the sliding glass doors that opened to the pool.

"Good. Busy. Two of my agents double-ended a deal, so that was pretty fantastic."

"Double-ended?" I asked, raising my brow. "Is that some crazy sexual position?"

She rolled her eyes, but she was smiling. "No. It's when

two agents from the same brokerage represent the buyer and the seller, meaning we get both commissions."

"Wow," I said. "That's awesome."

We rounded the corner to the backyard, and I tapped on my phone to cue the music. The candles—well, fake candles—were flickering along the edge of the pool, lighting the path to a table for two.

Alexis turned to me with a smile. "What is all this?"

"This—" I gestured widely "—is dinner."

"Wow. This is…" She held her hand to her mouth. "Nobody's ever done anything like this for me."

"Seriously?"

How had this woman not been wined and dined? On the one hand, I was grateful. Because it meant it was something special I got to do for her. But shame on the men she'd dated in the past. A woman like Alexis deserved to be wooed. And I was going to woo the fuck out of her. She thought this was a fling, but I wanted more. So much more.

I pulled out a chair for her and poured her a glass of wine before pouring one for myself.

"I'll be right back." I leaned down to peck her cheek, my hands lingering on her shoulders. "I hope you're hungry."

"Oh, I'm certainly hungry," she said with a seductive lilt to her tone.

"Don't tempt me." I tsked. "I could easily be persuaded to skip dinner and go straight to dessert."

I'd left the food in the pool house so it would stay fresh. And I returned a moment later with a large charcuterie platter as well as a caprese salad.

"This looks amazing," she said, taking a little bit of every-thing and putting it on her plate.

"I'm glad." It was a relief to know she liked what I'd chosen.

"How was Sophia today?" she asked, nibbling at her

cheese. "I hate it when I'm not home in time to wish her goodnight."

"She was good. Funny. She wanted me to buy hot-pink glitter candles for our dinner."

She laughed but then stilled. "Wait. You told her about our dinner?"

"Of course not," I scoffed. "I just told her I was planning a romantic dinner for a girl I liked."

She arched an eyebrow, crossing one leg over the other as she took a sip of her wine. "So, you like me, huh?"

I took her hand in mine. "You haven't figured that out yet?"

"Mm." She took another sip and then set her glass on the table. "No, I think you made that abundantly clear last night."

"And this morning," I added. "But if you need further proof of just how much I like you," I teased, "I'd be more than happy to oblige."

"Is that so?" She circled the rim of the wineglass with her finger, and just that simple action had my imagination racing into overdrive.

"Oh yeah. But first, I want to enjoy this meal with you."

She smiled. "So, what did you and Sophia do besides go candle shopping? This is beautiful, by the way. I would totally post it on my Instagram if I knew it wouldn't spark a million questions."

I chuckled. "Well, I'm glad I could design an Instagram-worthy moment." Not that that had been my intent. I just wanted to create something special for her.

"We went to the grocery store." I gestured to the platters of food. "And then we went to the park, and she made some new friends."

"That's good. I think she could use some more interaction with kids her age," Alexis said.

"I agree. I was actually wondering if she has any friends in town. She said a lot of them are at overnight summer camp or staying with their dads. But I was hoping to set up some playdates."

"I think her friend Brooklyn might be back from camp now. You could try reaching out to her dad, Nate."

"Great." I refilled our glasses with wine. "If you give me his number, I'd be happy to."

"Sophia will love that."

Music played softly, water splashed over the fountain into the pool, and the crickets chirped in the grass. It was perfect. And I could imagine us spending many nights together, eating dinner, laughing, sharing about our day.

"So, um, about earlier," I said. "I'm sorry for that bombshell I dropped on you this morning."

Alexis set down her fork, meeting my eyes over the table. I'd been afraid I'd find pity, but all I saw were compassion and love reflected back at me. She pushed back her chair and stood.

"I'm sorry if I came across as insensitive." She took a seat on my lap. I skimmed her thighs with my hands, relishing the feel of her silky-smooth skin. "And I meant what I said. I'm here if you want to talk."

I swallowed back a lump of emotion. She had no idea how much that meant to me. Just knowing she cared meant everything.

"You know what I really want to do right now?" I asked. She shook her head. "Relax in the hammock together."

"I like the sound of that."

We climbed into the hammock, and she nestled into my side. She fit perfectly in the crook of my arm, and I stared up at the sky, soaking in the moment. I picked up her hand that was resting on my chest, twirling our fingers. I'd never really opened up to anyone about my cancer, but for the first time, I found myself wanting to.

I cleared my throat. "I, um, was a sophomore in college when it started. I was tired, had lower back pain, and kept losing weight."

She kept our fingers moving, playing and dancing between us. It gave me something to focus on. A gentle comfort. A reminder that the past was in the past.

"At first, we thought it was just mono. But then, I was diagnosed with testicular cancer."

"That explains your prolonged degree program," she said.

I nodded. "Yes. For the next few years, my life was consumed with beating cancer. First surgery, then treatments. It was…difficult." Difficult was a definite understatement. "I tried to continue with school, but it just became too much."

I didn't mention the fact that the money my parents had saved for my education had been bled dry. They'd spent that and then some, willing to pay any sum if it meant I could live.

She gripped my hand, and when I glanced down at her, her eyes were filled with unshed tears. "Don't cry." A tear streaked down her cheek, and I wiped it away. "Please don't cry. I was lucky."

"Lucky?" she scoffed.

"Yes." I nodded. "Lucky. Unlike so many others, my story has a happy ending. I beat the fucker. I survived. And now I'm lying in a hammock with the most beautiful woman I've ever laid eyes on."

She nodded, but still, I heard her sniffle. "You're so strong. And I'm so, so sorry that I teased you."

I pulled her closer to me, holding her tight. "You didn't know. Honestly, I was nervous about having sex with you."

"Because of the uniball situation?"

I chuckled. "I'm a one-ball wonder, baby," I joked.

"That you are." And I felt her body shaking with silent laughter.

"That was part of it," I admitted. "And because I hadn't been with anyone in a while, and you're, well…you."

"What is that supposed to mean?" She sounded more curious than anything.

"Surely you realize how sexy you are? But it's more than that—you're intelligent, savvy, sophisticated, an amazing mom. You could have your pick of men. Men who are much more experienced than me."

"Experience is meaningless without chemistry, without connection. I feel that with you. I don't think I've ever felt so…alive. So cherished."

"I feel it too," I said, pulling her close to me as I stared up at the sky.

We lapsed into silence, both lost in our thoughts, until she said, "Can I ask you something?"

I tucked my hand behind my head. "Anything."

"You've been in remission for over a year. You really haven't dated anyone in all that time?"

"No. I—" My throat felt tight. "I was in a relationship when I got sick. She said she loved me, would stay by my side no matter what. But when it really came down to it, she couldn't handle it."

"She broke up with you while you were going through treatments? Fighting for your life?" Alexis's voice was calm, but I could hear the anger raging just beneath the surface. She was livid.

"Honestly, it was for the best."

"How can you say that?" She propped herself up on her elbow to stare down at me. Her hair fell across my face, curtaining us like a waterfall. Her scent surrounded me, perfuming the air like the jasmine that grew on the trellis outside my bedroom window.

"Cancer has a way of revealing who your true friends are. It sucked, but I can be grateful that it brought clarity to my relationships and my purpose."

"And what is your purpose?"

"To support and encourage the people I love. And to support those going through cancer themselves, specifically pediatric cancer patients."

"You—" she leaned in, nuzzling against me "—are an incredible man, Preston Hawthorne. And I'm lucky to know you."

"And you're about to get even luckier," I teased, needing to lighten the moment.

She rolled her eyes but laughed anyway as I pulled down the straps of her dress, kissing every inch of skin I could find. As she sank down on top of me, making love to me beneath the stars, I felt like the luckiest man alive.

CHAPTER THIRTEEN

Alexis

"Hey, Mom," Sophia said from her perch on a barstool. Her attention was on whatever concoction she and Preston were whipping up today. Pancakes, if I had to guess.

"Good morning," Preston said, his eyes lingering on my breasts, my hips. "Did you have a good workout?"

I nodded, taking a sip from my water bottle to cool myself off. Who was I kidding? Nothing was going to help the way he made me heat from the inside out. If I'd thought sleeping with him was the answer, it only seemed to fuel my addiction. It was like sugar—the more I got, the more I wanted.

"It was…hot." I smirked, dabbing at my forehead, then my neck, with a towel. I knew he was watching me, knew he wanted me.

"I can see that." He smiled at me over Sophia's head, and I smiled back.

"Guess what?" Sophia asked.

"What?" I rested my elbows on the counter, giving Preston a good view down my sports bra.

"You'll pay for that later," he mouthed, to which I merely smirked. *Good.*

"Preston's going to let me practice flipping the pancakes this morning. And then, we're going to the aquarium."

"That sounds fun. I love the aquarium." I picked a blueberry off a plate and popped it into my mouth.

"You should join us," Preston said.

I glanced at my phone, which was already blowing up with notifications.

"Yeah, Mommy. Please! Please!" Sophia chimed in. "It would be so much fun. The three of us could go together."

The idea was tempting, but still… I had clients I needed to call, agents to check in with, houses to follow up on.

"When was the last time you took a day off?" Preston asked. "Like really took the day off?"

I stopped to think about it, and I honestly wasn't sure. LA was a vibrant city, a busy city, and real estate was a fast-paced industry. There was a lot of competition, and you had to be on top of your game.

"Well, I think that answers my question," Preston said.

"Please, Mom. You've been so busy lately. Can't you just take part of the day?"

I considered it, scrolled through my calendar. "I mean, it is technically my Friday," I said, trying to justify it to myself. "So, maybe—"

Before I could finish my sentence, Sophia had wrapped herself around me like a spider monkey. I was positive I'd pay for this later, but at the moment, all I could think was that it would be worth it. It would be worth it to spend the day with my daughter.

I hugged her back and laughed. "All right, well, I guess I'll go shower so we can go to the aquarium."

"Yay! Yay! Yay!" Sophia danced around the kitchen.

Preston leaned his hip against the counter, watching her with a doting grin.

We spent the day exploring the aquarium, and it was perfect. I'd barely looked at my phone, and Sophia seemed to love spending time with both Preston and me. And Preston was great with her. He made me wonder if this was what it was like to have a partner, to have someone to co-parent with. Something I'd certainly never had with Cal.

After dinner, when we were putting away the dishes, Sophia said, "Time for family movie night."

"Well, I'll, uh, leave you to it." Preston turned, heading for the pool house.

I didn't want him to leave, but I wasn't sure how Sophia would feel about him watching movies with us. Typically, it had been a tradition for just the two of us. Not even Gabby had been invited.

"You can't leave now," Sophia said to Preston. "Please stay for the movies. Pretty please." She looked up at him with her pouty lips and big blue eyes.

"Are you sure?" He glanced to me for approval. "I wouldn't want to intrude."

"Nonsense," I said. "As long as you're okay spending *what should be* your night off watching *Annie*." I shrugged.

His eyes lit up. "I'd love to."

"Okay." Sophia turned, assessing the living room with the eye of a general preparing for battle. "Mom, you make the popcorn. Preston, drinks. I'll set up the pillows."

I laughed, ruffling her hair as I headed toward the kitchen. Sophia switched on the TV, and I could hear a commercial playing in the background.

I stepped into the pantry for popcorn, and a moment later, Preston's hands were on my hips, spinning me to face him.

My eyes went wide. "What are you doing?"

"Something I've been dying to do all day." He slanted his lips over mine, his touch demanding, punishing even.

My body instantly responded, desire washing over me. I'd kept it at bay throughout the day, but it was always there, humming beneath the surface. And now, I wasn't sure I could smother it again so easily.

"Better get the popcorn going before *someone* comes to investigate." He gave me one more peck on the lips.

I stared at him for a moment, dazed. Finally, I shook my head to clear it and emerged from the pantry, popcorn in hand. I placed it in the microwave and pressed *Start*.

"Sophia sure does take her family movie nights seriously," he teased, mimicking her posture and gestures from earlier.

I laughed. "Yeah. After the divorce, it kind of became our thing."

"I'm sure that was hard on her. Hard on both of you." Preston grabbed a few waters from the fridge.

"It was hard on Sophia. For me, it was more of a relief." I grabbed several bowls for the popcorn.

"Do you think you'd ever remarry?" He popped the tops off the bottles. The question seemed innocent enough, but it had my heart racing.

"You mean like *Christina on the Coast*?" I teased, trying to lighten the moment.

"Yeah. Like Ant and Christina and their four kids plus one on the way."

"Five kids are way too many for me," I deflected, not prepared to answer his original question.

"Still, they seem genuinely happy."

I nodded, relieved when the microwave beeped to signal the popcorn was done.

"Mom. Preston," Sophia called. "What's taking so long?"

I laughed. "Be right there, Soph."

We settled in to watch the movie, with me sandwiched

between Sophia and Preston. Every time he shifted, I caught a whiff of his cedar scent. It mingled with the popcorn to give me a sense of home, of rightness.

Sophia sang along with the movie, and Preston seemed to be enjoying himself. Though my eyes were trained on the screen, my attention was focused on the man next to me. Every time he moved, his thigh shifted against mine, his hand brushed against my knee. He was making it impossible to concentrate.

He kept his hand next to my thigh, moving his pinkie finger back and forth along my bare skin. My heart stilled, and I wondered if Sophia would notice. But she seemed too lost in the movie to care. I held my breath, shifting my hand so our pinkies were touching. It was the most innocent of touches, yet it felt practically erotic.

We stayed that way the rest of the movie, and I could tell Sophia was getting tired when she stopped singing. By the time the credits rolled, she was out. She looked so peaceful in her sleep, and I couldn't bear to wake her.

Preston picked her up, and I followed them up the stairs to her bedroom. Logically, I knew he took care of her every day. That he was paid to do so. But watching him cradle my daughter to his chest, carrying her up the stairs to her room, was so very different.

He gently set her on her bed, smoothing her hair away from her face. "Goodnight, princess," he whispered, kissing her forehead.

And that was my undoing.

He rejoined me in the hall, closing the door softly behind him. Without saying a word, I intertwined our hands and led him to my bedroom. I wanted him—not in the pool house or the backyard. Not in the living room or the gym. I wanted him in my bed, because he was certainly making his way into my heart.

"Are you sure?" he asked when I closed the door behind me. We had yet to actually spend the night together, and my room had always been off-limits. Until now.

I nodded. I was certain. "As long as you're gone by the time she gets up."

He grinned, stalking toward me. "I think I can manage that."

PRESTON BRUSHED MY HAIR ASIDE, BARING MY NECK TO HIM. With my eyes still closed, I snuggled deeper into the covers as he kissed the sensitive skin behind my ear.

"Good morning." His voice was deeper, gravelly. *Sexy.*

"Mm," I hummed as he continued kissing me. "Good morning."

A breeze carried the scent of jasmine in through my window, birdsong filling the air. Preston's arms were wrapped around me, bringing me a sense of security like I'd never known. His erection dug into my backside, and I wiggled a little, hoping to entice him to go for another round.

"You are insatiable." He kept his voice low, knowing Sophia was just down the hall.

"Can you blame me?" I asked, turning to face him and teasing his lips with mine. "I mean, it's not my fault you make me feel so amazing."

This man made me crazy. It was like my body had been dormant all these years until him. Preston turned me into this fiery ball of heat that craved nothing but him. He made me feel desired. He made me feel younger than my thirty-five years.

"Is that so?" He raised his brow and rolled us so he was on top of me.

With his arms bracketing my head and his body pressed to mine, the ache within me grew to unbearable levels. I arched my hips, needing to feel him against me, within me.

"Yes." I nodded, feeling less certain of my answer.

"So, it's my fault that your eyes are captivating?" He brushed his lips against the corners of my eyes, tracing the side of my face with his nose, nuzzling me.

"Yep." I warmed from his compliment, and the way he touched me with such reverence.

"And it's my fault that your lips are so gorgeous, I can't decide whether I'd rather kiss you or see them wrapped around my cock?"

"Uh-huh," I sighed as he moved down my body, dragging his long, hard cock against my inner thigh.

"I also suppose it's my fault that you have the most perfect tits," he said, using his nose to trace the outer edge of one, then the other. "And the most gorgeous nipples." He sucked one into his mouth, and I bucked my hips.

"That's, um… Yes, that's right." At this point, I wasn't even sure I knew what he'd asked me.

He chuckled, the sound rumbling across my belly as he continued his southward exploration.

"And, again, it's my fault…" I couldn't see anything, but I could feel his breath on my skin as he hovered over the apex of my thighs. "It's my fault that your pussy tastes even better than it looks."

"Exactly," I sighed, clutching the sheets as he began to lick and suck my clit. I could feel the orgasm building quickly, barreling toward me like a freight train.

"Mommy," Sophia called. "Mom," she said, dragging out the vowel.

My eyes snapped open, and I glanced at the door to

confirm it was locked. Preston had frozen beneath the covers, but I sprung to action, casting them aside.

"You have to get out of here," I whisper-hissed.

My heart was racing, and I scrambled to find my robe, a shirt, anything to put on that wasn't his.

"Coming," I called to Sophia, yanking a shirt over my head and trying to smooth my hair.

The doorknob rattled, and I shoved Preston toward the balcony overlooking the pool. "Go."

I glanced toward the balcony to confirm that Preston was out of sight. Then I sucked in a deep breath and opened the door. "Good morning, sweetie."

She walked into the room. "Have you seen Preston? I knocked on his door, but he didn't answer."

"It's his day off, baby. He doesn't have to answer."

"I know, but I was hoping he'd go to Juliana's office with us today. Is that okay?" she asked, as if the idea suddenly occurred to her.

"Of course," I said, ruffling her hair. "I think that's very sweet. Still, he might already have other plans."

What I didn't say was that he might not want to be involved in the over-the-top party-planning session we had scheduled. We were supposed to meet with my friend, and party planner to the stars, Juliana. The invitations had been ordered, but we needed to discuss decorations, the menu, and the cake.

Sophia glanced toward the open balcony doors and frowned. I turned to follow her gaze, relieved when I saw nothing but the flutter of white curtains and the view of the yard beyond.

"Mommy…" She tilted her head to the side. "Why was the door locked?"

I never locked the door, never had reason to. Until now.

"I, um, must have done it by accident." I hated lying, especially to my daughter. But for the time being, this was how it had to be.

I knew it was a mistake to let Preston sleep here, but I hadn't been able to help myself. Not after how sweet he'd been with Sophia. More than anything, though, I just wanted to know what it would be like to fall asleep in his arms. To spend all night with him.

"Oh. Okay." She shrugged, seeming to accept my excuse.

"Did you check the gym?" I asked, trying to buy Preston more time to get back to the pool house.

"That's a good idea." She skipped off toward the stairs.

I closed the door and sagged against it. Holy shit—that had been close. *Way* too close.

"Is the coast clear?" Preston asked, and my eyes popped open.

"What are you doing?" I rushed over to him. He was standing on the balcony in nothing but a pair of shorts. His dark hair was mussed, his lips shiny from my…*oh God.*

"I needed a kiss goodbye." He batted his lashes at me.

"Preston," I chided, attempting to push him toward the balcony. Man, he was solid. "You have to go."

Finally, he swung his leg over the railing. Standing on the opposite side, he held on with one hand while raising the other in the air. "Farewell, fair Alexis. Parting is such sweet sorrow."

"You did not just quote Shakespeare to me," I said, placing my hands on my hips, trying not to laugh.

"So what if I did?" He smirked. "With love's light wings—"

"Preston," I hissed, clutching the railing. Sweat prickled at the back of my neck. I was afraid Sophia would return at any moment. Even worse, that she'd see him from the yard. "This isn't funny. We're not teenagers, and if Sophia sees you…"

"Okay. I'm sorry," he said, looking contrite as he gave me a quick peck. "I'll go."

I watched as he disappeared down the trellis into the garden. And at that moment, I wasn't sure what I was most afraid of. The prospect of Sophia discovering me in bed with her nanny or that said nanny had used the "L" word, and I wanted him to mean it.

CHAPTER FOURTEEN

Preston

"Hey, Hunter. What's up?" I asked, answering the call. I clutched the phone between my shoulder and my ear as I buttoned my shirt.

"Have you been by the apartment lately?" he asked.

"No. Why?"

"I haven't heard from Kate in a while. And whenever I've tried calling her, it goes straight to voice mail." I could hear the concern in his voice.

"Huh. Okay. You want me to go check on her?" I asked.

He released a breath. "That would be great. Thanks, man."

"Aww, you do have a heart," I teased, knowing how protective Hunter was of his baby sister. "And it's no problem. I just need to make sure Alexis is good with Sophia tagging along."

"Alexis. She's the MILF, right?"

I gnashed my teeth. "Don't call her that."

"You slept with her." It was a statement, not a question.

How the fuck did he know that?

"I did not."

"Thou dost protest too much. How was it? Did she know

all these crazy tricks? I've never been with an older woman, but I imagine it could be a very…shall we say…*valuable* experience."

I closed my eyes and swiped my hand down my face. "I'm not talking about this with you."

"You banged your boss." I gripped the kitchen counter tighter, not sure I wanted to admit it to him. "Damn, she's getting quite the deal. Two-for-one services—nanny and fucktoy."

"Shut up, Hunter. Just shut the fuck up." When I glanced down, I realized my hand was shaking.

"Whoa." He was silent for a moment. "Okay. Sorry. I was joking. Wow, I didn't think you'd actually do it."

Alexis wasn't using me for sex, right? Maybe this had started out as just a fling. But for me, at least, it was so much more.

Still, I knew better than to push her. I'd learned that lesson the hard way, when she'd kicked me out of her room. I understood why she wasn't ready to tell Sophia we were seeing each other, but I was beginning to wonder if she'd ever be ready. We continued to have sex every chance we got, but I felt a distance between us, a coolness.

"Hey. You okay?" Hunter asked.

"Yeah." I dug my fingers into my hair. "Just stressed."

"What's going on?" Hunter might act like a tool at times, but he was a great friend. The best friend.

Where to start? "Sam's wife, Indy, called to say that he isn't doing well."

"Is the treatment not working?" Hunter was very familiar with the ins and outs of testicular cancer after watching me go through it.

"It's too early to say. It's more that he's struggling mentally. They were planning to have kids and…" I swallowed, emotion gathering in my throat. "His sperm counts are so low, it's been difficult to get a good sample to freeze."

"Shit," Hunter said. "That blows."

"Yeah," I huffed. "It makes my problems seem insignificant by comparison."

"What the hell is going on there? I leave for a few weeks, and LA falls apart without me," he joked.

"Kind of," I said. "Though I don't think you're responsible for Sam's issues or the fact that my scholarship was revoked. Not to mention, the Hartwell Agency still hasn't found a placement for me when this one ends."

I'd been calling Renata every week, and I knew she had to be sick of hearing from me. But with the deadline for my tuition looming, I couldn't exactly sit around and wait. Since I'd been counting on the scholarship, I hadn't applied for any loans. And when I'd tried contacting the school for information about student loans, I was politely informed that the deadline had passed.

While my position with Alexis paid well, it wasn't enough to cover tuition for my two remaining semesters plus rent. And I was running out of time to come up with a solution.

"I could loan you the money," he said, and I knew he would. Hunter had a trust fund plus his successful business, and he wouldn't miss the money.

"I know, man. And I so appreciate the offer, but I can't."

"Yes." His tone was more forceful. "You can."

I scratched the back of my neck. "You know I can't. I would never want to risk ruining our friendship."

"Okay. Well, the offer stands if you change your mind."

"Thanks."

"I'm afraid to ask, but is there anything else going on?" he asked. "You sound, I don't know, surprisingly down for someone who finally got laid for the first time in over a year. *Shit.*" He paused, and I could imagine him hanging his head.

"I don't know how you went without sex for as long as you did."

I laughed, relieved that we were back on more solid footing. "I bet you couldn't go a month without having sex."

"A month?" he asked in a haughty tone.

"Mm-hmm. Four weeks. Thirty days. And absolutely no sex." I grinned to myself, knowing Hunter would never be able to resist a bet.

"And what do I get if I win?" he asked.

"Besides the fact that you won't have gonorrhea?"

"Please. You know I always suit up. Speaking of, please tell me you and Alexis are being careful."

"Yes, Mother," I said in a singsong voice. I found it ironic that my manwhore of a best friend was suddenly concerned whether I was practicing safe sex or not.

"Well, we both know you're a bit out of practice."

"And there it is." I laughed, knowing he couldn't resist a good jab.

But I'd never divulge the fact that we weren't using condoms. That was a decision between Alexis and me. Just like I'd never tell him all the down and dirty details of our sex life. I respected Alexis, and that meant certain things stayed between us.

"Hey, man," he said in a pompous tone. "If you need any tips, I'm full of sex advice."

"I think I know how to please a woman just fine." I sniffed, lifting my chin. "So, are you going to accept my bet or what?"

"You have yet to define any terms. So, why don't I start? If I win, you let me pay your tuition."

"Since you're not going to win—fine. And if I win—" I tapped a finger to my lips "—you have to stop giving me shit about dating Alexis."

"Is that what this is—you're dating her now?"

"I will be."

"Damn." He chuckled. "I can't decide if you're crazy confident or just plain crazy."

"Maybe a bit of both," I admitted.

"And you have yourself a deal, motherfucker. But it starts after my birthday."

"Of course." I rolled my eyes, knowing he'd have to impose some additional condition. "You're coming home to celebrate, right?"

"Hell yeah."

"Good. We'll shake on it then." I chuckled, wondering if he'd ever be able to stick to it. Somehow, I doubted it. At least, I hoped so. Because there was no way I was accepting the money from him.

After we ended the call, I headed over to the main house. Sophia was eating breakfast in the kitchen.

"Hey, princess."

"Preston!" She leaped off the chair, bounding over to me for a hug.

I laughed, giving her a quick squeeze. "Your mom leave already?"

"Yep," she said, emphasizing the "p." "What are we doing today?"

"Well…" I pulled out my phone, sending a quick message to Alexis asking if I could take Sophia to my apartment. Alexis answered immediately, but all she wrote was "that's fine." I frowned down at the screen, even as I tried to reassure myself she was just busy.

"How would you like to run some errands with me?" I slid my phone into my back pocket.

"To the candle store?" She grinned, bouncing on her toes.

I laughed. "I think I'm good on candles. But maybe, after we swing by my apartment, we can get some ice cream."

"Okay!" She hopped off her stool and took her dish over to the sink. "I'm ready."

"Alrighty then. Let's go."

When we arrived at the apartment, Kate was just fine. In fact, she was delighted to have company, and we spent the day helping her with an art project she was working on. I texted Hunter to let him know she was okay. Though I left out the part about her having a new nose piercing. I knew better than to get in the middle of those two.

By the time we arrived home, the sun was dipping lower in the sky. Alexis walked in as Sophia and I were sitting down to dinner.

"Mommy! Come eat with us," Sophia said from her seat at the table.

"Sorry, baby." Alexis rushed over, placing a quick kiss on her head before darting toward the stairs. "I have to go. I have a phone call with a client."

"You'll put me to bed, right?" she asked.

Alexis was already halfway up the stairs when she called, "I'll do my best!"

Sophia and I had cleaned up the dishes and were winding down toward bedtime, but there was still no sign of Alexis.

"What are three things you're thankful for today?" I asked, going through our nightly ritual.

It was something my parents had always done with me, and it was a nice way to close the day. A reminder to be grateful and to appreciate everything, even the smallest things. Sophia's answers were always insightful and amusing, and I never knew quite what to expect.

"My mom."

I nodded. "Always good to be thankful for your mom. You should definitely tell her that." I knew Alexis would appreciate hearing it, considering how hard she worked to build this life for the two of them.

"The flamingo float," she said, and I laughed.

"It is pretty awesome."

"Can we go swimming tomorrow?"

I lifted a shoulder. "I don't see why not. What's your third thing?"

I spotted Alexis, leaning against the wall just outside the entrance to the kitchen. She'd changed into yoga pants and a T-shirt that hung off one shoulder. Her waves were piled in a loose knot, tendrils falling near her face. A soft smile played at her lips.

"Artists like your girlfriend, Kate," Sophia said.

"What?" I jerked my head back. "Kate isn't my girlfriend." How the hell had she gotten that idea? I needed to correct this and fast, because judging from the look on Alexis's face, she wasn't pleased.

Sophia frowned. "She's not? She lives at your apartment. And you bought all those candles for that romantic dinner."

"Yes," I said. "She lives there for the summer." I turned to Alexis. "Kate is Hunter's sister. Her apartment is being renovated after a fire, and she needed a place to stay. Since Hunter is in New York and I'm living here, it seemed like the perfect setup."

Alexis lifted a shoulder. "Sounds like a great compromise." She spun away from me. "Soph, time for a bath."

"Already?" Sophia whined. Fortunately, she hadn't realized that I'd never answered her question about the candles.

"Yes, already. It's nearly eight thirty."

Sophia dragged her feet, pausing at the entrance to the kitchen. "But I didn't get to hear Preston's three things."

"You, your mom, and spaghetti sauce," I rattled them off.

Sophia rolled her eyes. "The first two are always the same."

"Because they're always true." I grinned.

Sophia finally slunk up the stairs. Once she was out of

sight, I slid behind Alexis, wrapping my arms around her waist.

"I missed you today." I pressed a kiss to her neck, but she didn't sink into me like usual. She was stiff. Distant.

I knew she was tired. I knew she'd had a long day. I wanted her to look forward to coming home at the end of it all, knowing she'd see Sophia and me. Instead, it seemed like she'd rather be anywhere but here.

"I have to go do bedtime," she said, walking out of my arms.

"Hey." I tugged on her hand, pulling her back to me. "Are you upset with me?"

"Nope," she said. "Everything is fine, Preston."

Yeah, that was a sure sign everything was not fine.

"Can I see you…later?" I didn't care if we had sex or not, not that I'd complain if we did. I just wanted to be with her, hold her.

"Maybe another night. I have a ton of work to catch up on," she said, shutting me down.

"Is this about Kate?" I asked. "Are you jealous?"

"Jealous?" She scoffed.

I stepped closer, invading her space. "It's okay if you are." I placed my hands on her hips, sliding them over her ass. "It's actually kind of sexy. But really, there's no need. Kate is like a little sister to me."

I pulled her closer, wanting her to feel how turned on I was. "This—" I ground against her, enjoying the way her eyes darkened "—is what *you* do to me. No one else. You."

She opened her mouth to say something, when Sophia called, "Mommy. Are you coming?"

Alexis backed away from me, and I could feel the distance between us grow with every step. "I have to go."

I nodded, unable to stop watching her, even as she walked away. Alexis didn't strike me as the type of woman to get jealous. Which made me think something else was bothering her, something she wasn't telling me.

I walked over to the pool house and sat staring up at her bedroom window for a long time. The light was on, and I wondered if she'd stay up all night working. Or if she even was working. And I debated what to do as I drank one beer then another. Then another.

Finally, when she switched off the light, my decision was made.

I crept across the yard and climbed the trellis to the balcony outside her room. Though she hadn't been pleased with my last appearance as Romeo, I hoped this time it would be better received. I also hoped none of the neighbors would call the cops.

I was about midway up when my foot slipped on one of the rungs. "Shit."

I found my footing once more. And I finally made it to the balcony, hauling myself over the metal railing. She'd closed the doors, but they weren't locked. I pushed one open, only to realize that her bed was empty.

Light filtered in through the door to her bathroom, and I crept closer, wondering if this was a bad idea. But then I saw her staring at herself in the full-length mirror—naked—and all other thoughts fled my mind. She was fucking stunning.

But as she turned from side to side, tugging at her skin, trying to lift her breasts, the skin next to her eyes, there was a pang in my chest. She was looking for flaws, picking apart her beautiful body. She slumped forward, bowing her shoulders as she placed her hands on the marble countertop.

"You're so beautiful," I said, hoping she'd hear the sincerity in my voice, feel it in my gaze.

Alexis startled, jumping back from the sink and grabbing a makeup brush, which she brandished like a sword. When she glanced up and realized it was me, her shoulders relaxed. I laughed a little, feeling pleasantly buzzed.

"Preston." She held a hand to her chest. "What the hell were you thinking?"

"I wanted to see you. I wanted to be with you, to hold you."

She yanked her robe off the counter and wrapped it around herself. "Well, you scared the shit out of me."

"I didn't like how we left things earlier." I stepped closer. "Life's too short to have regrets."

Her eyes glittered with unshed tears, and I wondered what she was keeping from me. What was really going on.

"Talk to me." I traced the line of her jaw, smoothing my hand over her shoulders. "I want to know what's bothering you. Is this about Kate?"

"It's not about Kate, damn it," she said, her voice rising. "It's about what she represents."

I frowned, trying to follow her thoughts. "And what's that?"

"Youth. Vitality. Not—" she sighed, her movements agitated "—sagging breasts, a C-section scar, and gray hair."

"Is that what you see when you look in the mirror?" I asked, spinning her to face the full-length mirror. I placed my hands on her shoulders, gently rubbing up and down her arms.

"Because I see a woman who is tough, strong." I circled her, coming to stand so I was in front of her. "I see a woman who is loving and nurturing. Who carried a child and would do anything for her.

"And I see a woman who is so beautiful inside and out, it takes my breath away." I used my finger to lift her chin, forcing her to look me in the eye. "All I see is beauty and strength."

Tears streamed down her cheeks, and I knew I'd struck a chord. How could she not see how gorgeous she was?

"Thank you," she whispered, wiping away her tears. "I'm sorry. I'm sorry that I keep pushing you away only to pull you back in again. I'm just… I haven't dated anyone in a long time. And I've never dated anyone so much younger than me."

I smirked. "I haven't dated anyone in a long time either. And I don't see your age, I don't see your supposed flaws, I see you." I cupped her cheeks, weaving my fingers through her hair.

She blinked up at me, her eyes glittering with unshed tears. "I see you too. I see your heart and your potential. I see the way you interact with Sophia, the way you take care of our family."

I pressed my lips to hers, feeling even more connected to her than I had before. It was a sweet kiss—a kiss of promise and forgiveness.

I led her over to the bed and pulled back the covers for her. I tucked her in, so tempted to stay, to tell her I loved her.

As I was leaving, she grabbed my hand. "I know it's not fair to ask you this, but will you stay? Just for a little while?"

"Of course." I kicked off my shoes and lay on the bed next to her, gathering her into my arms.

I'd stay for as long as she'd have me.

CHAPTER FIFTEEN

Alexis

Lauren was on the phone when I arrived at the property for a walk-through, so I waited in the kitchen. As I was responding to emails, my phone chimed with an incoming text message.

Preston: Hope you're having a great day, beautiful.

I immediately smiled, typing out a response.

Not too bad. You?

Preston: Sophia and I are enjoying the pool.

A picture came through of Sophia waving from atop the giant flamingo float. Then another of Preston shirtless, wearing aviators and a sexy smirk. I wanted to kiss it off his face.

I wanted to do that and so much more. I'd never had so much sex in my life as I had the past few weeks, yet I was insatiable when it came to him.

You play dirty.

Preston: Only with you. ;)

I laughed, thinking of how much I was enjoying this little summer fling. It was fun, carefree. I'd never felt sexier or more desired. But there was more to it than that. Much as I wasn't prepared to admit it, I was falling for Preston.

He'd been through so much, yet he was still kind. He was loving and affectionate. And he was so sweet with Sophia, it made my heart swell to watch them together.

"Ooh, girl. Who are you texting?" Lauren asked, her heels clicking against the wood floor.

I opened my mouth, prepared to lie and tell her I was texting with a buyer, when she said, "And don't tell me it's Mateo. Because he told me you shot him down for a second date."

I bit my lip and glanced up at her. I'd been sleeping with Preston for weeks now and still hadn't told her. "I'm scared to tell you."

"As long as you're not getting back together with Cal, I couldn't care less who it is."

"Cal?" I cringed, recoiling at the thought. "Seriously, Lauren? Do you really think so little of me?"

She tapped her long, manicured nails on the marble countertop. "You're stalling."

"It's Preston," I blurted.

"Yes." She drew out the word, making it sound like a hiss. "Boy is fine." She snapped her fingers.

I squeezed my eyes shut. "Can we please not refer to him as a boy? It makes me feel like even more of a pervert."

She placed a hand on my shoulder. "First of all—you're not a pervert." Even with my eyes closed, I could feel her watching me. She gave my shoulder a good shake. "Repeat after me: I'm not a pervert."

I opened my eyes and shook my head. "*I* am not saying that. And *we* need to get back to work."

She mimicked the sound of a whip. "Oh, honey. Are you this much of a dominatrix in bed? Is Preston your sub?"

"Sub?" I laughed nervously. "I'm not even sure I know what that means."

She switched on her tablet, flashing me a devious grin. "I forget how innocent you are sometimes."

I put my hands on my hips. "I am not." She kept her attention focused on her tablet, but I saw that eyebrow rise. "I'm not!" I resisted the urge to stomp my feet.

"Mm-hmm. Have you ever done role-play? Bondage? Had sex in a public place?"

"I…" I frowned. Maybe she was right. Maybe I was boring.

I didn't realize I'd said it aloud until she spoke. "I didn't say you were boring. I said you were innocent, and I think it's refreshing."

"Yeah, but… Well, do you think Preston will expect me to have some tricks up my sleeve since I'm, you know, older?" I whispered the last word like it was a dirty secret.

"How has the sex been so far?"

My face split into a huge smile. "Ah-may-zing. Like, best sex of my life."

She grinned. "Damn, girl. You are so lucky. But hey, I'm happy for you. Not jealous at all. Maybe just a little. Does he have any hot friends?" She said it all so quickly, the words almost ran together.

I laughed. "I don't know. I haven't met them."

She arched one perfectly shaped brow. "Yeah. Because you spend all your time in bed with Preston."

"Hey now. I do other stuff. I spend time with Sophia. I work out. I have a demanding job."

"Is that why you've been passing off some of the smaller listings to your agents?" she asked.

I lifted a shoulder. "That actually has more to do with a need for better work-life balance—more time with Sophia. She's growing up way too fast. My agents work hard, and they deserve it. Besides…I have a newer, bigger listing to focus on."

"Mm, girl. Yes. Just how big is Preston's *listing*?"

I covered my mouth to hide my grin. "That was… Wow. I don't even know what to say to that."

"Give me all the deets." She held up her hands, wiggling her fingers as if gathering the information from me like a spider pulling in its web.

"Um, no. And I was referring to the Miller property."

Her eyes went wide. "Oh shit. You got the listing?"

"I did." My smiled spread across my lips.

This was bigger than I'd ever dreamed of—the opportunity to sell a twenty-million-dollar home in the Hills. It was insane. And I'd made it happen.

"Congratulations." She wrapped her arms around me. "I'm so proud of you."

I squeezed her back. "Thanks."

She released me, only to grip my shoulders. "You're going to hire me to stage it, right?"

"Obviously." I rolled my eyes.

"Damn… Twenty million dollars. And—" she gave me a devilish smirk "—you've snagged yourself a hot man. You're on fire, Alexis."

I laughed. "Whoa. Whoa. I did not snag Preston. There is no 'snagging.' This is just a fling."

"If you say so," she said.

"I know so." At least, that's what I kept telling myself, but even I knew it was a lie.

"Okay." I crouched before Sophia. "You're going to be on your best behavior, right?"

Sophia had been invited to a sleepover at Brooklyn's, and I was looking forward to a night alone with Preston. No sneaking around. No sleeping apart. We could spend all night together. I didn't want to admit it, but I was starting to depend on him more and more—and not just for help with Sophia.

"Yes, Mom."

"Brooklyn's dad knows about your food allergies, but it's always good to ask about the ingredients if you're unsure." She nodded. "All right. Give me a big hug and kiss." I opened my arms, and she stepped into them. "I love you."

"I love you too." Hearing that would never get old.

A car horn beeped, and she backed away, slinging her duffel bag over her shoulder. I couldn't believe how big she suddenly seemed.

"Where's Preston?" She glanced around. "I wanted to hug him before I go."

I tilted my head to the side, assessing her. I was surprised how attached she'd grown to him over the past few weeks. They spent a lot of time together, but she'd spent years with Gabby and Sophia didn't cling to her like she did Preston. And while it made me happy to see her forming that bond with a father figure, I also worried what would happen when the summer ended. I'd even started trying to think of ways to convince Preston to stay—and not just as the nanny—despite the fact that I knew Gabby was expecting to return to her job.

"Here I am," he called, jogging down the stairs. "You almost forgot Princess Sparkles." He held out her favorite unicorn stuffed animal.

"Thank you!" She wrapped her arms around Preston's neck, and he swung her around. I loved the sound of her giggles. I loved watching them interact.

The doorbell chimed, and I could see Brooklyn's and Nate's silhouettes through the glass. Sophia lunged for the door and pulled it open.

"Brooklyn Bridge!"

"Sopapilla!"

I laughed at their silly nicknames as I extended my hand to shake her dad's. "Hey, Nate."

"Hey, Alexis. Good to see you." He smiled.

"Same."

Nate's eyes darted between Preston and me, and I knew he was trying to figure out who Preston was to me.

"Hi," Preston said, extending his hand. "I'm Preston."

When he didn't explain that he was Sophia's nanny, I rushed to add, "He's been watching Sophia this summer."

A muscle in Preston's jaw ticked, but I turned my attention back to Nate and gave him a bright smile. "Any questions? You have the list of Sophia's allergies?"

"Wheat, gluten, and oats," Brooklyn chimed in.

I smiled down at her. "Perfect. You guys have fun, and we'll see you in the morning."

Nate said nothing, but his expression spoke volumes. He clearly suspected something was going on between Preston and me. And if so, he wasn't wrong. Still, I wasn't ready to share that we were together. Wasn't sure I'd ever be ready for that. I could only imagine the reactions of the other parents.

"See you tomorrow," Nate said.

Preston and I waved goodbye, watching as Nate's Land Rover disappeared down the drive before shutting the front door.

"Why did you do that?" he asked.

"I'm so sorry," I said, knowing I'd made a mistake, knowing I'd hurt him. "I panicked."

He frowned. "You don't owe Nate any explanation."

"You're right." I slumped. But that was easier said than done.

I hated the fact that we were finally alone together, and we were arguing. I leaned back against the door, flashing him a sultry smile. "Let me make it up to you."

"I like the sound of that." Preston inched closer, crowding me. I placed my hands on his chest, smoothing them over his shoulders so I could wrap them around his neck.

"But first," he said. "Dinner, drinks, and dancing." He placed his hands on my hips, shifting them from side to side, moving us to a beat only he could hear.

I arched a brow. "Dancing, huh?"

I was intrigued but also anxious. Typically, a fling meant no dates, right? I knew I was kidding myself by calling it a fling, but I wasn't ready to admit to my feelings. And, as much fun as it sounded, going out together in public was a big step. Our relationship was a secret, and I wanted to keep it that way.

"Mm-hmm." His eyes were on my lips. "And then, I'll spend all night making love to you." He pulled me closer, close enough that I could feel his hard-on.

"Mm." I hummed. "Maybe we should just order in and then skip straight to sex."

He chuckled. "Tempting as that is, I want to take you out. On a proper date."

"I don't know," I hedged. "What if someone sees us together?"

"What if I told you we'll be in disguise? Would that help?"

I nodded, a fluttering feeling in my stomach. Maybe we *could* do this.

"I want to be more than a fling." His expression turned serious as he smoothed his hands down my arms, taking my hands in his. "I want to go on dates. I want to fall asleep and wake up next to you. I want to be a family." He squeezed my hands.

His confession sucked the air from my lungs. I didn't know what to say. I wanted it too, but...

He placed a finger to my lips. "You don't have to answer now. Just...give me a chance to show you how good we could be together—and not just in bed. Say yes to one date."

I'd never had a man treat me like Preston did, never had a man make me feel like he did. He grounded me, gave me a sense of home. A sense of security more than money had ever provided. So, despite my reservations and my fears, I found myself agreeing.

His answering smile was brilliant. "You have no idea how happy that makes me. How happy you make me."

I pressed my lips to his. "Keep talking like that, and we really are going to skip the date and jump straight into bed."

When I leaned forward for another kiss and he backed away, I pouted. He gave me a cheeky smirk. "Don't worry, we'll still have plenty of time for that. Now—" He placed his hands on my shoulders, spinning me around. "Go upstairs and get ready." He smacked me on the butt, and I gasped, jumping away with a big grin.

"I have to know where we're going, so I can dress appropriately."

He backed toward the glass doors that led to the pool house. "There are two choices, with accessories for you, upstairs."

My jaw dropped. "What? When did you have time to do all this?"

He smirked. "No more questions. Up you go. I'll meet you back here at seven."

I hurried up the stairs to my room, eager to see what Preston had planned. He'd clearly put a lot of thought into this date, and he'd expected me to say yes. I liked a man with confidence, and he certainly had it in spades. But it wasn't the arrogance or cockiness of so many other men; it was a quiet confidence. And that was one of the sexiest things about him.

In my closet, there were two choices as promised. I'd wondered why he'd been so insistent on selecting my outfit, but I realized the moment I saw the vintage 1920s dresses. They were both so beautiful, so elegant. So glamorous.

I fingered the beading of the black flapper dress, tempted to pick it because it was classic—safe. But something about the gold sequined dress called to me, tempting me like the Hollywood screen sirens I wanted to emulate. And I had the perfect set of lingerie, a lace-trimmed silk bra and matching panties with a garter belt.

I took my time getting ready, watching a few YouTube tutorials for my hair and makeup. When I finally slipped into the dress, I could feel the rightness of my decision settle over me like the silk lining gliding over my skin. When I glanced in the mirror, I almost didn't recognize the woman smiling back at me. I'd certainly undergone an outward transformation, but it was the inner one that surprised me most.

I was happy—more than happy, I was glowing. And it was all thanks to Preston. He'd given Sophia and me the support we'd been lacking, making us feel more like a family than ever. And he'd given me a confidence boost I hadn't realized I needed. He made me feel incredible—like I could conquer anything.

I'd told Lauren this was nothing more than a fling, but I knew it was a lie. And that only became more apparent when I descended the stairs, the gold sequins swishing with every step. Preston stood at the bottom, peering up at me with such adoration and love, it had my heart careening down the stairs ahead of me.

I gripped the railing for support, pausing at the second to last step as I took him in. This was a moment I never wanted to forget. He stood tall, projecting confidence and sexuality. His black tuxedo seemed like it had been made for him. His hair had been combed to one side, and he looked like an actor straight off the set of *The Great Gatsby*.

In that moment, I imagined myself walking down the aisle to him in a white dress. And the idea that I'd not only fallen for him, but could envision myself marrying him, terrified me. This wasn't reality; it was fantasy. And while it might be fun for a night, or even a summer, I knew it wouldn't last. Nothing ever did.

But for the first time, maybe ever, I found myself wanting to believe it could. That it would.

CHAPTER SIXTEEN

Preston

Alexis turned back to smile at me as we walked through the gilded doors to the club, to an era when alcohol was prohibited but jazz reigned supreme. It felt like we'd stepped back in time. Everything from the light fixtures to the bar to the entertainment looked so authentic, it was impossible to know what was real and what was a replica. And the costumes were incredible—everyone was dressed to impress, including Alexis.

Kate had helped me select the two dresses, and while I liked both, I'd secretly hoped Alexis would choose the gold sequined one. I knew it would look flawless against her bronzed skin, showcasing her natural beauty. And I wasn't wrong.

I smiled down at her, relishing the feel of my hand on her lower back. To an outsider, it was nothing more than a simple gesture. But to me, it was a huge step forward in building a relationship with her. Toward being a couple and not just a fling.

"This is incredible," she said, and I had to agree.

The interior of the club was massive, spanning two

stories. Despite its large size, it retained a cozy, intimate feel thanks to the dark wood paneling. Large chandeliers glittered overhead, adding to the air of glamour and opulence. Everywhere I looked, there was something new to appreciate —intricately paneled ceilings and elevator doors, a long bar with bartenders dressed in period costume. Every detail had been considered, giving the club an amazing sense of authenticity.

"The couples—the way they move together. It's mesmerizing," Alexis said, drawing my attention to her.

Her eyes were glued to the front of the club, where couples spun, stepped, and flipped their way across the parquet floor, trying to one-up each other as they moved to the lively beat. And the band on stage was just as captivating, each musician performing with amazing skill and passion.

"It is," I agreed, though I was looking at her when I said it.

She was the most incredible woman I'd ever met, and I was still trying to wrap my head around the fact that she was here, with me. I'd meant what I'd said earlier—I wanted a future with her, her and Sophia. And I hoped this date was just the beginning. I'd half expected her to say no, so the fact that she'd agreed was encouraging.

"Why don't we grab a table, and then we can do some dancing?"

She nodded, allowing me to lead her over to one of the empty booths lining the dance floor. I opened the drink menu, trying not to cringe at the prices. Fortunately, the tickets had been relatively cheap. But between the costumes, an Uber, and now drinks and dinner, my bank account was bleeding cash like the gangsters in the St. Valentine's Day Massacre.

Still, I wouldn't trade this time—this opportunity to show Alexis what we could be like as a couple—for anything. Even if it meant I'd have to take on another job to afford my looming tuition bill. But I wasn't going to think about it tonight. Tonight was about Alexis and me and our future.

"I can't believe I've lived in LA all these years and have never been here," she said.

"Well, you've been busy—building an empire, raising a child."

"True, but this would be a great place to bring clients or even to celebrate our year-end with the brokerage."

I grinned. "I'm glad you like it so much. I hoped you would."

The waiter returned with our drinks, then took our order before disappearing once more. I held up my glass to toast, and Alexis did the same. "To taking chances and making love."

She laughed, her cheeks blushing with color. "Hear, hear."

We clinked our glasses together. She took a sip of her drink, closing her eyes to savor the flavors. "You have to try this Singapore Sling. It's delicious."

"Here." I slid my glass over to her. "Want to try mine?"

She took a sip, drawing my eyes to the long column of her throat. "Mmm. That is good. What's in it again?"

"Fresh mint, Pimm's, and lemon-lime soda."

"It's refreshing. I like it." She slid it back across the table, taking her own drink back.

"What do you think Sophia's doing right now?"

Alexis laughed. "I love that you asked—such a parent thing to do. To finally have a night out, but you're missing your kid."

"I do miss her," I said, sliding my hand over Alexis's. "I'm glad we get to have some alone time, but she's become a big part of my life."

She nodded, but I couldn't decipher her expression. "She's become very attached to you."

The waiter returned with our food, and it was just as delicious as the cocktails.

"She's a good kid," I said, cutting into my salmon.

"Completely spoiled," Alexis joked between bites. "But yeah, she's a good kid."

"I still can't quite wrap my head around her birthday party. The other day, she told me there was going to be a real-live mermaid in the pool." I chuckled, trying to imagine it.

Alexis rolled her eyes. "That was Juliana's idea. She thought we could hire an actress to dress as a mermaid for the afternoon. Apparently, it's the in thing right now."

"Still," I said, taking a bite of my salmon. "I can remember my birthday parties as a kid, and they were pretty low-key affairs. Some basic decorations in the back-yard, maybe a bounce house—if I was lucky—and a home-made cake."

She leaned back against the booth, taking a sip of her drink and meeting my gaze over the rim of the glass. "It might seem over the top, but it's what's expected."

I jerked my head back. "Expected?"

"Yes, Preston—*expected*." Her tone was stern, and I could see the passion blazing in her eyes. "I vowed that my children would always have what everyone else did. That they would never be made fun of for their clothes or where they live. And birthday parties are a big deal."

I frowned, wondering what Alexis's childhood had been like. She never mentioned her parents, and I realized I'd never met any of Sophia's grandparents. Even if they lived out of state, it seemed unusual that Sophia never talked about them either.

Now wasn't the time to ask, especially not when the waiter returned with dessert. Alexis had ordered the mixed berries, which were served in a martini glass with a mint leaf.

And while they looked delicious, I saw her eyeing my tiramisu.

I remembered Sophia's comment about Alexis never eating dessert. And I wondered why she denied herself something she so clearly wanted.

My fork slid through the creamy layers, and I scooted closer so I was sitting next to her. I held up the fork to her lips. She kept her mouth firmly closed even as she stared at the tiramisu with longing.

"Just one bite." I gave her a devilish grin. "You know you want to."

She stared at the dessert a moment longer before finally parting her lips. The moment it hit her tongue, she closed her eyes and moaned with pleasure.

I leaned in, pressing my lips to the sensitive spot behind her ear. "Better be careful," I rasped, drawing in a hit of her delicate perfume. "Or I'll be eating you for dessert."

She tipped her head back, which only encouraged me to place kisses down the column of her neck. She smelled of jasmine and sunshine and home. And I wanted to lose myself in her forever.

I slid my nose up her neck, along her cheek so that my lips were grazing the shell of her ear. "Mm," I hummed. "Maybe just a taste."

I'd expected her to say no, to protest, but instead, she parted her legs ever so slightly. Maybe it was the dimly lit club or the atmosphere that seemed to encourage hedonism. Or maybe she was finally ready to embrace that we were happening. Whatever it was, Alexis appeared to have shed her inhibitions tonight, and I was all for it.

The club was dark, and no one was paying us any attention. I slid my hand up the smooth skin of her thigh, pausing when I came to a narrow band of fabric.

"Fuck," I groaned. "A garter belt?"

She bit her lip and nodded. I caressed her skin, moving her panties aside so I could delve beneath them. Though she tried to maintain a calm façade, her hand gripped my thigh, her nails digging in. I swiped my finger over her slickness, then placed it in my mouth, loving the taste of her more than any dessert.

"Delicious."

Her eyes were hooded as she watched me. "You're such a tease."

"You're one to talk." I leaned back against the booth, placing my arm on the cushion behind her.

She held a hand to her chest. "Me? A tease?"

"Mm-hmm. Those yoga sessions on the lawn in front of the pool house. You knew what you were doing."

She laughed.

"Inviting me to work out with you." I peered down my nose at her.

"Just trying to make sure you have everything you need."

I held her chin between my fingers, leaning in close enough so my lips brushed against hers when I spoke. "The only thing I need is you."

"Can I get you anything else?" the waiter asked, suddenly appearing.

I turned to him and forced a smile. "Just the check, please."

When he returned with the check, Alexis reached for it. "Don't even think about it," I teased, placing my hand over hers. "This is on me."

"Preston." I sensed her hesitation.

I shook my head. "I'm a bit traditional when it comes to dates, I'm afraid. I invited you, which means I pay."

"Yeah, but..." She studied me with concern. "Are you sure? I really don't mind."

She released her grip on the check, and I slid the bill before me. "Positive."

As she settled back into her chair, I could tell something was on her mind. Still, I paid and left a generous tip, eager to get her out on the dance floor.

I stood, holding out my hand for her. "You ready?"

"I don't know. Are you going to step on my feet? I'm rather fond of these gorgeous T-strap shoes." She drew up the hem of her dress, pivoting one of her feet to give me a better look. "Where did you get them, by the way?"

"First of all," I said, helping her out of the booth and twirling her into my arms so her back was against my front. "I'm not going to step on your toes."

I spun her back out, enjoying the look of surprise on her face. "And secondly, I have a friend who works at a costume shop that caters to period films."

"Let me guess—Kate?" she asked, and I nodded. "Tell her she has good taste." She smiled, and unlike the last time we discussed Kate, I sensed no jealousy, no...reservations.

I led Alexis out to the dance floor, standing tall as I pulled her into my arms. She'd attracted the attention of other men all evening, but she didn't even seem to notice.

We spun and swayed, and I could honestly say it was the best date I'd ever been on. And the fact that Alexis hadn't glanced at her phone once all evening told me she was enjoying herself too. She rarely put it down, even at home. Though I'd noticed her trying to make more of an effort lately to unplug. I didn't know whether it was at my suggestion or just an attempt to spend more time with Sophia, but I was glad.

When we finally made it home hours later, my feet ached and my cheeks hurt from smiling so much. As she led me toward the stairs, our fingers intertwined, I asked, "What are three things you're thankful for today?"

She paused at the bottom step, turned to face me, and smiled. "Nate." I growled, but she merely laughed. "For giving us this opportunity to be together."

I lifted my chin as understanding dawned on me. "Good. I was wondering why you were listing another man as your first item."

She cupped my cheek. "You're the only man I want."

Her eyes were filled with such a look of adoration, I felt emboldened. "What else?"

"Sophia. And you, of course. What about you?" She smoothed her hands over the lapels of my tuxedo.

"How about three words, instead?" My heart was pounding so fast, I was positive she could hear it clanging against my ribs. I'd been holding it in so long, I was afraid I'd burst if I didn't say it. "I love you."

We stood there for a moment as if frozen in time, and I was afraid I'd made a terrible mistake. Even if she didn't say it back, I couldn't bring myself to regret telling her how I felt.

"Preston." She stared at my chest, gripping my lapels. Every second seemed to stretch for hours, and I held my breath, awaiting her answer. When she finally met my eyes, I braced myself for rejection.

Shit. I'd pushed for too much, too soon. I'd been convinced she felt the same, or maybe I'd just wanted so badly for her to feel the same about me.

"It's okay," I rushed to add. "You don't have to say it back. I just…needed you to know."

She pulled me to her, fusing her lips to mine. I told myself even though she couldn't say the words, I knew she felt them. For now, I'd have to be content to let her actions do the talking.

CHAPTER SEVENTEEN

Alexis

"Mommy?"

I dropped Sophia's duffel bag at the foot of the stairs. For one night away, she sure had a lot of stuff.

"Yes, baby."

"What's a cougar?"

"You know what a cougar is," I said. She'd known so many animals by name by the age of two, I wondered why she was asking. "You mean the big cat—wildlife?"

Sophia scrunched up her face. "I don't think so. Well, at least, I hope not. I heard Mr. Nate telling his girlfriend that he spotted a cougar when he picked me up."

I stilled, my blood whooshing through my ears. But Sophia continued talking, completely oblivious to my internal freak-out—thank goodness.

"You haven't seen one out by the pool, right?" She stared out the glass doors to the backyard as if she expected to see a big cat prowling the edge of the pool.

I would've laughed if I didn't feel like I was going to be sick. I was going to kill Nate. But really, could I blame him? I was the one who'd gotten myself into this mess in the first place.

I knew he suspected something between Preston and me. Knew it the moment I felt his shrewd gaze assessing, judging.

Sophia waved, and I spotted Preston smiling at her through the glass doors. He let himself in, closing them behind him. She rushed over to him for a hug, but his eyes were on me as he held her, silently asking if I was okay. I shook my head.

"You're back," he said to Sophia. "Did you have fun?"

"Oh my gosh! So much fun." She held out her newly painted fingernails. "We did mani-pedis, watched a new movie that's not even in the theaters yet, and got to make s'mores over the fire pit in their backyard."

Normally, I would've enjoyed hearing all about her adventures, but I was trying to hold it together. Nate had a younger girlfriend, sure. But he was a guy. People wouldn't judge him for their age difference. It was to be expected, something to be boasted about.

"Wow." Preston grinned, leaning his hip against the counter. "That sounds pretty epic. The graham crackers were gluten free, right?"

I loved that he was so conscious about her diet. Loved that he encouraged her to take charge of her allergies by teaching her to cook. Loved him, even though I couldn't bring myself to tell him that. But right now, all I could think about was the fact that everyone was judging me for falling for a younger guy.

Okay, not everyone, I thought. Just Nate. Who'd told his girlfriend. Who would tell someone else, and someone else, until everyone in our social circle knew. And when they realized Preston wasn't just younger, he was the nanny... I clamped my eyes shut, holding a hand to my stomach.

"Duh," Sophia's snarky tone cut through my thoughts.

"Sophia," I chided.

"Sorry. What I meant to say," she said in a tone I didn't appreciate, "was, yes, of course, they were." Where was this attitude coming from? She wasn't even seven, for crying out loud.

I pinched the bridge of my nose. I needed a drink. Several drinks. Something.

"Why don't you go unpack, and then we can go swimming," Preston said.

"Yay!" Sophia turned and headed for the stairs, but she paused before she reached the edge of the kitchen. "You haven't seen any cougars in the backyard, have you?" Her brow was furrowed with concern.

Preston glanced to me for answers, then back at her. "Um, no. I haven't."

"Okay. Well, could you check before I come down? Just in case."

He coughed into his hand to cover a laugh. "Of course."

She scampered up the stairs, and I slid my hands forward on the counter, resting my forehead against the cool surface. A moment later, I felt Preston's large hand on my back. He rubbed in a circular motion, leaning down so his mouth was next to my ear.

"Why does Sophia think there's a cougar lurking in the backyard?"

I lifted my head. "Because Nate told his girlfriend he saw one when he picked Sophia up."

Preston started laughing, but I glared at him, crossing my arms over my chest.

He held a hand to his mouth. "I'm sorry." He laughed some more. "It's just too funny."

"I don't find it even remotely amusing." I blinked back tears. "How can you laugh about what people are saying about me? About us?"

That caught his attention. "You're right." He pulled me into his arms, and I rested my head on his chest. "It's not funny."

In his arms, I felt safe. In his arms, I felt whole. And while it had been easy to escape last night, easy to believe the fantasy was real, it had all come crashing down with one comment. One seemingly innocent question from Sophia.

"Preston, I'm ready," Sophia called as her feet pounded down the stairs.

I backed away from him, putting some space between us. But he leaned in, speaking low in my ear. "You need to tell her about us."

His breath tickled my ear, and I wanted to sink into him. "I can't. Not yet."

He opened his mouth to respond, but he glanced at something over my shoulder and smiled instead. "Ready, princess."

"Nuh-uh." She pointed at his shorts. "Where's your swimsuit?"

"Oh right," he said with an exaggerated eye roll. "I need to change."

"What were you doing this whole time?" she asked.

"Talking to your mom."

"About what?"

"Your…birthday party." He strode toward the back door, opening it for her. When she hesitated at the threshold, he said, "There're no cougars. I promise. I checked."

I groaned and dropped my head on the counter, only to lift it a moment later when the doorbell rang.

"What now?" I padded over to the front door.

I was surprised to discover Christine, one of the agents from my brokerage, standing on my porch. I tilted my head to the side, one hand still gripping the edge of the door.

"Hey, Alexis," she said. "I'm sorry to bother you at home, but I've been trying to call and text and email."

She shifted her designer bag to her other arm, and suddenly, I felt incredibly underdressed in my scalloped shorts and tank top. My makeup was minimal, my hair was in loose waves, and I was positive from her expression that she'd never seen me look so…casual.

"You have?" I frowned, feeling a bit unprofessional. A bit —naked.

I glanced at my phone, realizing it was completely dead. No wonder there were no calls. I knew it had seemed odd. I hadn't thought to log in to my computer because my emails automatically forwarded to my phone. Now I was kicking myself for thinking I could step back, relax, unplug.

"What's going on?" I asked as I ushered her inside.

"Um, where to start?" She gestured wildly with her hands —always a tell that Christine was frazzled. "The seller for Miller stopped by wanting to talk to you. The escrow on Hummingbird fell through, and the buyer heard it from the bank before us. And…"

Her eyes were focused on something behind me. Even without looking, I knew it had to be Preston. A moment later, the glass door slid open, and he sauntered into the kitchen wearing nothing but his swim trunks.

He smiled, the white of his teeth almost as dazzling as the V of his waist. "Oh, I'm sorry. I didn't realize we had company."

I watched Christine, noticing how high her brows rose on her forehead.

"We forgot the sunscreen. I'll just—" Preston hooked a thumb over his shoulder.

I returned my attention to Christine, leaning my hip against the counter. So far, she'd only told me bad news. I was hoping it would improve, but I doubted it. I'd been gone for one day. *One.* And the office seemed to have completely fallen apart in my absence.

"Is there something else?" I asked, impatient to determine the full extent of the damage.

She cleared her throat, returning her attention to me. "And the buyers on the Trousdale house are insistent they won't close on the deal unless the light fixture in the kitchen is included."

"What is it? A grand? Two? Tell them to buy a new one and be done with it. They aren't going to get a better deal on that house."

"I know, but they're adamant. I'm afraid we'll lose the deal if we can't get the seller to agree."

"Then get the seller to agree," I said. "Try to find something else to sweeten the deal for them, and be done with it."

She nodded. "And the rest?"

"Give me fifteen minutes to get changed, and I'll ride with you to the office." I headed for the stairs. "Help yourself to a drink, and I'll be back in a sec."

When I got upstairs, I immediately plugged in my phone, dreading the moment all the calls, texts, and emails would finally come through. Preston was great about getting me to unplug and enjoy the moment, but it was unrealistic to maintain for hours at a time. Had I enjoyed the time off? Absolutely. But it came at a cost. And it could mean losing hundreds of thousands, if not millions, of dollars in sales.

I grabbed a dress off the hanger, shimmying into it before slipping into my favorite Jimmy Choo pumps. After a quick refresh of mascara and lip gloss, I tousled my waves, spraying in some dry shampoo. I was out of time; it would have to do. I'd never felt so disorganized, so unprepared, as I did in that moment.

Christine's laughter reached me from the stairs, followed by the deep timbre of Preston's voice. I gripped my phone, my heels clicking against the floor with every step. When I reached the kitchen, they were standing across the island from each other, and she was clearly into him.

"Ready to go?" I asked.

She whipped her head around to face me. "Yep. Whenever you are."

Preston walked over to me, pressing a soft kiss to my cheek. "Have a great day."

I stiffened, even as I forced a smile. What the hell was he doing?

"Bye, Soph," I called, stepping away from his touch.

"Bye, Mom." She waved from the pool.

"Shouldn't you be watching Sophia?" I asked him in a low voice, feeling conflicted about the kiss.

"I haven't taken my eyes off her the entire time," he ground out. And though I knew he was referring to my daughter, the green-eyed monster raging in my mind told me he was talking about Christine.

Who would blame him for looking? She was nearly six feet tall—even without the five-inch heels she often wore. She had platinum blond hair that hung like a waterfall down to her waist. And the most convincing pair of fake boobs I'd ever seen.

"It was nice to meet you, Christine." He padded over to the door. "I should get back to work." He gave me a pointed look, letting me know he wasn't pleased.

I followed Christine out to her car, my mood growing darker by the minute. I buckled in and started scrolling through the emails that had piled up, responding to each as quickly as possible.

"So, Preston…?" Christine finally asked as we neared the office.

I kept my attention on the phone, trying to keep my voice even when I spoke. "He's taking care of Sophia this summer."

"He's…the nanny?" She scrunched up her nose as if she smelled something disgusting.

"Yes. What's wrong with being a nanny?" I turned, watching her profile.

"Nothing, I guess." Even though she shrugged her shoulders like it was no big deal, she spoke the words with such disdain, it made me sick. "He seems too hot to be a nanny. Honestly, I thought he was your new boy toy."

"Boy toy? Me?" I burst out laughing, though her comment struck a little too close to home. "Christine, when have you ever known me to date? Let alone have a boy toy?"

"I wasn't trying to offend you," she was quick to say. "I thought it was a compliment."

"Is that so?" I resisted the urge to cross my arms over my chest.

We worked in an industry that thrived on reading subtle signals, body communication. And crossing my arms over my chest would send the wrong message—would make it abundantly clear just how pissed I was. Would reveal my weakness when it came to this man.

"Yeah. I mean, he's young, hot." She tossed her hair over her shoulder.

I'd always admired Christine's blunt manner, until now. She had to be close to Preston's age, but they were so different in their respective outlook on life. Where he was focused on family and giving back, her only thought was for appearances. Not that I was much better than her, but still.

"And I'm what—chopped liver?" I teased, though it was no laughing matter.

Christine was merely echoing some of my own insecurities. Ones Preston had tried to dismiss, yet I continued to cling to the notion that people wouldn't support our relationship. That there would be whispers behind our backs or snide remarks.

I'd worked too long and too hard to have people focus more on my personal life than my reputation as one of LA's top real estate agents, and now brokers. I'd earned that respect, and I wasn't going to give up now.

"Of course not." Christine placed her hand on my thigh. "Alexis. You know how much I respect and admire you."

At the moment, it felt more like hollow platitudes meant to placate her employer. But I was the boss, and I had a reputation to uphold. I had people relying on me—clients, employees, staff. Not to mention Sophia.

This thing with Preston was supposed to be a fling, nothing more. But I hadn't had this much fun in, well, years. I felt like I was finally living again—spending time with Sophia, going to the aquarium without thinking about work, movie nights sans my phone.

But now, I was paying the price. I'd missed calls, texts, and emails…potential sales because I'd been distracted.

I could fix these issues. I *would* fix them. But now, more than ever, I needed Preston's help with Sophia. And this was why I didn't mix business with pleasure. Because things could get messy.

CHAPTER EIGHTEEN

Preston

"Hey. How was your day?" I kissed Alexis on the cheek when she returned home from work later that week.

She'd apologized for snapping at me in front of Christine, and I'd forgiven her. Still, I sensed that she was pulling away, and I couldn't deny that it stung.

It was typical. Frustrating. Every time I thought she was letting me in, she stepped back. She clammed up. I knew she was busy at work, but still…I didn't know what more I could do to show her that I was there for her, that I loved her.

Alexis let out a deep sigh. "Long."

"I can show you something else that's long." I waggled my eyebrows, hoping my cheesy innuendo would help her relax and take her mind off work. If nothing else, I knew she couldn't deny our connection.

But she didn't bite.

"Where's Sophia?" She glanced around.

"Over at Brooklyn's," I said, gripping her hips. "And I'm pretty sure you'll be getting a call in the next thirty minutes asking if she can spend the night." I chuckled.

She smirked, and I could feel my shoulders relax at that small gesture. "I'm pretty sure you're right. Those two are as thick as thieves."

"So...I was kind of hoping you'd go out with me tonight, seeing as we have a babysitter." I grinned. "And tomorrow's your day off."

"Tonight?" She pinched the bridge of her nose. "I don't know. I have a lot of work to do."

"You've been working so hard lately, you deserve a break," I said, hoping to entice her to take one night off.

Instead, she stiffened, stepping out of my touch. "No." Her voice was hard. "That's part of the reason I'm in this mess, trying to put out all these fires—because I took time off."

I stared at her. She couldn't be serious. "You took one day to go to the aquarium. *One.*"

"Plus, all the time I usually spend answering emails at night, plus my days off."

"Then they're not really days off if you spend most of your time working," I teased.

Her expression hardened. "You might not understand, but there are a lot of people who depend on me—clients, agents, employees, Sophia, even you. I don't get a salary. If I don't work, if I don't answer emails and make phone calls and follow up, I don't get paid." She enunciated the last words.

"I understand that." I crossed my arms over my chest. "I understand the pressure of needing to make money."

She leaned forward, her expression hard. "Do you?"

I gnashed my teeth, but then I had another thought. *What was this really about?* Because it seemed like more than the normal stress related to work. I'd seen her negotiate multi-million-dollar deals without breaking a sweat. I'd watched her dress down a contractor without losing her cool. And I knew she thrived on the energy and the excitement of her job.

"Yes." I stepped closer, not wanting to get into a fight. Not when we finally had a night alone together. "I do," I murmured, tucking a strand of hair behind her ear. "But I also know that everyone needs time to decompress, to have fun. Even—" I held a finger to her lips when she opened her mouth to protest "—you."

She rolled her eyes, but she couldn't hide her grin. "I guess you're right. And we did just close another big deal."

"See," I said, rubbing my thumb across her lips.

"So, what did you have in mind?"

She toyed with the hem of my shirt, sliding her hand beneath the fabric and fanning her hands across the bare skin of my back. I massaged her shoulders, trying to get her as relaxed as possible before telling her my plans.

"Preston," she moaned, and my dick twitched with excitement.

She tilted her head back, eyes closed, mouth open in ecstasy. *Plans? What plans?*

I placed kisses down her neck, across her collarbone, between her breasts. She melted into me, relaxing into my touch as I smoothed my hands up her rib cage, beneath her bra. By the time I pinched her nipples, twisting the tight nubs, she was panting. I loved the effect I had on her.

I pushed up her shirt and bra, admiring her gorgeous tits before lavishing each with attention. She palmed me over my shorts, making me even harder if that was possible. I wanted so badly to give in, but I needed to taste her first. I sank to my knees, pushing her skirt up her thighs.

"Fuck," I groaned when I saw she wasn't wearing any underwear. I swiped my tongue along her slit, savoring her flavor.

"I know you're tired," I said, inserting one finger into her tight channel. Her eyes rolled to the back of her head. "But my best friend, Hunter, is in town, and I really want you to meet him."

"I thought we agreed we weren't telling anyone." She clutched the edge of the couch.

"*Yet*," I said, meeting her eyes. "We aren't telling anyone yet." It was important to me to make that distinction. "And we don't have to tell anyone anything."

I added a second finger, curving them toward that magic spot.

"Right there. God, yes."

I chuckled, knowing she was close. I could tell from the rosy hue spreading across her cheeks, to the way she squeezed my fingers.

"Yes, you'll go?" I asked.

"Can't," she panted.

I stilled, keeping my fingers inside her. I wasn't ready to give up, and I wasn't above playing dirty.

"What…?" She opened her eyes and stared down at me. "What are you doing? Why did you stop?"

"Do you want me to continue?" I asked.

She bit her lip and nodded, and I wanted to take her lip between my teeth. "Yes."

"You want an orgasm. I want you to go with me." I circled her clit with my thumb, reminding her how good I could make her feel. "I think we can come to a mutually beneficial agreement, don't you?" I circled faster, driving her wild before stopping again when she still hadn't answered.

She gripped my wrist. "Preston, I swear to god—"

I smirked, knowing I had her right where I wanted her. "All you have to do is say yes."

She let out a huff. "Fine."

"Fine, what?" I pressed, knowing she was a woman who paid meticulous attention to detail.

"Fine. I'll go."

"Yes." Warmth spread through my limbs. "But first, I'll make you come."

An hour later, our ride pulled up to the front of Apt. 608. Alexis glanced up at the loft-like space as I threaded my fingers through hers. Music and conversation filtered down to us from the rooftop bar, and I was eager to get inside.

A bouncer greeted us at the threshold. "ID?"

Alexis went to grab hers, but he held up a hand. "Just his."

I cringed, dreading how that comment would set our relationship back. For a woman who was so confident, she struggled with what other people thought. She forced a smile and closed her wallet, while he verified my age.

"Great. Up the elevator to the top floor," he said.

"Come on," I said, tugging Alexis's hand. "Let me introduce you to my friends."

Her bronze eyes, the eyes of a cat, peered into mine as we rode the elevator to the top floor. "I'm telling you, this is a terrible idea."

"Terrible idea or not, we're already here," I said, brushing her hair over her shoulder. "And we don't have to stay long. Okay?"

She nodded as the elevator doors opened to a bar that was more like a house party than a club. The décor had a hipster vibe and the music, a chill beat. Some people were even playing games on the large outdoor patio—darts, cornhole, and horseshoes. It was all very relaxed.

I easily spotted Hunter's blond hair across the bar. He stood out among the crowd—taller than most. I reached back for Alexis's hand, eager to introduce her to my best friend. She smiled, but her attention was elsewhere, scanning the crowd.

As we neared the spot where Hunter and a few of our other friends had gathered, Alexis removed her hand to dig for something in her purse. I tried not to let it show—how much that simple action pained me. She was here; she was meeting my friends. I reminded myself that I needed to respect her wishes, but it wasn't easy. It took every bit of my restraint not to do something stupid like pound on my chest and declare she was mine.

"Preston!" Hunter slung his arm around my shoulder. From his glassy eyes and loose limbs, I wondered how much he'd had to drink.

I grinned, patting his chest. "Hey, man. Happy birthday. I want to introduce you to somebody."

"Oh yeah?" He grinned, speaking low in my ear. "Tired of stalking the cougar?"

"I, uh." *Shit.* Fortunately, I didn't think Alexis hadn't heard that. "Hunter, this is Alexis." I gestured to her. "Alexis, Hunter."

Hunter extended his hand to shake, and I watched as he took her in with a smirk. She'd worn a gray romper that dipped low in front, bared most of her back, and showed a ton of her legs. It was sexy as fuck, and I couldn't wait to undress her later. Or at least, I'd loved it when it was just the two of us. Now that every other man in the club was eyeing her, I wasn't so sure.

"It's nice to meet you, Alexis." Hunter flashed her a brilliant smile, turning on the charm.

"Same." Alexis smiled.

I made the rest of the introductions, and Alexis seemed to relax more once she had a drink in hand. She was currently discussing vintage fashion with Kate. I frowned, wondering where Kate's nose ring had gone, or if I'd simply imagined it the last time I saw her.

Hunter leaned in. "Dude. She's the MILF, right?"

I gripped his shoulder, my mouth close to his ear when I spoke. "Call her that again, and..." I tightened my grip, knowing he'd understand my threat.

He nodded, and I released him.

"So," Kate said. "Preston didn't tell me. How did the two of you meet?"

My attention snapped to Alexis, my eyes pinging back and forth between her and Kate. This was her chance to embrace our relationship, to stop hiding what we were. I held my breath waiting for her answer.

Alexis smiled, but it was tight. "I, um, we…"

"We met at her daughter's school." I threaded my arm around her waist, wanting to do a fist pump when she didn't stiffen or try to shrug out of my touch.

"That's so cute," Kate gushed. "How old is your daughter?"

"She's six. Well, about to be seven in a week or so. Actually, I think you've met her—Sophia."

"Oh my gosh, yes." Kate smiled, brushing some of her long blond hair over her shoulder. "I can't believe I didn't see the resemblance before. She's adorable."

Alexis's cheeks glowed. "Thank you. Most people think she looks more like her dad. Probably because they both have those piercing blue eyes."

"Let's see," Kate said, setting down her drink. "Do you have a picture?"

Alexis pulled her phone out of her purse. It took her a minute, but she found a few. She handed the phone to Kate.

"Wait…Sophia's dad is Callum Kinnison?" Kate glanced between the image on the screen and Alexis. What was I missing?

"Yeah." Alexis chuckled, though she didn't seem surprised by Kate's reaction.

"You know him?" Hunter asked.

"Know him?" Kate's eyes were wide. "I love his music."

She stared at the phone a moment longer before passing it back to Alexis. "You have a beautiful family."

"Thank you," Alexis said. "We're divorced now, but we have a beautiful daughter together."

Hunter clapped a hand on my shoulder, steering me in the direction of the bar. "We'll be back," he called over his shoulder. "With a round of shots."

Everyone cheered. Alexis gave me a reassuring smile, returning to her conversation with Kate.

"Man, you are so screwed." Hunter chuckled as he led me to the bar. "Do you know who Alexis's ex is?"

I shook my head. "Should I?"

From what I knew of him, he'd bailed on Sophia for the summer. And it wasn't the first time. I didn't get the feeling he'd been the best husband either.

"This," Hunter said, typing on his phone, "is Alexis's ex."

He held up the phone, which displayed an image of a tattooed man holding a guitar. The muscles of his arms flexed as he played the instrument, his long, black hair falling into his face and covering his blue eyes.

"He's walking, talking sex appeal. He could bottle it up and sell that shit."

"And I'm not?" I shoved the phone back at him, not wanting to dwell on Alexis's past. "I think Alexis finds me pretty appealing."

"Yes, but...for how long?" he asked, echoing some of my own fears. "Maybe it's fun now, but I see the way you look at her. You want more."

He was right—I didn't want to be the nanny. I wanted us to be a family.

People bumped into us as they made their way to the bar. A beat thumped in the background, making my head throb. I massaged my temples.

"And what's wrong with that?"

"Nothing," he said. "At least, if you're both in the same

place. But she's older, established in her career, divorced, has a kid."

"Why are you telling me what I already know?" I grabbed one of the shots and tossed it back.

"Because you're at very different places in your lives. Plus, she may be hot now, but how old will she be when you're thirty? Fifty?"

"It doesn't matter." I was sick of having this argument—first with Alexis, now with Hunter. Age was irrelevant; we belonged together.

"You say that…" He placed a hand on my shoulder. "But what about kids? I know how much having your own would mean to you."

"First of all, she has an amazing daughter, whom I adore. And if we wanted more kids, we'd figure it out—together." I was so tempted to grab the empty shot glass and smash it to the floor. Instead, I shrugged out of his hold, annoyed with him. With this conversation. With everything.

"You've been through a lot, and I don't want you to get hurt."

"Yeah, well, what do you know about relationships? About love?" I snapped. "You never sleep with a woman more than once. You've never been in love."

His expression shuttered closed. "You know what? You're right. What do I know? I only spent two years watching you go through treatments, watching as you fought for your dreams, your fucking life."

He turned away, asking the bartender for something.

"Hunter," I said, once the bartender had gone. It wasn't fair to take out my frustration on my best friend, not when I was more annoyed with myself and Alexis than him.

He grabbed the tray of shots without giving me a second glance. "It's fine, man. Let's get drunk and celebrate being alive."

I followed him, but it was with a sinking feeling in my gut. Hunter was my best friend; he'd been at my side the entire time—through my diagnosis, treatments, recovery. He'd even shaved his head with me to show his support.

Considering how difficult it had been to get Alexis to take off time to do something fun like go to the aquarium with Sophia and me, could I honestly say I thought Alexis would have done the same? And if not, then what was I even doing considering a future with her?

CHAPTER NINETEEN

Alexis

"And this," I said, gesturing to a large, open space with pipes sticking up out of the floor, "will be the master bath." A saw buzzed in the background as I led Lincoln on a tour of the house.

"It looks great."

The house was shaping up, and I was getting excited. It was the first property I'd be developing from the ground up. I was making all the design choices and taking all the risk, but it was a great opportunity. And something I'd been wanting to do for a long time.

I leaned in so he could hear me over the power tools in the background. "Why don't we head out to the balcony?"

He nodded, gesturing for me to lead the way. I stepped delicately over a piece of lumber, mindful of my Valentinos. The balcony was large, but—like the rest of the house—still under construction. The railing hadn't been installed yet, so there was a temporary barrier.

"Great location. Great property. Great potential," I said, taking in the sweeping view of LA.

"Definitely." Lincoln nodded. "How much is it going for?"

"It's not on the market yet. You're actually one of the first people I've shown it to," I said, knowing how much he'd like that.

We'd been friends in high school but only recently reconnected. I had a feeling he was interested in more than just business, but I'd continue to show him houses in the hope that he'd buy. He certainly had the means to afford the multi-million-dollar homes.

"When complete, it will have five bedrooms, five baths, and a huge pool," I continued. "Not to mention, some of the best views of the city."

He nodded, tucking a hand into his pocket. "And the price?"

"Four nine."

"So, really, five."

I nodded. "Just under."

My phone rang, and I glanced at the screen to see Preston's name. He usually texted, so for him to call…alarm bells started ringing in my head. Something was wrong.

"I'm so sorry," I said to Lincoln, stepping toward the doorway to the house as I held up my phone. "I have to take this."

"Hey, sexy," Preston's deep voice rumbled over the phone.

"Preston," I hissed, glancing back over my shoulder to ensure Lincoln was a fair distance away. "You can't call me at work, not unless it's about Sophia."

"This is about Sophia. She misses you. I miss you."

I dodged a worker carrying a bucket of paint. "I miss you guys too. But I'm in the middle of a showing, and when you called…I worried something was wrong."

"Everything's fine, I promise."

"Hi, Mommy!" Sophia shouted in the background. "Will you be home for dinner?" she panted into the phone.

"Hey, baby." I laughed. "I'll do my best."

"Great!" she squealed. "Because Preston's making something special, and I get to help."

I smiled, wishing I could be there. I loved that he was teaching her how to cook. I loved seeing her sense of independence and pride grow with each new skill she mastered.

"I can't wait," I said, knowing that no matter what it took, I'd keep my promise.

That was the difference between Cal and me. Which reminded me, I needed to call to remind him about Sophia's birthday party.

"See you later. I love you," she said.

I could hear her giggles, the garbled conversation between her and Preston, before I finally disconnected the call. I longed to be there with them, whipping up something in the kitchen. Laughing. Watching movies.

"Everything okay?" Lincoln asked when I returned.

I smiled, smoothing a hand down my skirt. "Of course. Now, where were we?"

"I believe we were about to discuss the property over dinner and drinks."

I was flattered, but not interested. Still, I didn't want to piss off a potential buyer, and I was used to deflecting such attention. It was an occupational hazard.

"Unfortunately, I already have plans," I said.

He leaned against the makeshift railing. "Tomorrow night, then?" He was persistent, I'd give him that.

I tucked a strand of hair behind my ear. "I'm kind of seeing someone."

It was the first time I'd admitted it aloud, and I was surprised by how easily it rolled off my tongue. Maybe it was because he didn't know Preston, didn't know that he was my daughter's nanny and a younger man. But it was nice to be able to tell someone that I was in a relationship.

"Can't say I'm not disappointed." He turned for the front

door. "Whoever he is, he's a lucky guy. Another musician? A movie star?"

I laughed. "Um, no. He's actually training to be a counselor for pediatric cancer patients."

He smoothed a hand over his mouth. "Wow. That sounds…intense."

"It is," I said, wishing I knew more about it.

"Well…" He extended his hand to shake when we reached the front door. "Thanks again for showing me the property."

"Of course. It was my pleasure." I shook his hand, applying some pressure but not too much. "Let me know if you're interested, or if you'd like to see something else. I'd love to help you find your dream home."

After he left, I checked in with the contractor, making sure everything was on schedule for the property, before heading to my car. I slid into the driver's seat, navigating to the contacts on my phone and connecting the call to Cal before pulling out of the driveway.

"Hello." He sounded groggy when he finally answered on the third ring.

"Cal, it's Alexis."

"Oh." He paused, and I heard some shuffling in the background. Had he been asleep? "Hey, babe."

I rolled my eyes but didn't argue. I just wanted to get this conversation over with so I could move on with the rest of my day.

"I'm calling to remind you about Sophia's birthday party."

He yawned. "When is it?"

I closed my eyes and drew in a deep breath, holding it for a count before letting it out. I'd sent him an invitation by mail and email, as well as texted the date and time. I didn't know what more I could do.

"Next Saturday."

I heard him mutter "Shit," but I pressed on.

"Cal," I chided, though I wasn't sure why I was even surprised. "You promised Sophia you'd be there."

"Okay," he huffed. "Okay. I'll try."

"Which means you're going to disappoint her. *Again.*" I sighed, hoping that the party, the decorations, her friends, everything else would make up for the fact that her father wouldn't be there. Even so, I knew nothing could compensate for his absence.

"No," he ground out. "It means I'll do my best."

"Whatever, Cal," I snapped, gripping the wheel tighter as I approached a red light.

I didn't know why I was surprised. After all these years, I should've known better. Still, I always held out hope—for Sophia's sake.

"I have to go," he finally said.

"Yeah." There was a hard edge to my voice. "Me too."

My phone chimed with a calendar reminder, and I knew it was time to move on. I would continue to drive forward, regardless of what Cal did. And I would continue to put Sophia first.

By the time I arrived at Sophia's school, the parent-teacher meeting had already started. I slid into one of the empty seats, silencing my phone as they continued discussing the business at hand. There were a few men in attendance, and I marveled at what it must be like to have a dad who was so involved. A man who was actually present in his child's life, a man like Preston.

I shook my head. Preston was Sophia's nanny. Her nanny, *not* her father.

He claimed he wanted a future with me, with us. But I had to remind myself that this was a job. He was present, he took care of Sophia, fed her meals, and took her out for activities because he was paid to do so. And after talking with his friends the other night, I knew just how badly he needed the money.

Not that it took away from their incredible relationship. He was great with her, and she adored him. But it was a reminder that come the end of summer, he'd move on to another family. Just like Cal had moved on.

"Alexis, does that still work for you?" Margaret's voice floated to me from somewhere in the distance.

"Hmm?" I glanced away from the window, only to realize everyone was staring at me. *Right.* "Yes, that will be fine."

We'd been discussing the back-to-school plans as well as the fall carnival and silent auction. My brokerage firm would be donating a number of items for the auction, which would raise funds for a new gymnasium.

"Great. Unless there's anything else…" She glanced around the room, waiting for anyone to speak up. They didn't. "Then we're done."

Everyone started to pack up. A few parents dashed out, but many lingered, discussing their exotic summer travels or their children's latest accomplishments. Sophia was attending a music camp this week, and a STEM camp for girls next, but I didn't feel the need to brag about it.

"Hey." Margaret approached, speaking in a dulcet tone that told me she wanted something. "I wanted to talk to you about Cal."

I frowned, wondering where she was going with this. Sophia had been attending this school for two years now. Everyone knew that if they had a question about Sophia, they could ask Gabriela or me. Cal had *maybe* attended one performance when she was in kindergarten, and he never picked her up from school. In fact, I wasn't even sure his name was listed as someone authorized to give her a ride.

"What about him?"

"Do you think he'd be interested in donating something to the auction?"

I forced a smile as I struggled to get my tablet back into my purse. It was bursting at the seams, overdue for a much-needed purge. But I hadn't had time. Like everything in my life at the moment, it had been pushed to the back burner. Between work, Sophia's upcoming party, school starting soon, and struggling to fit in time with Preston where I could, I was always in a rush.

"I can see," I said. "But I wouldn't count on it."

She nodded. "Okay. Well, if you can persuade him." She gave me a devilish grin, and I tried not to visibly cringe. "We'd be most appreciative."

"Sure," I huffed, finally getting the tablet in. "Ava received the invite to Sophia's birthday party, right?"

Margaret nodded. "Oh yes. She's very excited about her mermaid party." She placed a hand on my forearm. "I'm sure it's going to be incredible. So much better than Bella's Shelle-bration." Her frown was disapproving. "I mean, come on. Talk about tacky."

Wow. I could distinctly remember Margaret making a big fuss about how adorable the party was. She'd practically fawned over the decorations; now here she was, ripping them apart. It wasn't entirely surprising, but it was disappointing nevertheless.

She patted my arm. "You always do everything with such style and grace that I'm sure it will be very…tasteful."

"Thanks," I said, knowing how much pressure there was to throw the perfect party, have the perfect child, the perfect house, the perfect life. If you wanted to do well, you had to fit in, you had to play the game.

"Did you hear about Hennessy and Staci?"

I shook my head, needing to get out of there. It was suffocating—the pressure, the expectations.

"Apparently, he was cheating on her with his assistant. Can you believe it?" Her smile was disapproving yet sinister. It was clear she relished the gossip, even if she pretended to be sympathetic. "What a cliché. And poor Staci."

Spots swam before my eyes. If she only knew…if she only knew I was falling in love with my daughter's nanny. Talk about a cliché.

CHAPTER TWENTY

Preston

Alexis slid an envelope across the kitchen counter. "This is for you."

We'd barely seen each other in days. She was gone before I woke, and she came home late, often long after Sophia had gone to bed. I knew she was stressed and exhausted, but a little hello would've been nice. Maybe a kiss. Or was a simple "How was your day?" too much to ask?

I tried to understand. Really, I did. I knew how much Alexis loved her job. I knew how important it was to her. I also knew that I didn't fully appreciate the pressure she was under, but I tried. I tried to be there for her, but it was difficult when it felt like she was shutting me out.

I picked up the envelope and opened the flap. "What is it?"

"Just a little something to say thank you for all the extra hours you've been working."

Inside, there was a check for five thousand dollars. I stared at the amount before placing it back in the envelope and pushing it away. There was no way I could accept that. It felt wrong—dirty. Like she was trying to buy me off or something.

"What's wrong?" she asked. "Is it not enough?"

I crossed my arms over my chest, my eyes wide. "Are you kidding? Not enough? It's way too much."

"Preston," she said. "You've been working on your days off, staying over late. I don't expect you to do it all for free."

"I do it because I love Sophia. I love you."

She didn't say it back, didn't look me in the eye. Finally, she sighed. "Look, I know what it's like to feel like you're being taken advantage of. I would never want you to feel that way."

She slid the envelope back across the counter toward me. "Please—take it. It's what I'd pay Gabby if she were working extra hours for me."

I shook my head, holding her gaze. "No."

She'd barely responded to my texts the past few days, unless it was to tell me she was running late. Now, *this*?

She threw her hands in the air. "I don't understand what the big deal is."

"What's the big deal? You avoid me for days, then come home and try to pay me off."

"I'm not paying you off," she huffed, her face turning red. "I'm paying you for services rendered."

"Services rendered?" I laughed, but there was an edge to it. "And exactly which services would those be—the babysitting or the fucking?"

"I—" She stared at me with her mouth open, before turning and storming off toward the stairs.

I marched after her. "Is this why you buy Sophia designer clothes and host elaborate birthday parties? To try to compensate for being gone?"

I regretted the words the moment I'd spoken them, but it was too late to take them back. She straightened, and it was then I saw her hidden strength. The fire that blazed in her eyes.

"I'm sorry," I sighed. "That was uncalled-for."

"Yeah. It was." Her voice was hard. "You have no idea what I've been through."

"Maybe that's because you won't open up to me," I ground out.

I kept trying. I'd thought we were finally getting somewhere. That she was finally letting me in. And every time I'd get a little closer, she'd retreat to work again.

I scrubbed a hand over my face. "I thought we'd agreed this was more than a fling. Maybe I was wrong."

"You're not wrong," she sighed, taking a seat on the stairs.

"Then talk to me." I sat next to her. "Don't vanish for days, only to come home and throw money at me. It makes me feel… I don't know…dirty."

She cringed, leaning her head on my shoulder. "That was definitely not my intent. I was trying to be fair. I was trying to do something nice."

"And I had to ruin it by being an asshole." I grinned, taking her hand in mine. "It's hard. We've missed you."

"I've missed you too. I've just been…busy."

"We have time now," I said, even knowing she was tired. "Tell me what's been going on."

She gave me a quick rundown, and I realized she'd been dealing with even more than I'd known. While part of me felt foolish for questioning her earlier, another part wondered if I was right to do so. Wondered if she'd ever fully let me in.

"How's Soph?" she asked.

"Good. Brooklyn came over today, and they had fun swimming. She missed you at bedtime. And…I think she's beginning to suspect something."

Alexis stilled. "Why do you think that?"

I lifted a shoulder. "I don't know. Just a few comments she made."

She was quiet.

"We need to tell her, Alexis."

"No." She jerked her hand through her hair, turning to look at me. "I mean, at least, not yet."

"When?" I wanted to respect her decision of when to tell Sophia, but I was tired of feeling like her dirty little secret. "The summer is almost over."

"I…I don't know. Let me think about it." When I didn't say anything, she added, "You understand, right? With your placement still in effect and her birthday coming up, we just…" She sighed. "We need to wait a little longer."

I nodded, but I didn't like it. And worry lurked in the back of my mind that she might never be ready to tell Sophia —or anyone, for that matter.

She stood, and I expected her to bid me goodnight. Instead, she asked, "Will you stay with me? I'm not ready to say goodnight."

I wasn't either, but I never was. Still, I understood and respected her wishes to have me sleep in the pool house, especially after Sophia had nearly walked in on us a few weeks ago. I couldn't wait to tell Sophia, to not have to sneak around anymore. I was so tired of trying to hide how I felt about this woman.

I followed Alexis up the stairs to her room, shutting the door quietly behind me. While she got ready for bed, I stripped down to my boxer briefs and paused when my phone lit up on the nightstand. I frowned at the screen, wondering why Sam was calling so late. I sent it to voice mail, promising myself to call him back in the morning.

I climbed between the sheets and tucked an arm behind my head, waiting for what felt like a long time. Finally, she switched off the bathroom light and meandered over to the bed. Even in a loose T-shirt, she looked incredibly sexy. And I smiled when I realized it was one of my shirts she was wearing.

She plugged in her phone and climbed between the covers, snuggling in. We were quiet for a while, and I'd almost wondered if she'd fallen asleep when she said, "Growing up, my family struggled." I stayed silent, waiting for her to continue. "It's not easy being the smelly kid at school or trying to hide the fact that you don't have a lunch or a home."

My heart ached for her, for the child that faced hunger and homelessness. For the woman who had overcome such obstacles, but was still haunted by her past. I held her closer to me, wanting her to know that she was safe. She was loved.

"I'm sorry. I had no idea." I felt even worse for my comment earlier about buying affection.

She sniffed. "No one does—except Lauren. It's not something I like to discuss. And it's not something I care for people to know about me."

"Thank you for trusting me with this." My tone was solemn.

Everything made so much more sense now. Her relentless drive to be successful, to make money. Her desire to give Sophia everything and more.

"I trust you with everything," she said, rolling so she was propped up on her elbow. "And I love you. But I'm scared," she whispered.

I cupped her cheek with my hand. Fuck if it didn't feel good to hear her say she loved me. But at the moment, I was more focused on the fact that she was scared.

"Why? What are you scared of?"

"I'm scared of losing you. I'm scared this won't last. And —" she dropped her head so that she was staring at my chest "—I'm scared of hurting Sophia."

"Do you think she would be upset by the idea of us together?" I asked. I didn't, but I was starting to wonder if maybe Alexis did.

"Maybe not at first—she's too young to really understand. But I'd hate to think that she'd be made fun of for our choices. You're her nanny. I'm—" she puffed out a breath "—so much older than you."

"Let me ask you something," I said, rolling on my side and tucking my hand beneath my head. "Those kids who made fun of you growing up…"

"Yeah?"

"Where are they now?"

She laughed, though it was devoid of mirth. "Honestly, I'm not sure."

"My point exactly. They don't matter."

"Yeah, but—" She stopped, shook her head. "It still affects me. I'm still trying to live that down. And I would never want that for Sophia."

"Nor would I," I said. "But she's strong and she's resilient. And we can get through this—together." I believed it. I just wondered what it would take for Alexis to see it too.

She rolled onto her back, staring at the ceiling with a deep sigh. "What about the Hartwell Agency? Your job?"

"Like you said, the summer's almost over. Besides, I can find another job," I said. "Those are short-term issues. In the long run, you and Sophia are what matter."

"You say that now, but what about in ten years, or even twenty? I'm not getting any younger, Preston."

I smoothed a lock of hair away from her face. "It doesn't matter how old you are, you'll always be beautiful to me."

I leaned in, needing to kiss her, needing to know I wasn't going to lose her. Perhaps I was pushing for too much, too soon, but life was short. You never knew what was going to happen.

She was quiet, and I so desperately wished I knew what she was thinking. "You were right," she finally said.

"Can you repeat that?" I teased, prompting her to slap my chest. "Okay, fine. But at least tell me what I was right about."

"Money. Sometimes, albeit unintentionally, I go overboard to try to compensate for not being around as much. I'm sorry for doing that to you, and I'll try to be more aware of it with Sophia."

I gathered her in my arms. "You know that Sophia adores you, right? That she'd love you even if she didn't have an insanely over-the-top mermaid party or the latest designer clothes?"

She nodded, but I wasn't sure she believed it.

"I love you too," I said, unable to resist telling her again. "And I would never, ever want you to feel like you have to buy my love."

She sighed, sinking farther into me. "I know," she sighed again. "I know that, but it's sometimes hard to believe."

"Because of Cal?" I asked, doing my best to keep my voice even.

"Cal, but mostly, my parents. After all the years they struggled, I was more than willing to give them money. I wanted them to have what they needed, to have a nice, comfortable life. But they just kept asking for more and more.

"Sophia is their only grandchild, and they only spent time with her when they thought it would benefit them. And when they started demanding money from me, expecting it…" She swallowed hard. "I'd had enough."

"So, they're not in her life at all?" I asked.

"My parents? No. I told them they could be, if they met certain conditions. But until then, they will not have access to her. The sad part is, I'm not sure they even care."

"That's really shitty." I smoothed my hand up and down her back, wanting to comfort her.

No wonder she struggled with trust—her ex-husband, her parents had all done a number on her. I could never in a million years imagine my parents treating me like that. And it only made me even more determined to show Alexis that she could trust me, love me.

THE FOLLOWING AFTERNOON, SOPHIA HAD JUST RETURNED from camp and was showing Alexis and me a new game she'd learned. The three of us were playing in the living room when the doorbell rang. Alexis went to answer it, returning moments later with a raven-haired man at her side—Cal.

"Daddy!" Sophia jumped up from her spot on the floor and ran over to him.

I stood, my eyes bulging at the sight of this tall, tatted musician swinging Sophia around. When he placed her back on the floor, I sensed he was assessing me. And I knew he was trying to determine who I was and what I was doing here.

A heavy feeling settled in my gut. What was *he* doing here? Had Alexis known he was coming?

"Daddy! I have so much to show you and tell you and..."

"Who's your little friend?" Cal interrupted, and I resisted the urge to roll my eyes. *Dick.*

Sophia jumped around, never letting go of his hand. "This is Preston. Preston, this is my dad."

"Ah." He jerked his chin toward me. Everything about him, from the long hair to the fitted T-shirt to the ripped jeans, seemed so contrived. Right down to the leather bracelets. "So, you're the new neighbor."

I frowned, holding out my hand to shake. "I live in the pool house. So yes, I guess, technically, that makes me their neighbor."

"Pool house?" He turned to Alexis, tightening his grip on my hand. Guess I wasn't the only one Alexis had kept in the dark.

"Yes, Cal," Alexis said. "Preston is living in the pool house for the summer."

Sophia bebopped around the room. "And he's my manny."

Cal choked. "He's your what?"

"My manny," she said. "You know—" she placed a hand on her hip "—man plus nanny equals manny."

Cal glared at Alexis, but Sophia was so excited to see her dad she didn't notice. "Come see the new game I learned at camp." Sophia tugged on Cal's hand, but he remained rooted to the spot.

Cal blinked at me a few times as if he hadn't heard her correctly. "This..." he finally said, gesturing to me, his eyes going wide. "He's..." he spluttered. "He's the new nanny?"

Alexis nodded. "Yes."

Unbelievable. It wasn't like I expected her to tell him we were dating, but seriously—she hadn't even told him I was watching Sophia for the summer? *What the hell?*

"Him?" His voice was strangled, and he glanced between the two of us.

"Yes, Cal," she ground out.

"You didn't think it was important to mention the fact that a guy was watching our daughter? Was spending time *alone* with our daughter." His voice rose with every word.

Sophia was now staring at them, and I bit my tongue, knowing better than to respond in front of her. Alexis went over to Cal and gripped his bicep, speaking low into his ear. I couldn't hear the words she said, but judging from the dark look on his face, he wasn't pleased.

"Come on, princess," I said to Sophia. "Let's go build a castle upstairs."

She eyed me warily, like she knew I was trying to distract her. But ultimately, my offer was too irresistible to deny. She complied, darting up the stairs ahead of me.

"Oh good. He's gay." I could hear the relief in Cal's tone, and I paused at the top of the stairs.

Was he serious? And why had he gotten the impression I was gay? Not that there was anything wrong with being gay, but if Alexis had told him I was…

I stewed over it while Sophia and I built her castle, imagining all the things Cal and Alexis could be saying or doing downstairs. I was on the verge of charging down there when they appeared in the doorway. Alexis cleared her throat, and Cal shifted uncomfortably.

"Preston," he said, and I pushed myself off the floor, standing before him. "I'd like to apologize for my earlier outburst."

"Thank you." I reached out to shake his hand.

As Sophia's father, I would show him respect, even if I sometimes imagined myself fulfilling that role. Not that I'd ever want to replace him, more that I hoped to soothe the damage he'd done in being an absent, often unreliable figure in her life. But for the moment, I had to remind myself, I was just the nanny.

"Alexis assures me you've been vetted by the best of the best, and I want you to know that you're welcome in our home."

I gnashed my teeth. *Our home?* This was more my home than his.

"Cal," Alexis said in a warning tone.

"What?" He shrugged, going over to Sophia. "I am staying, aren't I?"

I didn't like the way he was manipulating the situation, manipulating his daughter to get what he wanted. He'd been gone all this time, and then he waltzed in, acting like he owned the place. Still, I kept my mouth shut for Sophia's sake.

Alexis glared at Cal. "With Preston staying in the pool house, I think it would be best if you got a hotel room this time."

"But, Mommy—" Sophia pouted. "Daddy always stays for my birthday and Christmas. It's tradition."

I swallowed my tongue. Her ex staying *here*? At the house?

"What's the big deal, Lex?"

Lex?

Cal draped his arm over Alexis's shoulder. She bristled beneath his touch, but I kept my mouth shut. I wanted her to do something, say something.

"Yeah, Mom," Sophia said, tugging on her hand. "He can stay in the guest room down the hall."

Fuck no.

"I don't think that's a good idea," Alexis said, shrugging out of Cal's touch. The bands on my chest loosened, allowing me to breathe just slightly.

"Please, Mommy? Please. Please. Please." Sophia could be relentless when she wanted something.

A pregnant silence followed, a stretch of unspoken and unanswered questions. Alexis glanced at me, but I didn't know what she was expecting. After all, I was just the manny, right? And the manny wouldn't weigh in on something like this. At least, that's what was expected. Just like it was *expected* that I wouldn't be sleeping with my employer.

"Fine," she huffed. "You can stay in the room at the end of the hall."

I bit the inside of my cheek to keep from making a remark.

"Perfect." Cal grinned at me like he'd won a contest. "I'll grab my stuff." He paused when he reached Alexis, turning to face me so he was standing at her side, showing me exactly how they'd look together as a couple.

"Oh, and Preston," he said it casually, as if it were an afterthought. But the twinkle in his eyes let me know just how calculating he was. "You can take the rest of the day off. Alexis and I have it covered."

"Daddy's staying," Sophia sang, prancing around her room, looping a feather boa around her neck.

I turned to Alexis once he was gone. "Can I talk to you for a minute?"

She followed me out to the hallway, but I grabbed her hand and tugged her into one of the spare bedrooms. I closed the door softly, and she immediately started pacing. "I can't believe he actually decided to show up."

"I don't want him staying here."

"Neither do I, but what was I supposed to do? He always stays here. And you saw how excited Sophia was."

"Mommy. Mommy, where are you?"

"Coming," Alexis called before turning back to me and lowering her voice. "It's just for a few days, okay? Then we can go back to doing what we were doing before."

The problem was, I wasn't sure I could go back to that. I didn't want to be a secret anymore. I didn't want to watch from the sidelines.

But for now, I had to put my feelings aside and do what was best for Sophia. What was best for Alexis. And if that meant stepping back and allowing Cal to have time with his daughter, then so be it.

CHAPTER TWENTY-ONE

Alexis

"Someone's awfully excited," Christine said, peeking her head in the door to my office.

I'd been doing a happy dance when she discovered me, and I slowly lowered my arms to my sides. But I couldn't contain the smile that was overtaking my face or the excitement that was bubbling out of me like the champagne I hoped to be popping soon.

"I just got a call from an agent with a buyer who's interested in the Miller place, and they want to see it again. She's fairly confident they're going to make an offer."

Her eyes went wide. "Holy shit. The Miller place?"

I nodded. It was a twenty-million-dollar property, and after only a few weeks on the market, I'd found a buyer.

"Have you called the seller yet?"

I shook my head, shoving my tablet into my purse. "I will, but I'm heading over there now to show it."

"That's awesome," Christine said.

"Thanks. Well, I better get going, unless you needed something…"

"I have some news of my own." She grinned. "But it can wait."

"What? Are you kidding? Tell me."

"Jasper proposed last night." She flashed me a brilliant smile, and it was only then I realized she had both her hands behind her back.

"Oh, I'm so happy for you! Let me see the ring." I went over to her, holding out my hand. "Look at that," I said, admiring the large, round-cut solitaire diamond surrounded by smaller diamonds. "It's gorgeous."

I'd been about the same age as Christine when I married Cal. And while I couldn't say I regretted it, I'd definitely do things differently given another chance. Preston said he wanted forever, but I wondered if he really appreciated just how long forever could be. Especially if you weren't with the right person.

"He totally surprised me." Christine's diamond sparkled under the lights as she talked. "But he had everything planned out. And it was so romantic," she gushed.

I wondered if this meant she'd lose some of her competitive drive, that she'd be less focused now that her attention would be on planning the wedding. Christine was one of my best agents, consistently outselling the others. And I didn't want to lose her.

"You have to let me throw you an engagement party," I said, wanting her to know how much I valued her. My agents were a tight-knit group, and even though I was their boss, I liked to think I was their friend too. "Talk to Jasper and let me know what date works for you."

"I'd love that," Christine said. "Thank you, Alexis."

"Of course."

My phone rang, and she headed for the door. "I'll get out of your hair. And congrats on the Miller deal."

"It's not a done deal yet." I grabbed my phone off the desk, poised to connect the call to Shane, the general contractor for my Sycamore development.

"It will be." She grinned, shutting the door behind her.

I wanted to share her optimism, but I'd been in this business long enough to know better than to consider a deal done until the ink was dry.

"Hey, Shane." I cradled the phone between my shoulder and my ear as I headed for my car. "What's up?"

"We have a little issue over at the house on Sycamore."

"Okay." I started the car, connecting the phone through my Bluetooth. "What is it?"

"The ground beneath the pool is worse than we thought. And the city won't let us continue construction without an elaborate underground system."

I pinched the bridge of my nose. "How much?"

"To dig out the ground, add the new foundations, and…"

"Just tell me how much," I said, wanting to cut to the chase. I just needed to know how much it was going to set me back.

"Twenty."

"Grand?" I sputtered.

"Yes."

I sighed. "And there's no way around it?"

"Not unless you want to ditch the pool altogether. But you'd still be out a couple grand to cover the hole and shore up the groundworks."

Shit. I banged my hand against the steering wheel. That was a lot of money. Poof! Gone.

I could afford twenty thousand, not that I liked spending such large sums. But I wondered whether it was worth the investment. I wondered if I was making a huge mistake with this home that had been one obstacle after another. And I continued to sink money into it, my potential return dwindling the longer it took to get it on the market.

"Alexis?" Shane asked. "What do you want to do?"

I thought about the comps in the area, and I knew what needed to be done. "Fix the pool."

Another call beeped in, but I didn't recognize the number so I let it go to voice mail. I had a feeling Shane wasn't done. I turned on my indicator, taking a left and heading up into the hills toward the Miller property.

"There's something else," he said.

I braced myself, not liking the tone of his voice. "Okay. What is it?"

"You know the chandelier you ordered?"

"The Italian glass one?" I asked, already dreading whatever he was going to tell me.

"It, um, it was damaged when they tried to hang it."

"How damaged?" I ground out.

"Shattered."

Silence hung between us. That chandelier had been the pièce de résistance of the home. I'd planned the entire kitchen around it, and now... *Fuck.* I blew out a breath. There wasn't time to order another one, not if I didn't want to hold up the house for another three to four months while they custom-made it then shipped it to America. God, I wanted to scream or maybe cry. Which was ridiculous—I didn't cry over chandeliers.

"Please tell me you're joking," I said.

"I'm sorry, Alexis. The guys were really careful, but sometimes these things just happen."

"I have to go," I said, pulling up to the Miller property. The potential buyer and her agent were already waiting at the gate.

"What about the chandelier?" he asked.

"I'll..." I huffed. "I'll find another one, I guess." I mean, what other choice did I have? "I'll talk to you later."

I disconnected the call and took a deep breath. I needed

to get my head back in the game if I was going to make this deal happen. And with the costs mounting over on Sycamore and for Sophia's birthday party, plus her private school tuition coming due, I could definitely use a win.

I smiled and shook hands with the agent before she introduced me to the potential buyers. I let them into the house, when my phone rang again. I switched it to vibrate and sent the call to voice mail, not wanting any interruptions. I knew how some of these high-end buyers could be—high-maintenance. The smallest thing could set them off and ruin a deal.

But when my phone vibrated again—the same number for a third time—worry gnawed at my gut. I excused myself to a small outdoor courtyard, trying to keep my voice low.

"Alexis Black."

"Alexis, this is Amber with the STEM camp. Can you come pick up your daughter? There's been an incident."

"Sophia?" I asked, wanting to confirm she had the right child.

"Yes. Sophia Kinnison. I have her sitting here with me."

"Mommy." Sophia's voice came over the line, and I could barely understand her between her tears. "Can you...get me? Hurts..."

"What happened? Are you okay, sweetie?" I tried to remain calm, even as I panicked. What the hell was going on? And where was Preston?

I couldn't understand a word she'd said. "I'm on my way, okay? I'll be there as soon as I can. Can you let me talk to Amber again?"

A moment later, Amber came back on the line. I tried not to lose it on her, but I needed answers.

"Can you please tell me what happened?"

"Sophia fell on the playground, and we're concerned she's broken something."

My lungs were tight, and I found it difficult to breathe.

My only thought was of getting to Sophia, of making sure she was okay.

"I'm leaving now," I said. "Please keep her calm, and can you please call Preston and ask him to come. Tell him I'll be there soon."

"We've tried calling him," she said. "He's not answering."

I frowned, knowing it was close to the time Sophia normally got out of camp. He should be headed there. They wouldn't have known to contact Cal since I rarely listed him as an emergency contact. What would be the point? He was typically thousands of miles away and often unreachable.

"Please try again. I'll be there as soon as I can," I said before disconnecting the call.

"I'm so sorry," I said to the other agent. "My daughter had an accident, and I have to go."

"Oh." She frowned. "I hope she's okay. Is there any way I could return the keys to you later?"

I shifted from one foot to the other, wanting to wrap this up quickly. "Unfortunately, the buyers left strict instructions. I wish I could, but it's not possible."

"Okay. Sure." She spoke to her clients in hushed voices. As we said goodbye, I tried to smile and be professional, but my mind was elsewhere—with Sophia.

I raced across town, hoping Preston would be there by the time I arrived. But he wasn't. Instead, I found Sophia sitting on a bench, cradling her arm. There were still fresh tears on her cheeks and an ice pack covering her wrist.

Where the hell was Preston? And why hadn't he answered any of my calls? As the realization sank in of just how long Sophia had been sitting here alone, in pain and scared, the madder I got.

"Oh, baby. I got here as fast as I could," I said, helping her into the car. "It's going to be okay. We'll go to the hospital and get you all checked out."

She nodded, but her mouth was set in a grim line. For her to be so quiet, she must be in some serious pain.

"Where's Preston?" she asked. Not *Where's Daddy?* even though he was in town. But *Where's Preston?*

It surprised me that she wanted Preston to comfort her. But it also made complete sense. And I wished he were here, not just for her, but for me. I could really use his support.

"I don't know, baby." I gripped the steering wheel, trying to stay calm as I sped through a light as it changed from yellow to red. "I'll try to call him after we get to the hospital."

Fortunately, the pediatric emergency room wasn't very busy, and we were taken back to a room relatively quickly. Everyone treated Sophia with great care, and she thought the X-rays were pretty cool. She'd calmed down some since we'd arrived, though her pain didn't seem to have diminished much.

I was sitting on the bed with her, watching her favorite show on my tablet. I'd had to silence my phone when we'd entered the hospital, and I could feel my anxiety rising with every text that went unanswered. Every email that appeared in my inbox.

Not that I could see them. The hospital was a service dead zone. But I knew they were piling up. I could feel them growing like the anxiety stacking on top of me the longer we had to wait for the doctor to return.

The door opened, and a man in scrubs and glasses walked in. "Hi." He smiled. "I'm Dr. Carlisle. I'm a pediatric orthopedist, and you must be Sophia."

She nodded.

"Well, Sophia," he said. "I have good news and bad news. The bad news is that the bone is broken. But, fortunately, it's a clean break and won't require surgery. Just a cast."

I frowned. "That's the good news? Sophia's turning seven

tomorrow, and she's been looking forward to her mermaid pool party for months."

I was grateful, of course, that she didn't need to have surgery. But I'd been holding out hope that it wasn't actually broken.

"Considering the location, a fiberglass cast is an option—"

"Meaning it would be waterproof?" I asked.

"Ooh," Sophia chimed in. "Cece had one of those last summer. Can I have a pink one with glitter?"

I laughed, some of my earlier tension dissipating. "If it's an option, yes." I turned to Dr. Carlisle. "Please tell me it's an option."

"Yes, but not all insurance plans cover it. And, even if they do, it's typically more expensive than traditional plaster casts."

"Are there any other downsides?" I asked, knowing that Sophia's long-term health was more important than her mermaid party, even if I'd hate to disappoint her.

He pushed his glasses up the bridge of his nose. "Typically, they produce less sweat and odor. And lead to fewer skin problems."

"Great. Let's do it."

"Okay. Let me get the supplies, and I'll be back."

As I stood, I swayed on my feet, and Dr. Carlisle reached out to steady me. "Are you okay?"

I waved a hand through the air. "I'll be fine."

He frowned. "Are you feeling dizzy? Light-headed?"

"A little, I guess."

"When was the last time you ate something?" he asked, coming over and flashing a light in my eyes.

"Um…I'm not sure. Maybe breakfast." I hadn't had much of an appetite lately. Nor had I had much time to eat.

"Hmm," he hummed, taking my pulse, listening to my heart with his stethoscope. "I could run some tests…"

"I'm fine, really," I said, not wanting Sophia to worry. And, really, I was fine. A little tired maybe, but I'd been running like crazy.

Tired or not, it didn't matter. Sophia needed me. And if today's events had shown me anything—the only person I could rely on was myself.

CHAPTER TWENTY-TWO

Preston

"What were you thinking, man?" I asked Sam.

My only answer was the beep of the vital signs monitor, the rhythmic hiss of the ventilator pumping oxygen through his lungs. His eyes were closed, hands lifeless at his sides.

I'd just dropped Sophia off at STEM camp when Indy had called to tell me Sam was in the hospital. At first, I'd assumed he was suffering a complication—one of the latest of many from his treatments. But then she'd told me he'd tried to take his life.

"Fuck." I buried my face in my hands, wondering how I'd missed the signs. This was what I was training to do—counsel cancer patients. And I couldn't even help my own friend.

I'd been busy with my job, with Alexis. But that was no excuse. And when Sam had called the other night… I shook my head. I hadn't been there for him when he'd needed me most. I'd failed him.

I sat in the chair next to his bed, talking to him for a long time. I told him about Sophia. I told him about Alexis. I told him he would get through this—he had to. And that I would be there for him every step of the way.

I must have fallen asleep at some point, because the next thing I knew, someone was gently shaking my shoulder.

"Preston," Indy said. I blinked up at her, feeling groggy. "Hey, it's getting kind of late."

I rubbed my face with my hands and stood. "I should probably check in with Alexis."

She nodded, walking with me to the door. "Thanks so much for coming. I really appreciate it, and I'm sure Sam does too."

"You'll call me when he wakes up?"

"Of course." She patted me on the shoulder.

How could she be so strong? So brave? I considered telling her that Sam had called the other night, but I was afraid she'd blame me, hate me. And that would break me.

"Can I get you anything?" I asked. "A change of clothes? Some dinner?"

"I'm good. His parents should be here soon, and they'll want to stay busy."

I nodded, hesitant to leave, despite her insistence. "Seriously—" I gripped her shoulders "—call me if you need anything. Okay?"

She nodded. "I will. Thanks, Preston."

I shuffled out of the hospital toward my car. I didn't know where to go or what to do with myself. I wanted to go home. I wanted to see Alexis and Sophia, but… I clenched my fists. Cal was there. Cal was there with his easy laughter and his stories. Rubbing my face in the fact that he and Alexis had a shared past that included good memories, vacations—a child.

I slumped against the steering wheel. What the hell was I doing? Not just with Alexis, but with my life?

With a resigned sigh, I switched on the sound for my

phone and glanced at the screen. Why did I have six missed calls and several unread text messages? Half of them were from Alexis, and the others… *Oh shit.*

I'd forgotten to pick up Sophia from camp. Alexis had to be pissed. I sped home without stopping to listen to them. And when I tried calling her, it went to voice mail. I needed to talk to her, to apologize. To explain.

When I got back to the house, I threw my car in park, jogging over to the doors that led to the back of the main house. I held up my hand to knock when I saw them. Alexis was standing in the kitchen with her back to me, and Cal's arms were wrapped around her. He rubbed a hand up and down her back, speaking into her ear.

I stumbled backward, tripping over one of the lounge chairs and nearly falling to the ground in the process. Alexis whipped around to face me, and it was then I realized she'd been crying. She dabbed at her eyes with a tissue, and I frowned, trying to understand what was going on.

Cal placed his hand on her shoulder, glaring at me through the glass doors. And I'd never felt more like an outsider looking in. I tried to remind myself that it was temporary, that my banishment to the pool house was only for a few days. But it was easier to ignore the fact that he was part of their lives—and always would be—when he wasn't here.

"Alexis," I said, sliding the door open. "I'm so sorry I forgot to pick up Sophia. Are you okay?"

She scoffed. "Am I okay? Shouldn't you be asking if Sophia's okay?"

I tilted my head to the side, concern gnawing at my gut. "What are you talking about? What happened?"

I wasn't sure how much more I could handle in one day. I needed her to tell me.

"Sophia fell on the playground and broke her wrist."

I rubbed the back of my neck, aching to gather Alexis in my arms and hold her. But—I glared at Cal—*he* was here. And *he* had his hand on her shoulder.

I stilled. "Is she okay?"

"She will be, thank god. But she was distraught. And when they couldn't reach you, they…"

"They called you," I said, wondering if we were just going to ignore the fact that no one had attempted to call Cal. Maybe because he wouldn't know what to do or how to comfort Sophia.

"Yes." She nodded. "I was in the middle of showing the Miller property, and I'm pretty sure I may have lost the deal because of it."

I swallowed back a lump of emotion. "I'm so, so sorry, Alexis. I was visiting a friend—"

"You know what—" She sliced the air with her hand. "I really don't care what you were doing or who you were with." Her words, her tone, everything about her was hard. And it cut through me. "Sophia needed you, and you let her down." The words she didn't say, but I knew she felt were: "You let me down."

Her words fell with a thud, landing heavily on my heart. And the fight went out of me. It was no use trying to explain. We were both too upset. And I didn't want to make a bad day worse by telling her about Sam.

"Can I see her?" My voice cracked.

Cal pulled Alexis into his side, speaking for her. "Sophia needs her rest. You can see her tomorrow, at the party."

And what did Alexis do? *Nothing.*

I didn't know why I was even surprised. But the fact that she was going to keep me away from Sophia—it was as if she took the tattered pieces of my heart and ripped them to shreds.

"So, the party's still on?" I asked, considering her injury.

Alexis straightened. "Of course it is."

"Well, then…" I hesitated, wishing there were something more I could do or say. Yet again, I was at a loss. "I guess I'll wish you goodnight."

"Goodnight." Cal smirked, holding Alexis closer to him.

I flattened my lips, wanting so badly to ask Alexis what the hell she was doing. But again, just the nanny. Except, I wasn't. And the fact that I was being dismissed like I was nothing more than the hired help made me want to punch something, preferably Cal's smug grin.

I texted Indy, picking up some dinner for her and Sam's parents before heading back to the hospital. I spent the evening there, wishing I could go back in time to before Sam's suicide attempt, before Sophia's fall. Logically, I knew it wasn't my fault Sam had attempted suicide. Just as I knew it wasn't my fault Sophia had broken her wrist. But that didn't change the fact that I hadn't been there for the people I loved when they needed me most.

After a restless night, I awoke to the beep, beep, beep of a truck backing up. I peeked through the window to see a flurry of activity on the lawn. Decorations were being hung, tables were being set up, and balloons tied down.

I texted Indy to check in—no change. And then I showered and threw on some clothes before heading over to the house. I didn't know what to expect today, but I knew I wanted Sophia to enjoy her birthday party. I knew how excited she'd been, and I hoped her injury wouldn't put too much of a damper on her spirits.

As for Alexis, I fully intended to explain what had happened. But not today. Today was about Sophia and celebrating her life.

Sophia was sitting at the table with Cal and Alexis when I walked up to the sliding glass doors. They looked like the picture-perfect family, and I hesitated to interrupt their moment.

"Preston!" Sophia called, spotting me first.

She jumped out of her chair and ran over to the doors. Fuck if that didn't make my heart burst. She wrapped her good arm around me, squeezing me tight.

"Happy birthday, princess." I smiled, hugging her back. "Let me see this new accessory," I said, gesturing to her cast. It was hot pink—of course.

I crouched down to her level, needing to look her in the eye. "I'm sorry I couldn't be there yesterday. But you were very brave, and I'm glad you're okay."

She nodded. "I'm okay. Plus—" she grinned "—everyone's going to think my cast is so cool. Did you know it's waterproof?"

"Really?" I asked, feigning surprise. "That's so awesome. And you know what will make it even cooler?"

She scrunched up her face. "Sequins?"

I laughed. Leave it to Sophia to want to add sequins to her cast. Though, she wasn't too far off with her idea of embellishing it. "No. I was actually thinking you might like to have Kate decorate it with a mermaid or some scales or whatever you want, really."

"Really?" She hopped up and down.

I nodded. "As long as it's okay with your mom, that is."

Alexis smiled, but I didn't miss the dark circles beneath her eyes. "I think it's a great idea."

I hung around, hoping for a moment alone with Alexis, but it never came. Cal was always hovering nearby, or she was talking with her friend Juliana. When she disappeared upstairs to get ready, I briefly contemplated scaling the trellis just so I could talk to her. But the yard was crawling with people setting up for the party. And then guests started arriving, and I knew it was hopeless.

Still, I kept watching, waiting for an opening. Not to explain where I'd been—the middle of Sophia's birthday party wasn't the time or the place for that. But more to see if she was okay. Her makeup may be immaculate, but it couldn't disguise the fact that her smile didn't quite reach her eyes. I could feel the tension she carried between her shoulders as if it were my own. She put on a good performance, but she couldn't hide the truth from me—it was all an act.

Fortunately, Sophia was having a blast. And the cast didn't seem to be slowing her down one bit. She jumped into the pool, laughing and splashing with her friends, some of whom I'd met this summer, a few I recognized from her school.

"Hello, Preston," Margaret said, sidling up to me.

We'd met while I was nannying for Theo, and I always got the distinct impression that she was interested in me. Not that I'd ever done anything to encourage her. And the way she looked at me made my skin crawl.

"Margaret." I lifted my chin in greeting before taking a sip of my drink.

She, like most of the other moms, was wearing a bikini with a sheer cover-up. Though I knew for a fact that none of them would so much as dip a toe in the water. God forbid they mess up their hair or makeup.

"Listen, what are your plans for this fall?" she asked.

I tried to keep a blank face. What was she driving at? "I'm not sure yet. Classes start soon, and I have a few semesters left until I finish my degree."

"I love that—*love* a man who is intelligent." She dragged a finger down my arm.

I tried not to visibly react to her touch, though I could feel sweat trickling down my back. What was she up to?

"Well, if you ever want to pick up some extra cash…" She

trailed off, scanning the yard. "I'm sure we could come to an arrangement."

Surely, she wasn't implying what I thought she was... right?

When someone called her name, she waved and headed that direction. But not before glancing over her shoulder with a seductive grin that made my stomach turn. "Just think about it."

I turned, only to discover Alexis watching me, her jaw tight. Of course, she'd seen the entire thing. I let out a deep sigh and tried to go over to her, but Cal intercepted me.

"Alexis sure knows how to throw a party." He sipped his beer.

"Yep." I tried to move past him, but he kept talking, his eyes on the pool where Sophia and her friends were sitting on the edge, watching the "mermaid" perform.

"You know, Sophia breaking her wrist worked out even better than I could've planned."

"What?" I jerked my head back, feeling as if he'd slapped me.

"Yeah, well, with Alexis under so much stress, of course she'd turn to me for support. And who better to console her, who better to understand the pain she feels as a parent, than the father of her child." God, his tone and his entire expression made me sick. He was such a fraud.

"Wow." My mouth slackened as I tried to wrap my head around what he'd said. "Sophia deserves so much better. Alexis, too."

He crossed his arms over his chest. "And you think you're it, huh?" He scoffed, leaning forward and lowering his voice. "You've been here—what? All of two months? And you suddenly think you're an expert?"

"I'm not an expert," I said. "But at least I'm here. I'm

present day in and day out, which is more than I can say for you."

"You're paid to be here," he sneered.

I clenched my fists, my body tensing as if for a fight. "It's not about the money."

He barked out a laugh, crossing his tattooed arms over his chest. "It's not, huh?"

I shook my head. "I love Sophia, and I would love her whether I was paid to or not."

"*I* love her," he ground out.

"Then show her," I said. "You don't realize how much she craves your attention, your affection. And you don't see how disappointed she is when you don't call. Or how hard it is on Alexis to make excuses for you."

"And who disappointed her yesterday, huh?" He jabbed my chest with his finger, and it took everything in me not to snap it off his hand. "Who let her down?"

I gnashed my teeth. He had no idea how terrible I felt about that.

"I was…"

"Yeah. Yeah." He rolled his eyes. "'Visiting a friend.' Here's a little piece of advice." He leaned in, close enough for me to smell his aftershave. "I was here long before you, and I will be here long after. I was—and always will be—Sophia's father."

He didn't deserve the title, and my blood boiled with rage. Why could a piece of shit like Cal be a father, and someone like Sam not have that opportunity? Sam would make an amazing dad, given the chance. Yet he was fighting for his life, and his fertility was shot. The more I thought about it— the unfairness of it all—the angrier I got.

But Cal wasn't done. He tapped a finger to his lips. "I think the question now is…how long will it take me to get back with Alexis? And should I sleep with your little friend Kate to tide me over in the meantime?"

That's it.

I reared my arm back and punched him square in the nose. He didn't see it coming and stumbled backward. As I shook out my hand, I felt everyone's eyes on us, watching us. And a sick feeling pooled in my gut, only growing worse when I saw Sophia staring at the two of us, eyes wide.

What had I done?

Cal took a few steps back, covering his nose with his hand. But I saw what no one else did—the sparkle in his eyes, the smirk, that told me he'd played me. And I'd done exactly what he'd hoped I would.

Fuck.

CHAPTER TWENTY-THREE

Alexis

"Oh shit." Lauren's eyes—like those of most of the guests—were glued to Cal and Preston.

I marched over there with Lauren on my heels. Her presence gave me the support I needed. What the hell was Preston thinking? Punching Sophia's dad in the middle of her birthday party? I could kill him.

"Preston," I hissed, gripping his bicep. "Cal," I ground out. "Could you both please stop acting like a pair of two-year-olds and come with me?"

Cal continued to hold a hand over his nose, and I wondered what the extent of the damage was. I also wondered what had possessed Preston to punch him. The three of us were supposed to be responsible adults, role models. Yet only one of us was fulfilling that role. And now I was missing Sophia's birthday party because of their stupidity.

I led them into my office and shut the door. I thought I was going to be sick. "Sit."

"I want him gone." Cal lifted his chin, speaking to me as if Preston weren't in the room.

I ignored him, at least for the moment. "What the hell was that?" I stood behind my desk, resting my knuckles on the surface as I stared them down.

Preston glanced up at me from beneath his lashes. "I'm so sorry, Alexis."

"Shouldn't you be apologizing to me?" Cal asked.

Preston crossed his arms over his chest, and I could practically see the steam rising from his skin. He was pissed. "Why would I apologize when I'm not sorry for punching you?"

I jerked my head back. I didn't know what had gotten into Preston. First, completely forgetting to pick up Sophia yesterday. The fact that he was totally unreachable. And now this?

Maybe I didn't know him as well as I thought I did. Despite the fact that we'd spent a lot of time together the past few months, I wondered if I'd allowed my judgment to be clouded by lust. My desire to feel accepted and loved overriding reason.

Cal stood. "What are you waiting for Alexis? Fire him!"

I glanced between the two of them, trying to figure out how we'd gotten here. And why my nanny slash boyfriend had punched my ex-husband. When had my life turned into a complete circus?

"Can you give us a minute?" I asked Preston. He nodded, moving toward the door, and I hated seeing the wounded look on his face.

"I want him gone," Cal said again as soon as the door was closed.

I sighed. "Be reasonable, Cal. Sophia adores him. This will crush her."

He glanced between the door and me, his eyes wide. "He...he punched me." He jabbed a finger at his chest. "At our daughter's birthday party. In front of a backyard full of guests. He's damn lucky we're not calling the cops."

I rounded my desk, going to stand before him. "And *why* did he punch you?"

"Does it matter? He hit me in front of our daughter."

That was true, but still... Something didn't add up. Regardless, I had to think of Sophia. And the fear always lurked in the back of my mind that Cal would use something like this as ammunition to amend our custody agreement. I didn't think he'd actually go through with it, but it was enough of a threat nevertheless.

"I don't want more drama. I don't want that for Sophia." *Or Preston.*

"Then you need to fire him. Fire him, and I won't press charges."

Fire him? Press charges? I brought a shaky hand to my forehead, attempting to smooth back my hair. Cal watched my movements with concern, replacing my hand with his own.

"I just want what's best for Sophia." His tone rang with sincerity. As I looked at him with dried blood on his shirt, I knew he wasn't going to relent.

Shit.

"I'd like to talk to him alone."

Cal shook his head. "You think I want to leave you alone with that...that monster, after what he did to me?"

I resisted the urge to roll my eyes. Cal was being more dramatic than Sophia, and that was saying something.

"Cal." I placed a hand on his bicep. "I can handle this. I will handle this—*alone.*"

"Fine," he huffed. "But I'll be waiting just outside in case you need me."

I nodded, opening the door to find Preston leaning against the wall with a bag of ice on his hand.

"Preston." I inclined my head.

Cal brushed past him on his way out, and Preston bared his teeth. I braced myself for another confrontation, but Cal straightened and jutted out his chin before stepping aside.

Preston followed me inside the office, and I shut the door.

"You're firing me, aren't you?" he asked before I could even say the words.

I nodded.

He raked a hand through his hair. "Shit. I'm sorry, Alexis. I—"

"Look," I cut him off, needing to get this over with before I completely broke down. "I don't like this any more than you do. Luckily, Cal agreed not to press charges or report you to the agency," I sighed, already dreading what I'd tell Sophia. "Provided you leave immediately."

"So, that's it? You're just going to take his side?" he asked.

Did I want to fire Preston? No.

But it felt like my hands were tied.

I wanted to love him, to trust him, but he'd completely undermined that with his actions. First, forgetting to pick up Sophia. And now, starting a fight with Cal at her birthday party.

I gave a little shrug. "Things were never going to work out between us. We're at different points in our lives. We want different things."

"I can see you've already made up your mind, so there's no use trying to convince you otherwise."

His words struck me. And even though my heart was breaking and tears threatened to fall, I lifted my chin and put on a brave front. What could I say? I was afraid if I opened my mouth, the sobs I was desperately trying to hold back would come pouring out.

He gripped the arms of the chair, standing. "Though I guess I should've seen this coming." His denim eyes were flat when he looked at me. It felt as if he was seeing through me.

"You always had one foot out the door. You were always looking for reasons why we couldn't be together. And now you got your wish."

He marched toward the door, and I envied his confident, fluid strides. How could he be so strong when I was crumbling? He paused for a moment with his back still to me, hand poised over the knob. Time seemed to stop; my heart seemed to stop.

But then he opened the door and walked through it without looking back.

Oh god. My stomach hardened, a bout of nausea threatening to overtake me.

Juliana peeked her head in a moment later. "It's time for cake." She frowned. "You okay?"

I wanted to scream, to cry, to crumple to the floor, but I had a house full of guests and a birthday girl I couldn't disappoint. So, I straightened, steeling myself to make the most convincing sale of my life—that I was happy and everything was just fine.

"Of course." I forced myself to smile as I headed out to the backyard.

"Happy birthday to you," I sang, joining in with everyone else, trying to put my heart into it.

I had no idea how I was going to break the news to Sophia. Or even what I was going to do without Preston. Fortunately, I'd planned to take some time off from work to enjoy the last days of her summer vacation, and Gabriela would be coming back soon. But...still.

When one of the waiters sliced into the cake, the sickly sweet smell of the icing was overpowering. Bile rose in my throat, and I held a hand to my mouth, hoping I wouldn't be sick.

"I'll, um—" I forced a smile. "I'll be back."

Fortunately, Sophia had a lot to distract her—the cake,

her friends, the presents to open. I dashed up the stairs to my bathroom, ignoring the curious stares of the other parents. I didn't realize Lauren was following me until she entered the bathroom a few moments later.

"Are you okay?" she asked.

"I'm fine." I gripped the counter for support.

"You don't look fine." She held a hand to my forehead. "Seriously, you look like you're going to be sick."

I sank down on the toilet lid and fanned myself with my hand, but it did nothing. It felt like I was boiling alive.

"Did you get sweat gland injections?" I joked, needing a distraction. "I mean, here I am sweating like a pig, and you look…cool as a cucumber."

"Nah. I decided it wasn't worth it. But I also don't have two men duking it out over me at my kid's birthday party. Want to talk about that?"

I shook my head, finding it difficult to swallow even as I forced myself to stand. "I need to get back out there. I'm sure the rumors are already spreading like wildfire."

She grabbed a magazine and started fanning me. "You need to take a minute. Sit. Do you want some water or something? You look flushed."

I couldn't believe I was missing Sophia's birthday party. I could only hope she was having too much fun with her friends to notice.

"I'll get you some water. Don't go anywhere."

I barked out a laugh. Like that was going to happen. Any time I even considered standing, I was overwhelmed with dizziness. What the hell was wrong with me?

Lauren returned, but she wasn't alone. She gave me an apologetic smile as Cal followed her into the bathroom.

I stood, and spots swam before my eyes. "Get him out of here."

I needed to lie down, and I took a few steps toward the bed before Cal wrapped his arm around me. "Whoa."

Lauren's face was marred with concern. "Alexis, you need to go to the doctor."

"I'm fine." I waved a hand through the air.

"You know," Cal interrupted. "The last time I saw you like this, you were…"

"I was what?" I bit out as he helped me over to the bed. I slumped down on the edge, wishing I could lie down and go to sleep.

He glanced at Lauren, then back at me. "You were pregnant."

My eyes went wide. "I'm…" I couldn't breathe. "I can't be. There's no way. It's just…exhaustion."

Right?

Though, now that I thought about it, I was late for my period. Still, that didn't necessarily mean anything. At least, I hoped it didn't mean anything.

"Calm down," Lauren said, taking my hand in hers. "I'm sure you're right. I mean, you've been working like crazy lately."

"This can't be happening. I can't be pregnant. I'm on the pill. And…and he only has one ball, for crying out loud," I blurted.

"What are you talking about?" Lauren asked at the same time Cal said, "Well then, he's clearly less of a man."

I swung to face him, my entire body vibrating with rage. "He had testicular cancer, you jackass."

Lauren gasped. "Preston had testicular cancer?"

"Wait…" Cal furrowed his brows. "Surely you don't mean…?" He glanced back toward the door as if someone would appear. "Preston, as in the manny? The manny is your baby daddy?"

I covered my face with my hands, wishing the floor

would open up and swallow me whole. It was all too much—the fight, Preston leaving, the fact that I might be pregnant.

"It's time for you to go." Lauren's tone was sharp and left no room for negotiation. I heard shuffling as she ushered him toward the door. "Go keep an eye on Sophia. We'll be down shortly."

A minute later, I heard the door latch shut, and then I felt her hand on my back. "Hey." Her voice was calm, soft. "It's going to be okay. You know that, right?"

I shook my head, finally removing my hands from my face to grab a tissue. "How?" I asked. "How on earth is any of this going to be okay?"

"First, you need to find out if you're even pregnant. Then, we'll figure it out from there."

I stood from the bed, swaying a little as I went over to the mirror to check my makeup. I smoothed a hand over my pool cover-up, my eyes lingering on my currently flat stomach. Would it look the same in a few months, or would it be swollen with Preston's child?

Oh god. What had I done?

"Mommy?" Sophia asked, peeking her head in the door. "Are you okay?"

I forced a smile. "Of course. My tummy was just bothering me."

"Do you need some medicine?" she asked, suddenly concerned.

"No, baby. I'm fine. Let's get back to the party. What did I miss?" I gripped the banister for support as she led me down the stairs.

"I opened my presents. I got a new mermaid doll, some glitter paints, and come see the awesome float Preston got me." Sophia dragged me toward the sliding glass doors to the backyard.

She pointed at the pool, even though you couldn't miss

the gigantic pink shell float shimmering in the sun. Kids were climbing all over it, jockeying for the top position. No matter where I went, Preston was there. And now I might be carrying a reminder of him for the rest of my life.

Somehow, I made it through the rest of the party, which was relatively uneventful. At least, if you ignored the hushed whispers and the curious looks. Which I tried my best to. No one said anything to my face, but I knew they were all talking about me behind my back. And I shuddered to think of the gossip if I was, in fact, pregnant with Preston's child.

Finally, everyone left. The house was mostly back to normal, and Sophia was admiring all her new presents when my phone rang. Gabriela's name flashed across the screen, and a wave of relief washed over me. Thank god she'd be coming back soon.

"Gabriela, hi." I grinned, putting her on FaceTime.

"*Hola*, Alexis. How are you?" Her accent was heavier after an extended visit home. She leaned closer to the screen, squinting. "You look tired. What's wrong?"

"Nothing. We just finished Sophia's party."

"*Ay*," she sighed. "Yes. I was calling to wish her a happy birthday. Is she there?"

"That's so sweet," I said, genuinely touched by the gesture. "Soph," I called. "Gabby's on the phone."

She ran over, excited to see Gabby. I listened to them chatter and catch up. But then Cal asked Sophia something, and she darted off again. Despite the fact that it was almost bedtime, she was wound up thanks to all the cake and excitement.

"I'm so looking forward to your return, to restoring some much-needed order to our lives," I said to Gabby.

Her smile faded. "That's actually part of the reason I called. *Mi madre* fell and broke her—how do you say, *cadera*? —hip."

"Oh my gosh. I'm so sorry."

"Thank you." She bowed her head, taking a deep breath. "But it means I need to stay to care for her. I'm sorry, Alexis. I know you were counting on me."

The room spun. This couldn't be happening. First Preston, and now this? But what could I say? Gabby had been so good to our family, and now she needed to take care of her own.

"I completely understand," I said, trying to do some mental calculations on how long it would take to recover. "Take as much time as you need."

"That's the thing," she said with a sad smile. "I don't know when, or even if, I'll be able to come back."

My breath caught, and I teared up when she started to cry. "What are we going to do without you?" I asked.

She smiled through her tears. "*Hija*," she said, referring to me as she always did—*daughter*. "You and Sophia will be just fine. I know it."

I sniffled, wiping my tears as I nodded to reassure her. "You're right, but that doesn't mean we won't miss you terribly. Promise you'll visit when your mom is doing better?"

"I would love that. I'll let you go enjoy the birthday girl," she said.

"Goodbye, Gabriela," I said, feeling a sense of permanence to it.

"*Adios*, Alexis."

I sat there a moment, staring at nothing, really, until I felt a hand on my shoulder. "Hey," Cal said. "You okay?"

I nodded, wiping away a few tears. "Gabby's not coming back."

"I'm sorry, babe." I couldn't even find it in me to care that he'd called me babe. I simply didn't have the energy for anything more.

My eyes stung, and his nose was swollen. "Aren't we a pair?" I joked.

He took a seat next to me, wrapping his arm around my shoulder. "We always did make a good team."

I blew out a raspberry. "The only good thing we did together was Sophia."

He gave me a squeeze. "She's the best thing we did, and all the credit goes to you." He turned me so I was facing him. "You're a good mom, Alexis. I don't tell you that enough."

"You're going to make me cry again." I glanced toward the ceiling, trying to stem the flow of tears. It had been an emotional rollercoaster of a day.

He smoothed my tears away with his thumbs. "I love you. I never stopped loving you."

I looked away, unable to handle the intensity of his gaze. There were so many memories wrapped up in those blue eyes—both good and bad.

"I can't do this, Cal." I swallowed.

"I know." His tone was solemn. "I know I've already lost you. Hell, I lost you long ago. But I had to at least try."

"You're leaving, aren't you?"

"I can't miss any more of the tour," he said, standing.

"Well, I really appreciate you coming for Sophia's birthday. It meant the world to her." I smiled to myself, thinking of just how happy she'd been to see him. How proud she was to have him at her side when she blew out her candles.

And then it hit me—everyone was leaving. Preston, Gabriela, Cal. They were all gone. And I didn't know how I was going to survive.

CHAPTER TWENTY-FOUR

Preston

"Thanks for coming in today," Renata said when I arrived at the Hartwell Agency. "Please, take a seat." She gestured to the chair across from her desk.

I had a feeling I knew what this was about, and I didn't think it was a new position.

"Your placement with the Blacks ended early and unexpectedly. Would you care to explain?"

I crossed my arms over my chest. "Not really."

What was there to say? I slept with my boss. I fell in love. I fucked up. She chose her ex. Not really the type of thing I wanted to share with the agency.

"Preston." She leaned forward. "I'm really at a loss for what to do here. For the past year and a half, you've been an incredible asset to the Hartwell Agency. But now…" She huffed. "You assaulted a parent at a child's birthday party, and someone posted a video of it online. I assume you've seen it?"

I nodded. There was no use disputing it. I couldn't. The

video titled, "The Manny Strikes Back," had gotten hundreds of thousands of views. Fortunately, you couldn't see my face in the video, but it was still damning.

"I apologize for my behavior. I've apologized to the parents, and I'm deeply sorry for how my actions reflect on the Hartwell Agency."

Her shoulders relaxed slightly. "Thank you for saying that. Unfortunately, we're still going to have to let you go."

"I understand," I said, and I did. It didn't matter what Cal said—not that anyone knew the truth—I was the one who'd struck first. I'd punched him.

"Despite the incident, Ms. Black was generous enough to pay out the rest of your contract and then some."

I shook my head. "I don't want it."

She frowned. "What do you mean, you don't want it?"

"Exactly what I said. I don't want it." I stood. "Now, if we're finished here, I have somewhere else I need to be."

She stood as well, walking me to the door. "I believe you still have some belongings at the Black residence."

I nodded. "That's right."

I hadn't wanted to go back. Hadn't wanted to risk seeing Cal again. Or worse still—Cal and Alexis together.

"Can you pick up your things tomorrow—say between six and eight in the evening?"

"That's fine," I said.

"Goodbye, Preston." She extended her hand to shake. "I'm disappointed things turned out the way they did, but I wish you luck all the same."

"Thanks, Renata."

The door shut behind me, and I loosened my tie as I headed for my car. Traffic sucked, and by the time I arrived at the hospital, the meal I'd picked up was cold. Still, Indy seemed grateful.

"Thanks, Preston," she said, taking the bag from me.

"How is he?" I asked as we shuffled down the hall toward Sam's room.

"Better. They removed the breathing tube today. We're hoping he'll get to go home soon."

"That's great news."

She paused before we reached his room. "Preston." She placed her hand on my bicep. "I just want to thank you for all you've done. I can't tell you how much I appreciate it."

I kept my gaze on the linoleum floor. "I just wish there was more I could've done."

I still hadn't worked up the courage to tell her he'd reached out to me the night…the night when... I swallowed. I didn't know how to tell her. I didn't think I could. I felt like if I'd just answered the phone, maybe I could've talked Sam out of it.

"You don't think I wonder the same thing—about myself?" she asked. "It breaks my heart that he feels like life isn't worth living. And the thought of losing him—" She choked on a sob.

I wrapped my arms around her. "You're going to get through this." I squeezed. "You will."

She nodded. "Thanks to you and your friendship, we will."

I didn't think I could feel worse, but somehow, I did. My eyes were gritty from lack of sleep, but it was my heart that felt raw.

"Okay," Kate said the following afternoon as she placed another box in the trunk. "I think that's it."

"Thanks. And thanks for coming with me." I took one last glance at the house, surprised by how dark it was. Alexis's car wasn't in the driveway, and I was pretty sure no one was home. Where were they?

"Don't worry about it." She patted me on the back before climbing in the passenger seat.

"So…" she said as we drove across town. "You want to talk about it?"

"Not really." I turned up the radio, wanting some background noise other than the road. She was quiet for the rest of the drive home.

When we got back to the apartment, I kicked off my shoes and flopped down on the couch. I switched on the TV, and HGTV immediately came on. *Ugh.* I wasn't in the mood for *Christina on the Coast.* Anything but watching her and Ant and the—

"Hey, hey, hey," Hunter said when he emerged from the bathroom.

I whipped my head around to face him. "What are you doing here?"

"Kate told me you were moping."

I narrowed my eyes, glancing between the two of them. "I can't believe you told him I was moping," I said to Kate. "Traitor."

"Well, aren't you?" She shrugged, brushing her blond hair over her shoulder.

I rolled my eyes and turned my attention back to the TV. "No."

"Puh-lease." She plopped down on the couch next to me. "I know moping when I see it. And you, good sir, are moping."

"Have to agree." Hunter took a seat on the chair next to the couch. "Now, out with it. I didn't fly all the way from

New York to watch you shuffle around in your pajamas, watching Christina and Ant with sad, puppy-dog eyes."

"Please tell me that's not the only reason you flew here."

Kate's cell phone rang, and she disappeared to her room. Or Hunter's room. Whatever.

"You're special, but not that special." He grinned. "I have other news, but let's hear yours first, starting with why you punched Cal."

I groaned. "You saw the video?"

"I think everyone and their mom saw the video." Hunter chuckled. He quickly sobered when he saw my scowl. "So…"

"Fine," I huffed. "But don't say I didn't warn you," I said, before launching into the story.

I told him about Sam. About Sophia's broken arm. And when I got to the part about the party and what Cal had said, he was livid.

"You're fucking kidding me." He stood and started pacing. I shook my head, wishing I were joking. "I cannot believe that…that dick."

"He's a real piece of work," I said.

"And the fact that Alexis sided with him over you…" He clenched his fists, his feet pounding the floor with every step.

"What was she supposed to do? He's Sophia's dad. I punched him." Still, that didn't lessen the sting of it. Time and time again, Alexis had chosen herself over us. Had preferred to pretend our relationship didn't exist rather than own up to her feelings.

"Fuck that. She should've given you a chance to explain— for not picking up Sophia and for the fight."

"Whatever." I shrugged. I knew he was right, but I just didn't give a fuck. "It doesn't matter now."

None of it mattered. I'd nearly lost Sam. I'd lost my job. I was going to have to apply to defer my degree—again. And that was if they'd even let me. But worse than all that was the fact that I'd lost Sophia and Alexis. I was officially done.

"The hell it doesn't." Hunter grabbed me by the shoulders and shook me. "Preston, man. You have not come this far to give up now."

"What does it even matter?"

He took a seat on the couch next to me. "Look at me."

I turned to look at him, but my expression was blank. I felt numb, empty, void.

"Listen up," he demanded in a stern tone. "You are important. You matter. And the work you want to do—counseling cancer patients, *kids*—that matters. The world needs more people like you, Preston. And I did not shave my head, I did not sit at your bedside, missing out on all those college parties, for you to give up now."

I rolled my eyes, smiling despite myself. "You've more than made up for it since then—fucking every girl in LA."

"And that's another thing I want to talk to you about."

"Your manwhoring ways?" I asked.

"Yes. I believe we have a bet to settle." He sat a little taller, and I tried to determine what he was up to. "Kate," he called. "Can you come out here?"

She returned to the living room. "Yeah. What's up?"

"I have something to tell you—both of you."

"Okay," I said, drawing out the word.

Kate cocked her hip to the side, placing her hand on it. "This better be good. I was texting with one of the guys from school, and I'm hoping he's going to finally ask me out."

"Who? That Damien guy?"

She nodded, her long ponytail swaying from the movement.

Hunter shook his head. "I hate to break it to you, sis, but you've been friends for two years. If he wanted to ask you out, he would've already made a move."

When I saw her smile fall, I elbowed Hunter in the side.

"What?" He shrugged. "Don't waste your time on someone who's not all in—that goes for both of you."

"Are you done insulting me now?" Kate asked.

"I wasn't trying to insult you," he said, and her expression softened. "I'm trying to help you. I don't want to see you get hurt." He turned back to me. "Okay. Where was I? We got the New York office up and running. Which means, I'm moving back to LA full time."

"Who's going to run the New York office?" I asked.

"Toby. He's more connected in that region, and I realized how much I missed LA."

"You mean—how much you missed us," Kate teased.

"That too," Hunter agreed. "I have a few more weeks left in New York, but then I'll be back. So…we're going to need to figure out a new living situation."

"I can move out," Kate said. "It's no big deal."

"Like I said," Hunter said, not agreeing to anything. "We'll figure it out."

"Actually…" I stared at the floor, unwilling to meet his eyes. "Since I lost my job, I'm probably going to move back home."

"Like hell, you are." Even without looking, I could feel his eyes boring into mine. "And that brings me to my third point —our bet."

"What about our bet?"

He arched a brow. "I believe you remember the terms."

I nodded. "Yes, though it doesn't really matter now. Alexis and I are no longer dating."

"Tsk. Tsk. Tsk." He pointed his finger at me. "Always so quick to assume you won."

"Didn't I?"

"You…did not."

I stared at him, slack-jawed. "You're kidding, right? I

mean, there's no way that you—Hunter the manwhore Pruitt—lasted an entire month without sex."

"Shocking as it is," Kate said. "He did. He called or texted every night to confirm he was sleeping alone."

I shook my head. "And we're just going to take his word for it? He could have totally had a quickie in the bathroom—"

"Eww. Gross," Kate said.

"Or he could've fucked a girl in the elevator," I added with a shrug. "It wouldn't be the first time."

Kate waved her hands before her, screwed her eyes shut and shook her head. "Please stop. This is my brother we're talking about. I really, *really* do not want to know these things about him."

Hunter chuckled. "I won the bet, which means—"

"No." I stared him down. "Absolutely not. I will not let you pay my tuition."

"First of all, I want to. And second, you can think of it as a loan if you want. I'm investing in your future, in you. Because I believe in you."

"Aww." Kate held a hand over her heart. "You guys are too adorable. Bromance!"

"Shut up," we both snapped at the same time.

"Whatever. I'm out." She turned and headed for the door.

Hunter vanished to his room, returning a moment later with a blank check. "How much do you need?"

"I can't… I'm not going to accept it."

"You can, and you will. It's time to finish your damn degree. Eight years is long enough."

I blew out a breath, knowing he wasn't going to give up. He'd been offering for years, and now… Now, I was almost desperate enough to take him up on it.

"I will accept it on certain conditions."

He smirked, leaning his hip against the counter. "I'm not

sure you understand how negotiation works. You're not really in a position to bargain."

"First," I said, ignoring him. "I want you to have your attorney draw up a contract."

"Fine."

"Second, this is a loan. I *will* pay you back."

"But—"

"No." On this point, I would not waver. "You agree that this is a loan, or I will shred the check."

He rolled his eyes. "Fine. Geez."

"And third…"

"There's more?"

"Third," I said. "Thank you."

"Thank fuck," he breathed. "I mean, you're welcome, man."

We laughed, and he slapped me on the back. "Let's go out and celebrate."

"Celebrate what? The fact that my life is falling apart?"

"Celebrate the fact that you're *alive*. And, well, let's not forget the fact that you're now my bitch."

"I am not your bitch." I stopped and turned to face him. "That is not going in the contract."

"Oh, come on, man." He turned me in the direction of my bedroom and draped his arm over my shoulder. "You love it. And that," he said in a more serious tone, "was not the right answer. Going forward, you shall address me as 'Sir.'"

I laughed, but only to hide the pain. I could remember a time when Alexis jokingly said, "Yes, sir." And before I could stop it, I was flooded with a million other memories. Cuddling in the hammock. Sneaking kisses in the pantry. Whispering so Sophia wouldn't hear us.

"Hey…" Hunter paused. "You okay? You know I'm just teasing, right?"

"Yeah." I forced a smile. "Take me out and get me drunk…
Sir."

"That's more like it." He grinned.

I had a feeling alcohol would help at least for a little
while, but I knew nothing would numb the pain of losing
Alexis. I missed her—her and Sophia. And I didn't think any
amount of alcohol or time would heal that wound.

CHAPTER TWENTY-FIVE

Alexis

I was sitting on one of the lounge chairs, working on my laptop, when I realized that Sophia was quiet—too quiet. I straightened, my pulse quickening as my eyes darted around the pool. I let out a breath when I spotted her at the edge. She had her arms folded, one cheek resting on them so she was facing the pool house. It had been a few days since her party, a few days since Preston had left, and there was no denying she was in a funk.

"I'm almost done," I said, typing out a response to an email. "And then we can go grab some lunch and do some back-to-school shopping." I tried to infuse my voice with excitement, when all I wanted to do was crawl into bed and hide under the covers.

"Okay," she sighed.

I read through the email one more time before hitting *Send.* I shut my laptop and set it aside.

"Soph, are you not excited about starting school?"

She lifted a shoulder. "I guess."

"You aren't excited about meeting your new teacher and seeing Brooklyn every day?" I asked, knowing how much she'd been looking forward to it all summer. "You'll get to show off your new backpack, your new cast." I raised my eyebrows, knowing how much she loved the mermaid design Kate had painted.

Sophia was quiet a moment before she lifted her head and looked at me. Her hair was slicked away from her face, the water reflecting back on her blue eyes, making them seem even more brilliant. "Who's going to get me ready in the morning and take me to school? Who will pick me up?"

"I will." I smiled. "At least, until we find another nanny."

"I don't want another nanny." She pouted. "I want Preston."

She'd taken the news that Gabby wasn't coming back remarkably well. She'd accepted the fact that Cal had to leave in stride. But Preston...she seemed to struggle the most with the fact that he was gone.

I didn't blame her. I was struggling with it too. I missed him; I ached for him. And though I told myself our relationship had come to its natural end, I couldn't help but want more. Even if I was still mad at him for punching Sophia's dad in the middle of her birthday party.

"Well," I sighed. "Preston can't come back because he hit someone. And it's not okay to hit anyone, especially not a member of our family."

She furrowed her brows. "Yeah, but...what if? Well, I thought it was okay if you were defending yourself."

"Yes," I said. "An exception can be made for self-defense."

"What if Preston was defending himself?"

Huh. I hadn't really considered that option. I'd just been so upset. So shocked. I couldn't see past my emotions for any acceptable reason to justify his behavior. All I knew was that he'd punched Cal in the middle of Sophia's birthday party, in front of all our friends.

"What if he was defending himself, and…and he said he was sorry? Could he come back then?" Sophia pleaded.

"I don't know." I didn't want to promise something I wasn't sure I could deliver.

Who knew what his excuse would be, or if it would justify his actions? All I knew was that he deserved a chance to explain. That was…if he even wanted to talk to me.

"Preston might be working with another family this fall," I said, hating the thought.

I would be happy for him, of course. I knew he needed the money, but still…the idea of him moving on… Without me? Without us? I hated how we'd left things. What if I never saw him again?

"Call him, Mommy. Please call him. You have to try."

"I wish it were that simple," I said, needing more time to think it over.

"Hello," Lauren called from the gate.

"Hey," I said, relieved for the interruption. "Come in."

"What are you girls up to?" She took a seat next to me, looking stylish in her turquoise dress and cork wedges.

"Well, we were thinking lunch and then some back-to-school shopping. Want to join?"

"Girl, you know it. If it's okay with Sophia," she said, turning to Sophia.

Sophia's eyes were wide, and she nodded her head quickly, causing some of her hair to fall over her face. "Yes, please."

"Soph," I said. "Why don't you get ready, and then we can go."

She hopped out of the pool, drying off before disappearing inside the house.

Lauren glanced at the doors one more time before leaning forward. "So…?"

"So…?" I asked, mimicking her tone and inflection.

"Please tell me you took the test."

I shook my head. "I haven't even had time to buy a test, let alone take it."

She rolled her eyes. "Girl. This is classic Denial 101. The sooner you know, the more options you have."

"There really is only one option for me. If I'm pregnant…" Just saying the words aloud was enough to make my heart race and my skin heat. "*If* I am, I'm keeping the baby."

She squealed, taking my hands in hers. "Can I do the nursery?"

"Oh my god. We don't even know if I'm having a baby."

"But still…can I decorate it?" I appreciated her enthusiasm. I wished I could share in it. My life was too much of a mess at the moment to be cause for celebration.

"Of course."

"What about Preston?" she asked.

I let out a deep sigh. "What about him?"

"Have you talked to him?"

I slumped my shoulders, crumpling in on myself. "No."

"Aren't you at all curious why he punched Cal? If I had to bet money, I'd say it was totally justified. Cal can be such a dick."

I laughed. "Yeah, I know. No love lost between you two."

"Divorcing him was one of the best things you've done. And I'd never seen you happier. At least, not until Preston."

I blew a raspberry, staring out at the pool. "Preston did make me happy. But when push came to shove, he wasn't there for me when I needed him most."

"Alexis," she said, taking my hand in hers. "He let you down, sure. But people make mistakes. Don't you think he deserves a second chance?"

I lifted a shoulder. "I know you're Team Preston, but I have to consider what's best not just for me, but for Sophia." And, if I was pregnant, this new baby too.

"He was amazing with her. Don't let one mistake erase all the great things he did."

"Two mistakes."

"Whatever." She threw her hands in the air. "I think you and I both know that whatever happened that weekend was out of character."

I nodded, considering it. It was extremely out of character. He'd always been punctual, kind, patient. And I'd lost count of the times he'd gone above and beyond to help Sophia or me. Thinking back on it, I didn't know what more he could've done to show me he loved me, us.

"I'll think about it," I said.

And I did. Over lunch, I thought about it. While Sophia tried on clothes for school, I thought about it. In fact, I couldn't stop thinking about it.

I was grateful for Lauren's company because I was distracted and exhausted. But she kept us busy, and she made sure we had fun. And when she joined us for dinner, it made the house seem a little less empty.

"Time for bed," I told Sophia.

"I'm going to run a quick errand, and then I'll be back," Lauren said to me before hugging Sophia and wishing her sweet dreams.

I helped Sophia get ready for bed, and when she climbed between the covers, she asked, "What three things are you grateful for today?"

"You, Lauren, and—" I wanted to say Saltine crackers, but instead, I said, "Mermaids."

"Mermaids?" She giggled.

"Yeah. Because they always seem to make you smile. All right." I tucked the blanket around her. "What three things are you grateful for today?"

"Hmm. You, our swimming pool, and… Hey, will you tell me the bedtime story about the beautiful mermaid princess?"

I furrowed my brow, trying to figure out which story she was referring to. "I'm not sure I know that one. You want to show me?"

"No. It's not in a book. It's one Preston made up. It's my favorite."

"Well," I said, scrambling to come up with something that might appease her instead. "How about the story of the dragon queen?"

"No." Her lip began to quiver. "I want to hear the beautiful mermaid princess story."

"Well, I don't know it," I sighed, feeling like Preston could comfort my child better than I could.

Without him, I felt lost. And I had no idea what I was going to do when school started next week and my vacation was over. It wasn't just about his role in Sophia's life, but his role in mine. He grounded me, kept me sane, made me feel like the confident, successful woman I wanted to be.

Without him, I felt like a shell of myself. Without him, it felt like our family was incomplete.

And being in this house—where everything reminded me of him—was going to drive me insane. Lauren wanted to decorate the nursery; I wanted to move. Because when I padded across the rug in the living room, I felt his hands on my skin. When I sat by the pool, I remembered the feel of his lips on mine, savoring that moment in the hammock. When I lay in bed at night, his scent lingered on my pillow. And when I woke up in the morning… I remembered that he was gone.

"Mommy, are you okay?"

I sniffled, not even realizing I was crying until I touched my cheeks and found them wet with tears. "I'm fine."

She peered up at me with her wide, blue eyes. "It's okay if you miss Preston. I do too."

I pulled her into me, inhaling the scent of her shampoo. "He was pretty awesome, wasn't he?"

"He was…the best." I could hear the smile in her voice as she yawned. "I miss his pancakes."

I missed everything about him.

I'd made a huge mistake, and the more I thought back on our relationship, on my actions, the worse I felt. How many times had I pushed him away? How many times had I placed a greater emphasis on appearances than his feelings?

At this point, I was pretty sure I was the one who needed to apologize—for not hearing him out. Not giving him a chance to tell his side of the story. Looking back on it now, I realized that both the night Sophia had broken her arm and the day of the party, I'd jumped to conclusions. I'd shut him down because I was scared.

"Maybe we can try to make some in the morning." I kissed the top of her head. "Happy dreams, baby girl. I love you."

"Sleep well, Mommy. I love you too."

I switched off the light, and when I reached the door, Sophia said, "Wait. I forgot to say my third thing."

"What is it?" I whispered, knowing she'd never go to bed without telling me.

"Preston." She yawned. "I'm thankful for Preston."

Me too, I thought, grateful it was too dark for her to see my tears.

I closed her door softly, pausing at the top of the stairs for a moment as I struggled to catch my breath. I used my fingertips to wipe away the tears and walked back downstairs to discover Lauren had returned and was drinking a glass of wine.

"No more excuses." She shoved a box of pregnancy tests at me. "Do you know how many different pregnancy tests there are—digital, smiley face, two lines, one line, blue line?"

I laughed. "Yes. There are a lot of options, but they're all pretty much the same."

"Thanks. A. Lot," she said. "I just spent ten minutes staring at the boxes, trying to decide which one you would choose."

"Aww." I teared up. "You're such a good friend."

"That's right. You have no idea what I went through to get you those tests," she huffed.

I frowned. "What you went through?" I wasn't sure I followed.

"Funny thing," she said, and she seemed flustered. Which was weird because Lauren never got flustered. "I was on the 'family planning aisle' at Target, staring at the tests when a super tall, super hot guy passes by. He paused, clearly checking me out. Or at least, that's what I thought he was doing. And what did I do?"

I shrugged. "I don't know. What did you do?"

"I held up two boxes of pregnancy tests and told him they were for a friend." She groaned.

I laughed. "That's what everyone says."

"But they really *were* for a friend—for you," she huffed, her cheeks turning pink. "I made a damn fool of myself. So now, you really do have to take the test."

My stomach churned. "I don't know…"

"Exactly," she said. "You don't know if you're pregnant. You might not be. And if you're not, we'll drink some wine."

"I just… I'm not ready for this."

"Ready or not." She pursed her lips.

"Fine," I huffed. "You're right. I know you're right."

I tore open the box, and several tests went flying across the floor in the process. I grabbed one and tried to rip it open, but my hands were shaking so badly, I couldn't.

"Here," Lauren said, taking it from me. "Let me."

"Do you want to take the test for me too?" I teased.

She wrapped her arm around me. "I can only imagine what you're thinking and feeling right now. But I'm here for you. Okay?"

I nodded. "Thank you."

She gave me a squeeze before releasing me. "Now, go pee on a stick. You got this."

I laughed and headed for the bathroom, feeling like I might throw up. *You got this. You got this,* I chanted to myself.

When I was done, I set the test on the counter and washed my hands. I didn't know what the results would show: one line or two. But as I waited for them to appear, I knew one thing for certain. Pregnant or not, I wanted Preston back in my life. I wanted us to be a family.

CHAPTER TWENTY-SIX

Preston

I drove up the winding road, impressed by the other homes in the neighborhood. Most of the houses had been redone, but some were more modern than others. I was curious to see what style Hunter was interested in. And I was still trying to wrap my head around that fact that he wanted to buy a house. He'd told me it was because it was a good investment, but I sensed there was more to it.

I reached the top of the drive and confirmed it was the address he'd given me. The exterior was a bit modern for my taste, and it was all very…white. Still, it was a nice house, and the location couldn't be beat—just minutes from the Sunset Strip, but still far enough away from the hustle and bustle. And I could only assume there would be some amazing views off the back.

The gate was open, and I let myself in, wondering if I was the first to arrive. I rapped my knuckles on the door, and it opened slightly.

"Hello," I called, peeking my head around the door. "Hello?" I stepped farther inside, closing it behind me.

"Is anyone here?" I glanced around the space, my footsteps echoing on the Travertine floor. I was drawn toward the living room, where a wall of windows overlooked the pool and the city beyond.

Holy shit.

The views at this place were sick. I stood there a moment, taking them in, when I heard a noise from down the hall. I headed that direction. "Hello?"

Light trickled out from beneath a closed door. There was the sound of water running, and then the door swung open. Caramel-colored hair, sun-kissed skin, and curves for days… curves I was intimately familiar with. She lifted her head, her bronze eyes meeting mine.

"Alexis?"

She froze, her eyes going wide. "What are you doing here?"

"Hunter asked me to come look at a house." My heart was pounding so hard, I'd be surprised if the neighbors didn't hear it. "I had…" I swallowed, trying to gather my thoughts. "I didn't know you were the real estate agent."

"So, he's not coming?"

I shook my head. "He's in New York, but he'll be back soon. And he wants a bigger place."

She tilted back her head, showing me the long, delicate line of her neck. I traced it with my eyes, trailing down to her breasts, which looked fucking amazing. Her narrow waist. Her… God, this was awkward. And so incredibly painful.

I didn't care if Hunter was truly interested in the house or not, there was no way I could stand here—with her.

She swayed on her feet, and I reached out a hand to steady her. "Hey. Are you okay?"

"I'm fine," she snapped, waving off my concern. As always —pushing me away. Nothing had changed. I didn't know why I'd expected anything different.

"Maybe I should just go." I turned for the door.

"No. Wait." She grabbed my wrist, her small hand encircling my skin, lighting me up.

I closed my eyes and forced myself to take a deep breath in, then blew it out. I hated that she still had such a profound effect on me. That I could be such a fool when it came to this woman.

"I'm sorry. I…I've been meaning to call you," she said.

"Is that so?" I turned back to face her, crossing my arms over my chest.

I couldn't think straight when she was touching me. But now that I took a moment to look at her, really look at her, I noticed how pale she seemed. There were dark circles beneath her eyes, and she looked as if she was going to be sick.

She closed her eyes and held up one finger, asking me to wait. What was she even doing showing houses when it was obvious she should be in bed?

Despite my anger, my gut twisted with concern. "Can I get you something?" She shook her head. "Here." I placed my hand on her shoulders and steered her toward the couch. "Sit. I'll find you some water."

"There's a bottle next to my bag."

"What—no green shake?" I asked before I could stop myself.

"Oh god," she groaned. "Please don't mention those right now."

I frowned. For as long as I'd known her, she had one nearly every morning. And she always seemed to enjoy them, or at least, not have quite that reaction to them. I grabbed the water bottle before rushing back to her.

She took a few small sips before setting it on the coffee table. "Thank you."

"You should be at home, resting."

"I'm fine," she said in a breezy tone I didn't buy. "It'll pass."

An awkward silence descended on us, and I didn't know what to say. I didn't like to leave things unresolved, not since I'd had cancer. And especially not since what had happened with Sam.

"I'm sorry for punching Cal. I hope he's okay," I said, needing closure, if nothing else.

She blew out a breath. "He's fine. If you ever wondered where Sophia gets her drama queen side from, it's him."

We both laughed, but there was an undercurrent of anxiety running through it. As if neither one of us knew quite what to do or say. I remained there for a moment, pleasure mixed with pain. I didn't know if I could sit here and talk to her as if nothing had happened, when my entire world, my heart, was shattered.

I stood, dragging my fingers through my hair. "What are we doing?"

"We're talking. We're finally doing what we should've done before. I'm sorry I didn't give you a chance to explain what happened the weekend of Sophia's birthday. I know it's probably too late, and that I probably don't deserve it, but I'd like to hear your side of the story now."

I went to the window, surveying the city. "What's the point?" I muttered, more to myself.

I'd apologized for punching Cal, but I didn't know how much more I could take. Especially when I wasn't sure it would make any difference.

"Preston." Her hand was on my back, her touch reawakening the ache for her I'd tried so desperately to ignore. "Talk to me, please. I want to know."

"I'm not sure you do," I said, knowing how difficult it would be for me to tell her the truth—and for her to hear it.

"You're not…" She withdrew her hand, and I turned to see her holding it to her mouth, her eyes wide. "You're not sick, are you?"

"No." *Thank god.* "But my friend Sam is." I led her back over to the couch, knowing this was a heavy conversation. "Are you sure you feel up to this?"

"Yes. Please, talk to me."

I nodded. "The day Sophia broke her arm…" I drew in a shaky breath. "Well, I got a call from Sam's wife that he tried to commit suicide."

She held a hand to her mouth again. "Oh my god, Preston. I'm so sorry. Is he—" Her eyes searched mine. "Is he okay?"

I nodded. "He'll be discharged from the hospital soon, but he has a long road ahead of him."

She placed her hand on my bicep. "I'm so, so sorry."

"He'd called me the night of—the night when it happened, but I didn't answer."

"You can't blame yourself for what happened," she said.

I didn't say anything—couldn't. Instead, I stared straight ahead and focused on finishing the story. "I lost track of time and there was no cell service in the hospital, so I had no idea what was going on with Sophia. As soon as I found out about Sam, I should've called you. At least then you could've had Cal or someone else pick her up. I can't tell you how terrible I feel that she broke her wrist and I wasn't there."

She lifted a shoulder. "You couldn't have prevented it. No one could."

"I know. But every time I think of her sitting there alone, scared and in pain…" I cleared my throat.

"I know." She hung her head. "But even if you'd gotten there first, I would've left work to be with Sophia. She loves the mermaid Kate drew, by the way."

I grinned, feeling a little lighter. "I'm glad. I kind of thought she might. How is she? Is her arm healing okay?"

Alexis nodded, taking another sip of water. "She's doing well. She was excited to start school."

"Does she…" I swallowed, turning my attention to the

view. It was much easier than looking at Alexis. "Does Sophia hate me?"

"What?" Alexis gasped, taking my hand in hers. "No. She doesn't hate you. She misses you. She loves you." Something released in my chest, a tightness I'd been holding in.

"I love her too." Saying the words was as easy as breathing.

"So, do you want to tell me why you punched Cal?"

I groaned. "Not really."

I would never want her to know just how hurtful his comments were. How insensitive. I wasn't even sure he'd really meant them, but they'd certainly hit their mark.

"Okay, then," she said, and I sensed her frustration. "Will you at least answer one question?"

I nodded.

"Did you hit him to defend yourself?" She held her breath, and everything seemed to hinge on my answer.

I shook my head. "No." Her face fell, the color draining from it. "But I was defending someone else."

Her eyes were filled with hope when she met my gaze. "Preston…I want another chance. Sophia wants you to come back—I want you to come back."

"What about Gabby?" I blurted. I wasn't sure I could go back to being Sophia's nanny, mostly because I wasn't sure I could be around Alexis after everything that had happened.

"No." She scooted closer. "Not as the manny, nanny, whatever," she huffed. "I want to be together. I want to be a family."

I didn't know what to say. How many times had I hoped she'd say those words? And now…

"Please say something," she finally said.

"Do you know how often I dreamed of hearing those words from your lips?" I asked, feeling my chest rise and fall. "But I'm done being your dirty little secret. And I will not be in a relationship with someone who's ashamed of me because of my age, my job, whatever. I deserve more."

"I agree," she said. "I shouldn't care so much about what other people think, but I do. It's ingrained in me. But—" She took in a jagged breath. "It's something I'm working on. Something I will continue to work on.

"I promise never to take you—or our relationship—for granted again." Her voice vibrated with sincerity, and I knew she meant every word.

Still, doubt lurked in my mind. It was easy to promise something when we were alone, only to turn around and pretend something else in front of her friends. How many times had she told me she loved me in private, only to act like we weren't a couple in public?

"What about Cal?" As much as I didn't want to admit it, he was still very much a part of Sophia's life.

"I'll handle Cal," she said.

"And what about the other parents—Nate, Margaret? Or anyone else who judges our relationship?"

She lifted a shoulder. "Their words only have the power I give them. I don't want to be the type of woman who bases her life on other people's opinions. That's not the example I want to set for Sophia."

Those words were the ones I'd needed to hear. They meant more than any "I'm sorry" or "I love you." Because I'd needed her to admit what I already knew—she was strong, and she didn't need anyone to tell her how to live her life.

"If you want to be a family, we have to tell Sophia," I said, knowing how much she'd fought me on it in the past. But if she wanted to be together—to truly be a couple—I needed to know she was all in.

"I promise." She crossed her heart. "We will tell Sophia, and I want you to move back in—but not to the pool house," she added with a watery smile. "Preston, I love you."

My heart was racing, and I was pretty sure I had a dopey smile on my face. I didn't think I'd ever been happier than in that moment. She loved me, and she was willing to back up her words with actions. We were going to be together—for real, this time.

"You're going to make space for me in your closet? You really must love me," I teased.

"Is that a yes?" Her golden eyes glistened with unshed tears as she grinned up at me.

"It's a hell yes." I crashed my lips to hers, pouring all my love, all my hopes, all my desire into the kiss. And she met me stroke for stroke, my body tingling with anticipation.

My hands were in her hair, caressing her skin, brushing over her breasts. I needed to touch her, to possess her.

She broke the kiss, panting as she rested her forehead against mine. "There's something else I need to tell you."

"Can it wait?" I kissed my way down her neck to her collarbone, relishing the taste of her skin on my tongue. I smoothed my hands up her rib cage to her breasts, squeezing them once more. She moaned, and the sound went straight to my dick.

"God, your breasts are amazing."

"Ugh." She groaned. "I don't want to stop, but…"

That got my attention. I frowned, suddenly concerned that whatever she had to tell me was serious. I stopped kissing her, but I kept my hand on her thigh. I needed to touch her, couldn't stop touching her.

She twisted her hands together in her lap. "You know how you wanted to be a family?"

"Yes." I nodded. "I want it more than anything."

"Well…" She swallowed, and my chest tightened. "How would you feel about expanding our family?"

"You mean Gabby?"

"No. Gabby had to stay in Colombia to help her mom."

She was quiet a moment, her shoulders tight. "I meant…a baby."

I jerked my head back. "You want to have a baby?" I'd always gotten the impression she didn't want more kids. I was trying not to get my hopes up.

"I—" She swallowed, taking my hands in hers. "We're having a baby. I'm pregnant."

My eyes went wide, and I blinked at her a few times. P-pregnant? She was pregnant? How was that even possible?

"I know," she said, making me realize I'd asked the last question aloud. "I had a hard time believing it too at first. I mean, I was on the pill. And you…"

"Only have one testicle," I finished for her. "Though it's not uncommon for fertility to return."

And suddenly, it all made sense. The nausea, her pale skin, the fact that she was repulsed by the idea of her green smoothies.

I cupped her cheeks, kissing her lips, her cheeks, her jawline. "That has got to be the best news ever." She laughed, and I sensed her relief. "I love you, and I'm so fucking excited."

I clapped a hand over my mouth. "Shit. The baby probably heard that, didn't she?"

She laughed some more and patted my cheek. "You're adorable. I'm only about eight weeks pregnant, and we won't know if it's a he or a she until we have the twenty-week sonogram. And that's only if we choose to find out the gender."

I wrapped my arms around her, thrilled to be holding both the woman I loved and our child. "Oh, it's definitely a she."

"You're convinced, huh? Are you going to be disappointed if it's a boy?"

"Of course not." I kissed the top of her head. "I will love

the baby, no matter what. But Sophia will probably be disappointed if it's a boy."

"Oh god." She held a hand to her chest. "I didn't even think about that—how am I going to tell her?"

I took her hand, holding it mine. "How we will do everything from now on—together."

"Together," she said, as if she were testing the word. "I like that."

So did I.

Alexis

"God…" Preston rubbed his hand over his face. His facial hair had grown out, leaving a nice layer of scruff. It looked good on him, sexy. "I can't tell you how happy I am. How excited I am."

It was such a relief to tell him about the baby, such a relief that he was happy. Not just happy—over the moon. And the fact that he still wanted us to be a family was… It was everything. I only hoped Sophia would take the news as well. Of Preston coming back, I had no doubt. But the fact that she was going to be an older sister—I wasn't so sure. It was a lot of big changes happening at once, and I never wanted her to question how much I loved her.

"How are you feeling?" Preston asked.

"Better now," I said, and I meant it. Some of my earlier nausea had subsided, and I really did feel better. "I haven't done as many showings lately—passing them off to my agents instead. And I wasn't going to do this one, but my assistant said the client insisted on having me."

I'd looked at the financials my assistant had sent over. Hunter could definitely afford the house; I just didn't know

now if he was actually in the market for one. Or if this was all part of an elaborate ruse to bring Preston and me together.

"And now I think we know why." Preston chuckled. "I can't believe he set this up."

"You really had no idea?"

He shook his head, but I already knew the answer. I'd seen the surprise written on his face when I came out of the bathroom.

"Though I do think he's genuinely interested in the house," Preston said. "But I'll text him to verify." He typed on his phone.

A minute later, he chuckled, turning the screen to face me.

Preston: Did you set me up?

Hunter: Set you up?

Preston: Sending me to look at a house, knowing Alexis was the agent?

Hunter: That would be pretty ingenious.

Preston: Are you even interested in the house?

Hunter: Yes. I'm not a complete asshole. Tell her I want to put in an offer, assuming you think everything looks good.

Hunter: And you can thank me later for giving you both the nudge you needed. Be sure to name your firstborn after me as a token of appreciation.

I stared at Preston. "You didn't tell him, did you?"

"No." His eyes went wide. "Of course not. He was just teasing."

"Okay." My heart was racing. I was still getting used to the idea of being pregnant. I wasn't ready to tell anyone. Besides, it was early in the pregnancy, and I was older now. I didn't want to share the news for a while. "I'm not that far along, so we should probably wait to start telling people."

"Of course." Preston set his phone on the coffee table. "Whatever you want, beautiful." He tucked a strand of hair behind my ear. "Though I can't tell you how excited my mom is going to be."

My face and ears felt incredibly hot, and I knew it wasn't from the excess of hormones surging through my veins. "Your mom?"

I was trying not to care what other people thought about our relationship, but his mom was different. What if she thought I'd taken advantage of her son? What if—

"Yeah. I can't wait for her to meet you. But," he said, perhaps sensing my freak-out. "There will be time for that. No rush."

"No rush?" I sputtered. "Preston, we're kind of on a schedule." I pointed at my still-flat stomach as if to underscore my point.

"I know." His tone was calm, soothing. "But let's just focus on enjoying this moment. I want to celebrate the fact that I'm going to be a father." His eyes were watery. "I didn't know if I'd ever get the chance to be a dad, and to have not one, but two kids..." He held a shaky hand to his mouth. "I can't tell you how excited and proud I am."

I'd always known Preston would be a good father, and I found myself getting more excited about our little one. I swiped at the corners of my eyes, overcome with emotion.

"Dang pregnancy hormones," I joked.

"Well, if you need midnight ice cream runs or sex on demand..." He grinned. "I'm your guy."

"Good to know. Now, come on." I stood, needing to move

before I did something crazy like have sex with him on the couch of a house I was supposed to be showing; that was more Lauren's style. "Let's tour the house, so you can report back to Hunter."

He stood, taking my hand in his. "Lead on."

"Typically…" I glanced at him over my shoulder as I led him up the stairs. "I don't hold hands with a client."

He chuckled. "Now that we're together, you better never hold hands with a client. Though I do like the idea of being the boss in this situation." He leaned in, his breath tickling my ear. "That you're trying to please me," he rasped.

His words, his touch, awoke a desire within me, a yearning for him I'd been trying to ignore.

"I always strive to ensure that my client is satisfied." I grinned, pausing at the top of the stairs. "Here's a bedroom that would be great as an office."

The room had been staged as an office, and I leaned against the desk, admiring the view. Preston stalked over to me, placing his hands on the surface and trapping me in his arms.

"This desk is very…solid." He pressed his hips against mine, letting me feel just how solid he was. He leaned down, nuzzling my ear. "You're so sexy."

"Preston." I angled my head back, granting him access.

I'd missed him. God, how I'd missed him. The way he touched me, lighting up my body. The way he kissed, making me feel as if he'd captured my soul. The way he made love to me, making me feel as if we really were one person. Despite how much I was tempted to, we couldn't… Not here.

I straightened. "Moving on. We have a lot more to see."

"Yes, we do." He gave me a wicked grin.

"Come on." I dragged him down the hall, quickly showing him the other bedrooms and bath.

I could feel his eyes on me the entire time, and he didn't

stop touching me once. When we made it to the master bedroom, I told him about the blackout shades that could be lowered at the push of a button, the safe hidden in a discreet wall panel, and the TV that could be disguised to look like a work of art. He seemed impressed, but I knew we were both distracted. And every time he grazed my arms with his fingers or brushed past me, I thought I might combust.

"Let's head back to the kitchen," I said, once I'd finished showing him the master bath.

I tried to pretend he was just another client, even though I knew he wasn't. And while I hoped I might be able to sell Hunter a home, I honestly couldn't care less. Having a second chance with Preston was worth more to me than any commission.

"Kitchen is all stainless-steel appliances, gas range—" I glanced over at him, and he was watching me with a dazed expression. "Are you even paying attention?"

"Mm-hmm. I'm thinking about all the ways I can fuck you on the Carrara marble."

"Preston." I slapped his bicep, feigning outrage. "And it's not Carrara, it's Calacatta."

"Calacatta, Carrara, still serves the same purpose." His eyes were hooded when they met mine.

"So, what do you think?" I smiled brightly, holding my arms wide.

He grabbed me by the waist, lifting me up on the Calacatta countertops as if I weighed nothing. "I think the house is beautiful, though you're even more so. But we have a little problem because I'm still not satisfied."

"That's unfortunate," I said, playing along, unable to resist anymore. I tangled my fingers in his hair. "What can I do to remedy the situation?"

"I have a few ideas." He pressed his lips along the swell of my cleavage, cupping my breasts from below. "Seriously, did your boobs get bigger? Because they look amazing."

"Yes." I laughed, knowing that my bras and dresses were already getting a little tight in the bust. "They are a little bigger. Side effect of pregnancy."

He smoothed his hand over my breasts, coming down to rest on my stomach.

"Fuck." He bit his lip, leaning back a little to admire me. "I can't wait to see your belly swollen with my child."

A bolt of desire shot straight to my core, and I could picture it. I could envision our future together, and I didn't want to wait any longer to be with him. I never wanted him to doubt my love; I wanted him to know. I wanted to show him.

I cupped his cheeks, feeling the love, the power, vibrating between us. "I love you."

His blue eyes sparkled with unspoken promises, with hope. And I knew I was responsible for it. Our baby was responsible for it.

"I love you." His voice was rough, fractured. "So fucking much."

He crashed his lips to mine, and the kiss was a celebration. It was all our hopes and dreams, our happiness wrapped up in one. It was a confirmation and a revelation; it was everything. And his hands were everywhere—in my hair, cupping my cheeks, caressing my breasts, gripping my hips.

"Wait," he panted. I frowned, wondering what was wrong. "This won't hurt the baby, will it?"

I furrowed my brow. "Sex?" He nodded, and I couldn't help but laugh. "No. It won't hurt the baby. You can be as gentle or as rough as you want."

"Thank fuck." He gripped my hips, pulling me to him so there was no space between us.

I tugged on the hem of his shirt, and he pulled it over his

head in one fluid movement. His body was…unreal. And it was all mine.

"Though I have to warn you," I said as he pulled down my dress and bra to reveal my breasts. It felt so good to be free from those confines. "My nipples are extra sensitive."

"Good to know." He glanced up at me, one eyebrow quirked as he absently traced a circle around my nipple, never quite touching it despite coming close. Already driving me wild. "Anything else you want to tell me?"

"I love you."

He chuckled, his blue eyes dancing with mirth. "Was that a question?"

"No. There was never a question about it—I love you." It felt so freeing to say it without hesitation, without reservation. And I sensed there'd been a shift between us, and not just because of the baby.

"I love you." He pressed his lips to mine. "I love you, and I love Sophia, and—" he kissed my stomach over the material of my dress "—I love you, little one."

I melted into a puddle of goo. He was going to have to pick me up off the floor because the love he had for me, Sophia, and our new baby was overwhelming.

I unzipped his pants, and his erection sprang out, bobbing against his stomach. His eyes were dark, the pupil nearly swallowing the iris as he ran his thumb over my lower lip. I sucked it into my mouth, swirling my tongue around the tip as I pulled it deeper inside.

"I want you," he rasped, his eyes intent on my mouth.

"So take me," I said, leaning back on the heels of my hands. "I'm yours."

"Always?" He pushed my underwear aside, teasing my clit with the tip of his erection. I leaned my head back, already anticipating the connection, the release.

"Alexis."

"Hmm?" *God, that feels so good.*

"Say it," he growled.

I lifted my head to look in his eyes. "Always," I said in a solemn tone.

He took his time, sinking into me inch by delicious inch. I'd never felt so full, so content, as I did in that moment. We might not be in our house, or lying in our bed, but it certainly felt like coming home.

CHAPTER TWENTY-EIGHT

Preston

"No." Sophia shook her head at the latest design Lauren had shown us. "Not blue. I'm not having blue in my baby sister's room."

"We don't even know if it's a boy or a girl," Alexis sighed.

"And blue is a soft, peaceful color that can transition nicely whether the baby is a boy or a girl," Lauren said. "Besides, this is really closer to mint in color."

Sophia placed her hands on her hips. "Stop talking about having a boy. I'm getting a baby sister, and her name is Seraphina. No…Anastasia."

I smirked, watching it all play out. I loved how excited Sophia was about her baby…whatever. She'd taken the news in stride, and she loved brainstorming baby names—well, so long as they were girl's names. She refused to entertain the idea that the baby could be a he, not a she. But I was cool with it. I secretly hoped it was a girl, too. Though, honestly, I didn't care what the baby was, so long as it was healthy.

"What do you think, Preston?" Alexis placed her hand on my thigh, and I stared down at her bare ring finger. It was taunting me.

"I think they're all great designs. I want whatever makes you happy," I said, and I meant it. It really didn't matter to me, so long as Alexis was satisfied.

"Aww," Lauren said. "That's so sweet." She leaned forward, her expression hardening. "But really, which one do you like best?"

"Umm…" Sweat prickled along my forehead, and I felt like I was taking a test I hadn't prepared for. "Well, I like the rug in this one. It looks fluffy but still easy to clean. A wooden rocking chair has a classic feel to it, but I want to make sure whatever chair we get is comfortable. As for the crib, as long as the paint is nontoxic and it meets all the safety criteria and then some, I'll be happy."

Alexis smiled up at me, and I knew I'd passed with flying colors. She kissed my cheek. "Good answers."

"You liked them?" I asked.

She lowered her voice, speaking into my ear. "Yes, and I'll show you just how much I liked them later."

"Mmm," I hummed. "I like the sound of that."

Ever since I'd moved in, she was insatiable. If I'd thought she was horny before, she was even more so now. Not that I was complaining. She wanted sex, and I was more than happy to oblige. Sex and, well, Starbucks breakfast sandwiches. She was obsessed with them, and she still couldn't stomach the thought of her breakfast shakes.

Lauren cleared her throat, and I glanced at the time on my phone. It was getting late.

"Well, ladies—" I stood, knowing Lauren and Alexis could discuss the nursery plans for hours. "If you'll excuse me, I have to get ready for my date with Sophia."

I climbed the stairs two at a time, restless with nerves and excitement. Tonight was important, and I wanted to get it just right. It was time for phase one of my plan.

I showered and dressed in a suit and tie before slipping

the box into my pocket. After one last glance in the mirror, I headed across the hall to Sophia's room and knocked on the door.

It swung open, and she grinned up at me. "You look very handsome."

"Thank you. I love the glitter," I said, smiling as she twisted from side to side, making her skirt sparkle as she twirled. "Do you have your stuff packed for Brooklyn's?" That was phase two.

"Yep!" She tried to lift her duffel bag, but she couldn't.

I hefted it onto my shoulder. "What on earth do you have in here?"

"Just…stuff. Okay?" she huffed.

"Okay." Far be it for me to understand the needs of a seven-year-old girls' slumber party. "Let's go say goodbye to Lauren and your mom."

She skipped down the stairs and into the living room. I could hear Lauren and Alexis gushing over her outfit and her hair. When I stepped into the room, all eyes shot to me. Lauren gave me two thumbs up, and Alexis stared at me as if she couldn't quite believe her eyes.

While Sophia was saying goodbye to Lauren, Alexis crossed the room to me. "You look hot," she said, wrapping her arms around my neck. "I can't wait for you to get home."

She pressed her lips to mine, and I loved that she no longer shied away from showing affection. I loved the fact that we no longer had to hide our relationship—from anyone. Sophia, my parents, Cal. I didn't get the impression he was my biggest fan, but he was no longer hostile toward me. Not that we saw him much—he was still on tour, and it was going so well, it had been extended.

"Me either." I grinned, swatting her on the butt. "All right, princess," I said to Sophia. "Your carriage awaits."

"Goodnight, Preston." Lauren waved.

"Night."

I drove across town, hoping Sophia would like the place I'd chosen for dinner. She talked about her plans with Brooklyn and her hopes for the baby. She told me about her latest history assignment, and we brainstormed ideas for it.

I was no longer her nanny, but Alexis and I had decided not to fill the position. Instead, I'd structured my classes so I could take Sophia to school and pick her up. And we'd settled easily into a new routine. We did our homework together in the afternoons before cooking dinner. We had it ready by the time Alexis arrived home, and then we'd eat together as a family. And I loved it. I loved the new life we'd made for ourselves, our family.

Alexis had transitioned to working fewer hours and actually enjoying her days off—and not just because she was pregnant. She'd really made an effort to find more balance in her life, to prioritize days at the aquarium and family movie nights.

As the host led us through the restaurant, I hoped Sophia felt as special as she was. Dinner passed by quickly, and after dessert, it was time to pop the big question. I tugged at my collar, hoping I was doing the right thing.

"Sophia," I said.

"Yes, Preston." She folded her little hands on the table, meeting my gaze. She was so serious. So mature.

"You know that I love you, right?" She nodded. "And I'd never want to replace your dad. But I have to ask—how would you like to be my daughter too?"

She scrunched up her face. "Would I call you Daddy?"

I lifted a shoulder. "Only if you want to. But Preston's good too."

"Okay. Cool." She seemed to relax. "I love you too, Preston."

I smiled. "Which brings me to my next question. I want to marry your mom. Would you be okay with that?"

"Okay?" She nearly leaped out of her chair, drawing curious looks from nearby diners. "This is so awesome. Do you have a ring? When are you getting married? Can I be the flower girl? What about my baby sister?"

"Whoa. Whoa." I chuckled, thrilled by her reaction. "Slow down.

"I do have a ring. And, of course, you can be the flower girl. As to the rest, it's up to your mom."

"Yes. Yes. Yes," she hissed.

"I also have a present for you," I said, wanting something to commemorate this moment. I pulled out the velvet box and slid it across the table.

Her eyes were wide, and when she opened it, she squealed. "Thank you, Preston." She pulled out the delicate chain with a heart locket engraved with the letter "S." "I love it."

"You're welcome. I thought we could put pictures of our family inside. I already added one from the baby's sonogram."

She rushed over to me and threw her arms around my neck. "Thank you. And thanks for making my mom so happy."

My heart swelled with happiness, and I only hoped my proposal to Alexis would go as well. Sophia didn't seem to care that I was younger than her mom, or her former nanny; she loved me. And I was relieved that most of the kids at her school didn't seem to care either. If they'd teased Sophia about it, she certainly hadn't mentioned it to Alexis or me.

When I dropped Sophia off at Brooklyn's, she stood at the door and gave me two thumbs up. The entire drive home, I rehearsed my speech, relieved to find Alexis still awake.

"Hey." She glanced at me over the back of the couch, typing something on her laptop. "Did you have a good time?"

She was already in her pajamas, and I removed my suit jacket and tie before heading over to the couch. *Christina on the Coast* played in the background, and I smiled to myself, thinking it was a good omen.

I grinned. "Always."

"I think it's super sweet that you took Sophia on a date. I bet she absolutely loved it."

I nodded. "I think she had fun. I definitely did."

"Let me just finish this email about the Miller property," she said, returning her attention to her laptop.

Despite having to cut the showing short because of Sophia's broken wrist, Alexis had sold the twenty-million-dollar property. It was closing soon, and I was so proud of her. And I knew having the extra money in the bank gave her a sense of security with the new baby coming.

When she shut the laptop, I sank down onto the cushions with a heavy sigh, hoping I wasn't about to make a huge fool of myself. As long as she said yes, I didn't really care.

"This," I said, gesturing between us, "isn't working for me."

I hoped she'd remember those words, remember the night she'd spoken them. The night everything changed.

"Is it because I got mad at you for leaving the toilet seat up?" she asked, not looking away from the TV.

I shook my head. I couldn't care less about that. I honestly felt bad I'd forgotten to put it down, but I was still getting used to living with a woman.

"If you want to redecorate so it feels more like 'our' home instead of 'my' home, I'm sure Lauren would be happy to help," she said. "Oh man, look at their new pool."

"Nope. That's not it either." I tried to school my face into a stern expression. Man, this was hard—hard to act like I was upset when I was bursting with excitement.

"Preston." She lowered the volume on the TV and turned to face me. "What's going on? I thought everything was great. Please, just talk to me. Whatever it is, we can find a solution."

"This isn't working because I want more. I don't want to be just your boyfriend or your baby daddy. I want to be your husband."

I knelt to the ground before her, smirking to myself when I heard her gasp. "I love you. I love our family, and I want to spend the rest of my life with you."

I reached into my pocket to pull out a small velvet box. I fumbled, nearly dropping it.

"Alexis Black, will you marry me?"

She stared at the rings for a moment without saying anything. All the while, my heart was pounding, blood whooshing through my ears.

"Oh my gosh." She held her hands to her mouth. "Those rings are...stunning."

"I'm glad you think so." I grinned, pleased that she was so taken with the stacking rings I'd chosen. I removed the rose gold band with diamonds from the box and held it up. "This one represents my love for Sophia. She gave me her blessing, by the way."

She held out her left hand, presenting it to me so I could slide the ring on. A tear fell down her cheek, and I wiped it away with my thumb.

"This one," I said, holding up the black gold band with diamonds. "Represents my love for you. I chose it not only because of your last name, but because black is required for all the other colors to have depth and variation of hue. Much like you give depth and richness to each of our lives."

I slid it onto her finger before removing the final ring, a white gold band with diamonds inlaid in a scalloped edge.

"And this one is for our child—our future. It represents the hope you've given me."

She cupped my cheeks. "Every time I think I couldn't possibly love you more, you go and do something like this." She laughed through her tears. "I love you. I'm so incredibly in love with you. And yes, I absolutely will marry you."

I was flooded with relief, overwhelmed with excitement, and just in awe of this incredible woman. I slanted my lips over hers, needing to seal the moment with a kiss. I poured all my hopes and dreams, all my love into it.

I loved her. I loved her, and I couldn't wait to marry her. I gathered her in my arms and carried her up the stairs to our room, where I spent the rest of the night making love to my future wife.

CHAPTER TWENTY-NINE

Alexis

"Ooh, girl." Lauren stood behind me, meeting my eyes in the reflection in the mirror. "You look amazing."

I smoothed my hands over my stomach, which had popped in the last month. "Despite the baby bump?"

"*Because* of the baby bump. This dress is perfect for your curves, and Preston is going to lose his shit when he sees you."

I grinned, knowing she was right. He was going to love the cream gown that flowed over my body like water. It dipped low in the front, showcasing my larger breasts, but gathered around my stomach. It was the perfect mix of retro and modern, and it made me feel incredibly sexy. And it was perfect for the venue—the 1920s jazz club where we'd had our first date.

Sophia skipped into the room with Juliana on her heels. "Oh, Mommy." She came to a halt when she saw me, and I turned to face her. "You look sooo pretty."

"So do you, baby." She looked so sweet in her blush-colored dress with a sparkly headband. The locket Preston gave her dangled around her neck, and I knew she couldn't wait to walk me down the aisle.

"Everyone's in place," Juliana said. "So, whenever you're ready."

"I think I changed my mind," I blurted.

Juliana gasped, and Lauren's eyes went wide. "Are you having second thoughts?" she whispered.

This wasn't my first time walking down the aisle, but it would be my last. We'd planned the wedding in less than a month, and it had been a whirlwind of excitement. But now, I wanted to savor the moment. And I wanted to take a moment to be with Preston.

"Juliana, can you get the photographer? I want to have a 'first look' after all."

I could hear the collective sigh of relief, and I laughed. "Wait...did you guys think I was having second thoughts about marrying Preston?"

"If you were," Juliana said, pausing at the door, "I was going to step in. I planned a kick-ass party, and your groom looks hot."

I laughed, placing a hand on my belly. "Well, we wouldn't want to ruin *your* party, Juliana," I teased, knowing how hard this had to be for her—planning a wedding less than a year after she'd lost her fiancé in a tragic accident. But she'd been insistent.

"And keep your hands off the groom—he's mine," I said, hoping to keep the mood light.

"Oh, there's no doubting that," Lauren said. "That boy is so in love with you."

"Not a boy," I chided.

"Mm, girl. I know." She waggled her eyebrows, placing her hand on Sophia's shoulder and steering her toward the door. "Come on, Soph. Let's give your parents a moment alone."

"Why can't I stay?" she asked as they passed through the door.

"Because this is a special moment just for them. One day, you'll understand," Lauren said.

I turned back to the mirror, checking my teeth, adjusting my earrings. I couldn't believe I was getting married—again. But this time, I knew I was making the right decision. I couldn't imagine my life without Preston. I couldn't imagine our family without him.

A moment later, there was a knock at the door. "Alexis?" Preston called.

With a shaky hand, I twisted the knob, opening the door just an inch or two. "Are you ready?"

"So ready," he said. "The photographer is here."

The photographer took some shots, framing us on either side of the door, holding hands. We still hadn't seen each other, and I was growing impatient.

"Okay," the photographer said. "I'm going to have Preston wait for you at the end of the hall with his back turned." A moment later, he said, "You can come out now, Alexis."

As promised, Preston was standing at the end of the hall. It was the first time I'd seen him all day, and I admired the way the custom tuxedo draped over the muscles of his shoulders and back. And when he turned to face me, I felt the rightness of my decision settle over me. Not only was I happy we got to share this moment, but I was thrilled I got to share my life with him.

His jaw dropped, and I dipped my head, gratified by his reaction. All the while, the silk train swished behind me, the material flowing over my body as I glided toward him.

"You," he breathed as he drank me in. "I-I don't even know what to say." He rubbed a hand over his mouth. "I can't believe you're going to be my wife."

I grinned. "I can't believe you're going to be my husband.

That I get to wake up to your handsome face every morning. That I get to fall asleep in your arms."

"You look absolutely stunning," he said, settling his hands on my hips, resting his forehead against mine. "And I love you."

"I love you too." Our breath mingled, and I stared into his blue eyes, seeing my future written there.

"I'm dying to kiss you, but I don't want to mess up your lipstick."

I laughed. "It's lip stain, and it won't smear. But if you're worried about it, you can kiss me somewhere else."

"Alexis," he chided, pretending to be outraged. "What are you suggesting?"

I bit back a grin. "I was suggesting somewhere like my cheek or neck. What were *you* suggesting?" I asked, knowing full well what he had in mind.

I'd forgotten all about the photographer at that point, but he continued to snap away, taking picture after picture.

Preston gently brushed my hair aside, placing a kiss on the sensitive spot behind my ear. "I guess you'll just have to wait until later to find out."

I sighed, losing myself in his touch. He grazed the shell of my ear with his teeth and goose bumps erupted across my body. I wrapped my arms around his neck, needing more.

"Stop. That tickles." I said, holding my belly as I laughed.

He leaned back and frowned. "Me or…" He glanced down to where my hand was resting on my stomach. "The baby?"

I nodded. I took his hand and placed it over my stomach. "Here." We waited, and I hoped she'd move again. We'd been playing this game for days. She'd recently started moving, and without fail, every time Preston put his hand on my belly, she stopped. "There," I said, when there was another little flutter. "Can you feel her?"

"Her, huh?" He glanced up at me. "So you're referring to the baby as a girl now."

I shrugged. "It seemed easier than fighting you and Sophia every time I mention the baby."

"You know we're just teasing, right? I'll be thrilled either way."

"I know, though Sophia might be a tad disappointed." I held up my thumb and pointer finger.

The baby moved, and Preston sucked in a quick breath. He glanced up at me with watery eyes and a huge smile. "That's so cool." He beamed down at my stomach. "Hi, baby. It's me, your daddy."

I ran my nails over the short hair at the back of his head, soaking in this moment. This man.

"Does it hurt?" he asked.

"No." I laughed. "It tickles. As the baby gets bigger and stronger, it can hurt."

"Is it weird that I really want to have sex with you right now?"

I glanced down at his tuxedo, noticing a prominent bulge. "Are you hard?"

"When I'm with you? Always." He smirked. "Want to go have a quickie in the dressing room?"

"Preston." I slapped his chest, backing away. "We have thirty guests waiting downstairs, including your parents and our daughter. We are not having a quickie in the dressing room."

"You know you want to," he taunted, and he wasn't wrong. I also knew he was joking—at least, I thought he was.

"All right, people." Juliana clapped her hands. Where had she come from? "It's time to get this show on the road."

"You ready?" Preston asked. "Because there's no turning back now."

"I think we're well past the point of no return," I teased. "But I wouldn't have it any other way."

"Okay. Preston, you and the photographer can head downstairs. Take your place at the front like we rehearsed."

He nodded then turned to me. "I'll be waiting for you."

When I reached the bottom of the stairs, Sophia was already there. Juliana handed me my bouquet with a watery smile, and I took a deep breath. She spoke into her headset, and then it was time.

The doors opened to reveal the dark-paneled club I remembered, but it had been transformed. Chairs flanked a central aisle, and white flowers perfumed the space, while candles cast a warm glow. It was romantic and sophisticated, yet relaxed all at the same time.

Family and friends smiled as we passed, including Sam and Indy, but I only had eyes for one person—Preston. He stood at the altar, hands clasped before him and a grin that split his face. After Sophia "gave me away," we recited our vows. The entire time, I felt as if I were living a dream or someone else's life. And when we were pronounced husband and wife, well, I didn't think I'd ever been so happy.

Preston scooped Sophia into his arms, carrying her down the aisle as he held my hand. After we'd posed for some family pictures, it was time for dinner and dancing. Though we'd kept some traditional wedding elements, we'd ditched others. There were no bridesmaids, no groomsmen, and there would be no tossing of the garter.

The food had just been served when Hunter stood, clinking a fork against his glass to get everyone's attention.

"Preston may have opted out of having a best man, but we all know who he would have chosen." With his hand still wrapped around the microphone, he pointed at himself, and everyone laughed. "You know, when Preston started working as a manny, I gave him so much shit."

"When did you stop giving me shit for it?" Preston asked, drawing another wave of laughter.

Hunter waved a hand through the air, his movements loose from the alcohol. "But I have to say, after watching Sophia for a day—love you, girl—I do not know how he did it. And—" he turned to Preston "—I have a newfound respect for you.

"You are an incredible man. I've watched you overcome so many obstacles. And I'm honored to call you my friend. Alexis—you're good for him. And I wish you both so much happiness. So please raise your glass to toast the bride and groom."

Everyone lifted their glasses, and I raised my glass of sparkling water.

"To Alexis and Preston—health, wealth, and happiness."

"Health, wealth, and happiness," everyone repeated.

Dinner was delicious, and the cake...the cake was the same tiramisu I'd tasted the night of our first date. Though the club had made it gluten free so Sophia could enjoy it as well. The dessert was just as good as I remembered, and this time, I didn't hesitate when Preston raised his fork to my lips. I licked off the excess cream, noticing the way his eyes darkened.

"Keep doing that," he said. "And we'll be leaving our reception early."

"Tempting." I smirked. "I just hope I don't pass out on our wedding night." I patted my belly, knowing that I tired more easily now that I was pregnant. And today had been a big day.

"Don't worry." He grinned, smoothing his hand up my thigh. I tried to keep my expression neutral even as my breathing quickened. I had a flashback to the last time we were here. "I promise to keep things interesting."

"Was that part of our vows?" I teased. "Spice up the sex life?"

"No, but it should be." He removed his hand, and I immediately missed his touch.

I laughed. "Deal."

"Now…" He stood, offering me his hand. "I believe I owe you a dance, my beautiful wife."

"I believe you do, my handsome husband," I said, allowing him to lead me to the dance floor.

As he twirled me around, I saw the faces of friends and family. Juliana, Lauren, and Harper, but also, Preston's friends and even his parents. I'd been worried they'd freak out when they found out about us, but they'd only ever been supportive. They didn't seem bothered about our age difference or the fact that he'd been Sophia's nanny. And they adored Sophia, doting on her and giving her the type of love only grandparents could.

Before I'd met Preston, my life was perfect—at least, from the outside looking in. I had money and success, but I was lonely. Perhaps even more than I'd realized. It wasn't until Preston showed me what I was missing that I knew what I really wanted—a partner.

Someone who would be there, cheering me on when I was struggling. Someone to celebrate the highs and commiserate the lows. Someone to love, and who loved me in return. And that was what I'd discovered in him.

He picked up Sophia, holding her in one arm as he wrapped his other around me. I smiled up at him, pressing my lips to his, with our child fluttering in my stomach. And I knew that no matter my age or what challenges life threw my way, I didn't have to do it alone. Because I knew without a doubt that he would be at my side, every step of the way.

Sophia dropped her head against his shoulder, and the three of us swayed to the music.

"What three things are you grateful for?" I asked Preston.

"They're right here—in my arms. And I'm never letting go."

I pressed my lips to his, my heart near to bursting with happiness and love. Preston had shown me the value of slowing down and savoring every moment. And this was definitely one I never wanted to forget.

CHAPTER THIRTY

Preston

A *few months later*

Everyone held their breath, waiting for the fateful cry.
And then there was a loud wail, and I grinned at Alexis, holding her hand.

"It's a girl!" cried one of the nurses.

"Did you hear that, beautiful?" I asked, smoothing her hair away from her face. She was lying on the operating table, and I was so incredibly proud of her. So in awe. "It's a girl."

She smiled, but it was a dazed smile. One that spoke of exhaustion and a cocktail of drugs swirling through her system. "Sophia's going to be thrilled."

I stayed there with her while the doctors finished stitching her up, watching as the nurses fussed over our daughter. *Our daughter*, I thought, letting those words sink in.

"We did it," Alexis, said, but her eyes nearly fluttered closed.

I leaned down and pressed my lips to her forehead. "I'm so proud of you. You are amazing."

"I don't feel amazing. I feel like I've been run over by a Mack truck," she muttered.

I combed my fingers through her hair, watching as her eyes closed and her face relaxed. "Just rest."

They wheeled us to our room, and then rolled in a tiny bassinet with a little bundle of pink nestled inside. The nurse carried our baby over and set her on Alexis's chest, helping her move the hospital gown aside.

"She's beautiful," the nurse said with a soft smile.

"Just like her mother," I said, drinking in the scene. Alexis was so fucking beautiful. And she was my wife, the mother of my child.

"I'll give you some alone time. Page me if you need anything," the nurse said before disappearing to the hallway.

I stood there a moment just watching them before taking a seat on the bed next to Alexis. I could already see the immense love she had for this baby, and I felt it too. We'd waited to find out the baby's gender, and discovering that she was a girl after all had been the sweetest surprise.

We stayed there, cocooned in our own little world with our new baby girl. "Do you want to hold her?" Alexis finally asked.

"I've been dying for you to ask," I said, eager to hold our baby but not wanting to rush her.

Alexis carefully swaddled our daughter and then handed her to me. I stared down at her, cataloging her features—the blue eyes, the tuft of brown hair, her rosy lips. My voice was clogged with emotion, my heart overflowing.

"Hello, little one," I cooed at her. "I'm your daddy."

One of her little fists emerged from the blanket. "She's so tiny," I said, marveling at the size of her hands.

"Hard to believe Sophia was once that little." Alexis looked down on her with a wistful grin.

"What do you want to name her?" I asked, unable to take my eyes off my beautiful daughter. My miracle.

Alexis pursed her lips. "I don't know. I'm not sure any of the names we were considering suit her. Do you know what I mean?"

I nodded, understanding exactly what she meant. "She doesn't really seem like an Ava or a Madison to me. We have time to decide, right?"

"Yes, but I'd like to decide sooner rather than later. I don't want to keep referring to her as the baby or baby."

"Agreed." I studied my daughter. "Who are you, little one? Are you an Amelia?" She didn't say anything. "Or maybe a Sloan."

"Not Sloan," Alexis said.

"How about Alice or Everly?" I asked.

There was a knock at the door, and the nurse stuck her head inside. "Mom, are you okay with having visitors? Your daughter is asking if she can see you and meet the baby."

Alexis smiled. "Send her in."

A moment later, Sophia peeked her head around the door. "Mommy?"

"Come in," Alexis said. "Come meet your baby sister."

"Yes!" Sophia fist-pumped, which only made me laugh. A tear leaked out, and I wiped it away. "I knew it was a girl. You're naming her Charlotte, right?"

Charlotte had always been Sophia's first choice. She liked how regal it sounded, and I had to agree. Though, I still wasn't entirely sure I was sold on it.

"We're still deciding," Alexis said. "Why don't you sit on the couch with Preston, and you can hold her."

"Really?" Sophia's face lit up, and I knew she was excited she'd get to hold the baby so soon.

"Yes, but wash your hands first."

Sophia did as Alexis asked and was soon settled on the couch. I could tell from the way she squirmed that it was a struggle to remain still. I carried the baby over to her, sitting next to her on the couch. "Remember to support her head, like this." I showed her.

"Okay." She nodded, and I placed the baby in her arms. "Hi. I'm Sophia, and I'm your big sister."

I grinned, glancing up at Alexis to see her watching us with a smile.

"Your face is kinda scrunched up, but I'm sure you'll get cuter with age. I certainly did."

I coughed into my hand to cover a laugh. This kid—she was hilarious. I hoped her little sister would be just as independent and precocious.

I wrapped my arm around Sophia's shoulder, holding her close as we stared down at the newest addition to our family. "I love you," I said, pressing a kiss into her hair. "Both of you."

"I think we should name her Blair," Alexis said. "Blair Elizabeth."

"Blair." Sophia glanced down at the baby. "Are you a Blair? I think I like Blair."

"Preston?" Alexis asked.

I grinned, feeling a sense of rightness settle over me. "I think I like it too."

We stayed that way for a while, until Blair started crying. Her face was red, and she shook her little fists, showing her displeasure. I handed her off to Alexis, while ushering Sophia out to the waiting room where a crowd had gathered.

My parents were there, along with Hunter and Lauren, though they sat on opposite sides of the waiting room. Everyone cheered when I told them it was a girl, announcing her weight and height with pride. Sophia ran over to my dad, excited to tell him all about *her* new baby. Lauren and Hunter offered their congratulations and said they'd stop by the house once we'd settled in. Then it was just Sophia, my parents, and me.

Mom wrapped her arms around me. "I'm so happy for you. To be able to know the joy of parenthood—it's everything."

She pulled back, cupping my face in her hands. "I'm so proud of you, Preston. You went through hell, but now you're married, you're a father. And you're about to graduate." She shook her head, pressing her fingers to her lips. "It's everything I ever could've wanted for you."

"*Mom*." I wrapped my arms around her once more. "Thank you. And I love you too."

"Preston." Sophia tugged on my shirt. "I'm hungry."

"Okay. Okay." I chuckled. "You guys know the drill, right?" I asked my parents.

They'd generously offered to come and help when the new baby was born. And with me in the middle of finals and Sophia's school year coming to a close, we needed all the help we could get.

Though Sophia would be spending a few weeks with Cal for the summer, we'd all agreed she could spend some time with her new sibling first. Cal wasn't my biggest fan, nor was I his. But he had apologized for his behavior at Sophia's party, and we'd reached a sort of tentative peace.

"We've got it covered," Dad said, clapping a hand on my shoulder. "I'm proud of you, son."

He wasn't an emotional man, but his watery smile told me everything I needed to know. He was proud to be my father, to be a grandfather. And he loved me.

"Thanks." I gave him a big hug. After all the shit we'd been through with cancer, it was nice to finally be at the hospital for such an amazing reason.

I crouched down before Sophia. "I'll see you tomorrow. Okay, princess?"

"Okay. Take good care of my baby."

My parents and I laughed. "I will. I promise to take very good care of Blair."

"You chose a name?" Mom asked.

I stood, ruffling Sophia's hair. "We did. Blair Elizabeth."

"It's beautiful," Mom said. "Strong yet feminine. It's perfect."

"Thanks." I smiled. "I better get back to them."

"Yes, of course. Go." She pushed me in the direction of Alexis's room, and I gave the three of them one last wave.

"Goodnight."

"Goodnight," they called. "We can't wait to see Blair tomorrow."

When I returned to the hospital room, Alexis's eyes were closed, and Blair rested on her chest. They looked so peaceful, I couldn't help but stare. My whole world was wrapped up in Alexis, Sophia, and now, Blair—my girls.

Alexis's eyes fluttered open, and I stood from the chair, going to her side. "Do you want anything? Something to eat? Are you comfortable?"

She glanced down at Blair before meeting my eyes once more. "I have everything I could ever want."

I pressed my lips to hers, so incredibly grateful for this woman. "I know the feeling."

"What three things are you grateful for today?" she asked.

"You, Sophia, and Blair," I said without hesitation.

She grinned. "You say that every night, except now we know this little one's name."

"I say it because it's true. And it will be true every night for the rest of my life."

She removed one of her hands from Blair's back and placed it over mine. "Thank you for taking a chance on me, for being patient and kind and loving. You showed me what love could be. What family could be. And for that, I will be forever grateful."

I touched my forehead to hers, needing to feel that connection to her. "I love you."

"I love you. So, so much." She placed her hand on my cheek, pressing her lips to mine.

Blair stirred, and I peered down at her sweet little face. And I knew that life wasn't made up of the big moments like weddings or graduation, it was lived in the small, quiet moments. The tender kisses we shared. The times Sophia wrapped her arms around my neck or told me she loved me.

I considered myself lucky, not only because I'd survived cancer. But because I'd been given the chance to live life—an amazing life. And I intended to savor every moment.

LOVE NOTES

My Beautiful Wife,

What three things are you grateful for today?

My answer, as always, is you, Sophia, and Blair.

I know Sophia makes fun of me for having the same answer day in and day out, but it's true. I couldn't be more grateful for my three girls. For you— the love of my life, the mother of my children, the keeper of my secrets. You give me a sense of home, a contentedness, that was missing from my life. And I've never been happier.

I'm grateful for Sophia—our darling, precocious girl. She's too smart for her own good, and she's growing up way too fast. Can we keep our princess little forever?

And Blair. Our beautiful, unexpected, miracle. She's more than I ever could've hoped for—you all are. Every time I look at her, I see hope, joy. I'm beyond proud to raise these girls, to be their daddy, to be your husband.

I know life is hectic right now—between running your brokerage firm, expanding the developmental side, and raising two small children. But I'm so proud of you for all your hard work. For taking care of our family. For kicking ass in real estate and racking up the sales and awards. If anyone deserves them, it's you. You are so incredibly smart, savvy, and beautiful. And did I mention sexy as fuck?

I can't wait for this weekend. My mom is watching the girls, and I have plans for you. Plans that involve chocolate syrup and lots of time in bed, the shower, and anywhere else we want.

I feel like the luckiest man on the planet that I get to spend my life with you.

Thank you for opening your heart to me. Thank you for trusting me and loving me. I'm grateful that I get to wake up to your beautiful face every morning, your fingers dancing across my skin, your lips soft against mine. The way we come together, our bodies moving as if in a dance where we know all the steps.

I love that we've made a home together, a family. It was something I always wanted and never expected. Something I dreamed of but never believed was possible.

And all because you took a chance on me—the nanny. Manny? Fuck, I still don't know what to call a male nanny. Nothing fits. But you know what, it doesn't matter.

What matters is that we're together. And we're a family.

As we recited in our wedding vows, that magical evening when you promised to be mine: With this ring, I give you my heart. I have no greater gift to give. May you feel deeply loved, for indeed you are. I'm honored to call you my wife and blessed to call you mine.

Those words were true that day, and they are true every day. I love you. I love our daughters. And I'm privileged to share this life with you. To share every moment with you—big or small, bad or good.

All my love,
Preston

Princess Sophia,

Happy Valentine's Day! I can't wait to hear about your adventures at school.

I know you like Jason, and he says he wants to be your boyfriend, but no kissing! Even if he does give you the stuffed kitty cat with the heart you've been eyeing at the school Valentine's store. I don't care what he gives you—no kissing until you're thirty. No—forty!

What do you need those silly boys for anyway? I'll always be your valentine.

When you get home, we'll make some yummy heart cookies for Mama! I always have the best time baking with you.

I love you.

Love,
Sir Preston

Blair,

Happy Valentine's Day, baby girl! You can't read yet, but I like writing to you all the same. One day, I hope you'll look back on all the notes and cards I've written you and smile. Most of all, I hope you'll always remember how loved you are.

We're going to have so much fun today! Your giggles are the most beautiful sound I've ever heard. You bring joy everywhere we go, making strangers smile with your happy demeanor and sweet coos.

I love you more than you could ever know.

Love,
Daddy

A TASTE OF HOME

My daughter and I love cooking together. We view her food allergies not as a limitation, but an invitation for creativity and innovation. I hope you and your loved ones will enjoy cooking these recipes as much as we do.

There's nothing better than slowing down, taking the time to make something from scratch. It doesn't have to be fancy, it just needs to be made with love. And I've found that kids love helping out in the kitchen, and they often are more excited to try new foods when they do.

I sincerely hope you'll enjoy this collection of recipes. They are meant to be easy, delicious, and allergy friendly (not to mention kid-approved)! But you can easily substitute regular all-purpose flour, if that's more your jam.

Happy cooking!
Preston

PANCAKES

What's your favorite breakfast food?

My wife, Alexis, wasn't much of a fan of breakfast before I came along. Well, we all know she secretly craved pancakes but was too busy sucking down those disgusting protein shakes. No more!

Now, she's the first to scarf down my homemade pancakes. With two little ones and a full-time job, time is at a premium. I strive to find recipes that are both easy to execute and delicious! These were inspired by a recipe on the blog <u>A Cup of Jo</u> a while back, but I've added my own twist!

The original version is even easier—just two ingredients! But I found it lacked the texture and flavor I wanted. After messing around with them a bit over the past few years, this is the best version I've found. One that strikes a balance between flavor/texture and ease.

They're super easy and great to make with kids (bonus: they're gluten free and nut free!).

Pancakes

Makes 2 servings

Ingredients

- 1 banana, mashed
- 2 eggs
- pinch of salt
- 1/8 tsp. cinnamon (Honestly, I just sprinkle a thin layer over the top.)
- 1/2 tsp. Olive oil (plus more to oil the pan) or a tablespoon of melted butter
- 1/2 tbsp. Gluten-free Rice flour
- Toppings of your choice

Instructions

- Preheat pan to medium-high, add some olive oil.
- In a bowl, mix all the ingredients together. Batter should be relatively thin. Drop some into pan and flip when the edges start to firm. Cook fully, then serve with toppings of your choice.

Variations

There are endless variations on these. My recent (and so far, most favorite), is to substitute 1/2 tablespoon of shredded (desiccated) coconut for the rice flour and add the zest of half a lemon. Serve with blueberries and slivered almonds, and it's heaven on a plate!

WAFFLES

Lately, Sophia, Blair, and I are OBSESSED with these waffles (okay, Alexis too). They're delicious, relatively healthy (no added sugar, other than the maple syrup you might drizzle on top), and super easy. They're also great frozen and reheated in the toaster, for those mornings when you're short on time or patience!

*Gluten free and nut free.

Makes about 5 waffles

Ingredients
- 1.5 bananas, mashed
- 2 eggs
- pinch of salt
- 1/2 tsp. cinnamon

- pinch of nutmeg
- 1 tsp. vanilla extract
- 3 Tbsp. Olive oil (plus more to oil the waffle iron)
- 1/4 to 1/3 cup of milk (2% or a substitute such as rice, soy, or a nut milk)
- 1/2 tsp. baking powder
- 1/2 tsp. baking soda
- 1 cup gluten-free flour (I use Bob's Red Mill One-for-One Gluten-Free Flour)
- Toppings of your choice

Instructions

- Preheat the waffle iron on desired setting. We use a spray olive oil to make sure nothing sticks.
- In a large bowl, mash the bananas, then add all the wet ingredients and stir until incorporated. Then add the dry ingredients (baking powder, baking soda, and flour) and combine.
- Once the waffle iron is heated, drop half a cup on the griddle and close the lid. Cook fully, then serve with toppings of your choice.

GUACAMOLE

This recipe is so ridiculously simple, I'm not even sure it should be in here. But honestly, simple dishes, prepared well are often the best. Fresh and flavorful, guacamole is incredibly easy and adaptable.

*gluten free, nut free, and vegan

Ingredients
- 1 avocado, mashed
- lemon juice
- garlic salt
- salt
- pinch cumin

Instructions
- In a bowl, mash the avocado with a fork or potato masher (if you're making a big batch!). Add a pinch of cumin,

a light layer of garlic salt, and a pinch of salt. Give a generous amount of lemon juice—about half of a lemon. I find the sweetness of the lemon tastes even better than lime, but try it out and see what you think!

• Taste and adjust seasonings as needed. Serve!

Variations

If you want to spice things up, add diced jalapeño. Fresh cilantro can also be a nice addition. If you're getting really fancy, you can add diced tomato and/or onion as well.

I find that kids seem to like it plain. And they love mashing the avocado and even playing with the pit after you've cleaned it. Blair loves to roll it around on the floor and listen to the sound it makes.

I recommend waiting to make the guac until just before you need it so it's freshest. Though the lemon juice will help slow browning, it won't prevent it. Which is why I recommend eating it all in one sitting—as if you could help it!

PIZZA

There's nothing better than a make-your-own pizza party! It's easy to set up, and the kids love it! It keeps them occupied for a while, and there's no fighting over toppings. Win-win!

This recipe comes from my mother, who graciously agreed to share it!

*gluten free, nut free, vegan

Pizza

Dough Ingredients

• 2 1/2 cups gluten-free flour (I use Bob's Red Mill One-for-One Gluten-Free Flour)
   • 1 tsp. salt
   • 2 Tbsp. olive oil
   • 1 cup warm water + 3 tsp. yeast (1 sachet) + 1 tsp. sugar

(This must be done together before adding it to the flour and oil, as sugar activates yeast.)

Instructions

- Pre-heat oven to 425 degrees Fahrenheit.
- Mix dough ingredients. I usually start with about 2 cups of the flour and then slowly add more as necessary. You don't need to knead it long, just until it's pliable and smooth. Let rise if you want (Though I don't find it's necessary, or that I have the patience.)
- Roll out on pan or lightly floured surface, add sauce/ toppings.
- Bake for 20 minutes or until cheese is sufficiently melted.

Variations

Top with whatever you like! Are you a fan of Canadian bacon and pineapple? An olive lover like Sophia? My personal favorite is sautéed onions, mushrooms, and pepperoni. And I love mixing parmesan, Havarti, and mozzarella. Mmm. Melty goodness.

For the sauce, we typically use a can of crushed or pureed tomatoes. We add dried oregano, salt, and garlic salt. But you could use a pesto or even a sun-dried tomato paste, and it would be delicious.

Want to make it feel extra fancy? Add some fresh basil AFTER it comes out of the oven, not before.

SOPHIA'S SUGAR COOKIES

My girl has a sweet tooth, and she loves baking cookies for her friends and family. Over the years, she's progressed from stirring the dry ingredients and helping roll and cut the dough, to measuring the ingredients and cracking the egg herself. Cooking is a great exercise for kids. It teaches them math skills, patience, and helps give them a better appreciation for the food they consume. Plus, doesn't everything taste better when you've made it yourself?

*gluten free and nut free

Sugar Cookies

Cookie Ingredients

• 3 1/4 cups gluten-free flour (I use Bob's Red Mill One-for-One Gluten-Free Flour)

- 1 1/2 teaspoons baking powder
- 1/2 teaspoon salt
- 2 1/2 sticks salted butter, softened
- 1 cup granulated sugar
- 1 large egg
- 1 tablespoon milk (or milk substitute)
- 2 1/2 teaspoons vanilla extract
- 1/2 teaspoon (or more) of fresh lemon zest

Plus, for the icing, you will need powdered sugar, water, food coloring, and any sprinkles your heart desires.

Instructions

- In a medium bowl, whisk together the gluten-free flour, baking powder, and salt. Then, set aside.
- Using a mixer, beat the butter and granulated sugar until fluffy and well blended.
- Add the egg, milk, vanilla, and lemon zest to the butter/sugar mixture and beat until well combined. Gradually add the flour mixture and beat until well blended and smooth.
- Scoop the dough out of the bowl and form a ball. Divide dough in half and wrap in plastic wrap. Chill in fridge until slightly firm (at least thirty minutes, ideally one to two hours).
- Preheat oven to 375 degrees Fahrenheit.
- Remove from fridge and roll out to no more than 1/4 inch thick. Cut with whatever shapes you like. Roll scraps for more. Refrigerate if too soft to handle.
- Place cut-out cookies on prepared baking sheet and place in the oven on the center rack for nine to twelve minutes until lightly browned on bottom.
- Remove from the oven and allow to cool before decorating.

Frosting

- Combine powdered sugar with water until you get the right consistency. You want it to be spreadable and not too runny.

Acknowledgments

This book was so much fun to write. Inspired by Charlie Puth's song, "Boy," the characters sprang to life. I loved the idea of a woman who was confident yet struggled with insecurities. And a man who was young, but so much wiser than his years.

Thank you for reading *Unexpected.* I love writing for the pleasure of it, but seeing readers' reactions, reading your comments and reviews is definitely a highlight.

Thank you to all the amazing readers, bloggers, and bookstagrammers who helped spread the word about this book. You guys are awesome, and I so so appreciate every post, every comment, every "like," and every share. Seriously, I'm honored and humbled by your response to Alexis and Preston's story.

To my editor, Lisa with Silently Correcting Your Grammar. I so appreciate your attention to detail, and your patience with my questions. You always go above and beyond. And your comments crack me up! Thank you for helping me create a thoughtful and well-polished book I can be proud of.

Thank you to LJ for designing such a gorgeous cover that really captures the feel of the story and characters. And a huge thanks to Linda and Alissa for everything you both do. You're rockstars!

Thank you to Ellen for taking this journey with me. Thank you for being so supportive and positive, for being a friend. Thank you for helping me rediscover myself at a time that I felt very adrift in my life. And thank you for sharing your incredible eye for detail.

Thank you to Kristen for being such an amazing friend. I

value your judgment and honesty, and I so appreciate your support. We've been through so much together, and I treasure your friendship and advice. Seriously, I cannot thank you enough for all that you do. Thank you for getting me through those last few chapters. I had a loose idea, but you helped me find the way.

Thank you, Kirsten. You are thorough and fast, and I so value your opinion. Your comments made Preston the man he is today! I appreciate you having the courage to point out his shortcomings.

Thank you, Jade. You make me a stronger writer, and you challenge me on pacing. You are so clever and always provide great insight. And you are always so on top of cover reveals, teasers, etc. Thank you so much for promoting me on Instagram.

A huge thank you to all my beta readers. Thank you for making me a stronger writer, for offering your unique insight and advice. You each seem to bring something different to the table, and I'm always amazed and impressed by your suggestions. I'm honored to have you on my team!

Thank you to my husband for always encouraging me. For always supporting my dreams. You are better than any book boyfriend I could ever imagine. And to my daughter, for always putting a smile on my face. You are spirited and independent, and I wouldn't have it any other way. Dream big, my darling.

A big thanks to my parents and my in-laws for taking such good care of our daughter while I write. And to my mom for always being my number one fan.

If this list of people shows you anything, it's that dreams are often the effort of many. I'm grateful to have such an awesome team. And I'm honored that you've taken the time to read my words.

About the Author

Jenna Hartley is USA Today bestselling author who writes feel-good forbidden romance, much like her own real-life love story. She's known for writing strong women and swoon-worthy men, as well as blending panty-melting and heart-warming moments.

When she's not reading or writing romance, Jenna can be found tending to her growing indoor plant collection (pun intended), organizing, and hiking. She lives in Texas with her family and loves nothing more than a good book and good chocolate, except a dance party with her daughter.

www.authorjennahartley.com

Also by Jenna Hartley

<u>Love in LA Series</u>
Inevitable
Unexpected
Irresistible
Undeniable
Unpredictable
Irreplaceable

<u>Alondra Valley Series</u>
Feels Like Love
Love Like No Other
A Love Like That

<u>Tempt Series</u>
Temptation
Reputation

For the most current list of Jenna's titles, please visit her website www.authorjennahartley.com.

Or scan the QR code on the following page to be taken to her author page on Amazon.com

SCAN ME